NEVER SAY NEVER

JUSTINE MANZANO

NEVER
SAY NEVER
JUSTINE MANZANO

*You're enough,
no frills needed!*

[signature]

Copyright © 2021 by Justine Manzano

All rights reserved. Except as permitted under the U.S. Copyright Act of 1976,
no part of this book may be reproduced or used in any manner without the prior
written permission of the copyright owner, except for the use of brief quotations
in a book review.

Sword and Silk Books
105 Viewpoint Circle Pell City, AL 35128
Visit our website at SwordandSilkBooks.com

To request permissions contact the publisher at
admin@swordandsilkbooks.com.

First Edition: June 2021

The characters and events in this book are fictitious. Any similarity to real
persons, living or dead, is coincidental and not intended by the author.

Ebook: 978-1-000-0000-0

Edited by Jennia Herold D'lima
Cover Art by Lucy Rhodes
Layout by Laynie Bynum

To all of my many sisters, both by blood and by bond, but most especially--

To Megan, for inspiring so much of who Brynn needed to be. I will never forget the way you knew what Brynn would do before she did it.

To Joy, for always being the Nina to my Brynn. May you never waste another second of precious time.

CHAPTER ONE
THE TRUTH ABOUT LOVE

WHEN I WAS EIGHT, I told my best friend Nina I wished my parents would get a divorce. She hadn't understood then, and she still didn't. Her parents loved each other.

But true love is a relationship unicorn. You either find it, or you spend your entire life searching for it, like a dog digging up the entire yard for something buried next door.

I had experience with people who had destroyed their yard and came up empty. They were sitting at my kitchen table.

Dad stared blankly at his newspaper, holding it up like a wall between himself and Mom, who drew her spoon through her cereal at a speed that would surely make her Cheerios soggy before they ever made it to her mouth. Both grunted their good mornings at me, shiny happy people as usual.

As I grabbed a yogurt from the fridge, I yawned. Loudly. Somewhat uncontrollably. I thought my jaw might crack, but I survived unscathed. Thinking about the reasons for my exhaustion, I regretted my life choices.

"Very ladylike," Mom commented, finally finding her cereal appetizing enough to eat.

Dad spoke over her. "Stay up late?"

I nodded, digging into my yogurt. "Homework."

"Uh-huh." Dad turned the page of his paper. "How much of that time was spent reading that book you got in the mail yesterday?"

"Minimal."

"Minimal," Mom parroted. "Translation——you completed your homework by seven and were up 'til midnight reading the book."

It was so much more humorous when they played off each other, despite not being able to look at one another. That kind of unity took commitment.

Although playing off each other was always better than them playing off me. They could use teamwork just fine when they needed to scold me, but could they manage a mature conversation like one of those fairytale couples on television? Not a chance.

Dad pushed his chair back from the table, the legs scraping against the linoleum.

Mom didn't miss a beat. "Tell your father he needs to lift his bottom off the seat to stand or he'll peel the linoleum."

Oh, here we go. It was like playing referee in a boxing match with a broken bell.

And me without my striped shirt.

I turned to Dad, who was just a few feet away, putting his dishes in the sink. "Mom said you have to stand and move the chair back more gently or you'll destroy our flooring."

If I repeated their statements word for word, I'd have lost my mind a year ago when they'd started this round of ridiculousness. When I thought about it, I couldn't find many memories where they smiled together, laughed together——hell, even talked to each other.

"Well, tell your mother I'm sorry. I wouldn't want to ruin anyone's perception of our perfect kitchen."

"Dad expresses genuine regret at his transgression and promises never to commit such a horror again." I shot a bitter

2

smile in Dad's direction, my way of informing him he was the ass in this situation.

No matter whose fault the argument was, I was always in the middle——the expired meat in their misery sandwich.

"You need a ride to school, kid?" Dad wandered out of the room before I could answer, heading towards the living room.

"Maybe?" I called after him. "Just a sec." I pulled my phone from my pocket and texted Nina.

We getting a ride today? Need an answer STAT.

I finished my yogurt while waiting for a response. Instead of a message from Nina, I got one from her foster sister, Val.

We'll be there in about five minutes. Nina needs you!

Val had moved in with the Lopezes in August and had immediately clicked with Nina in a way that could have made me jealous ... if she wasn't insane. Which was why I didn't blink at the drama of the text message. It was just Val being Val.

"Don't need a ride." I stood carefully——so as not to scratch the damned linoleum——and cleared the table.

"Is that Adam boy driving you again?" Mom asked. "I need to talk to his father and see if he's a good enough driver to be carpooling you all to school."

"That Adam boy" was Val's boyfriend, and he was nothing to worry about. Probably the most responsible guy ever created. And maybe, someday, Mom would actually talk to his father, instead of just asking me about it every other week since the beginning of the school year.

I made my way behind Mom, leaned over, and wrapped my arms around her, making sure to catch her eye. "Adam's fine. It's Val that's trouble." I waggled my eyebrows and managed to get a smile from her and a playful smack on the arm.

"You kids stay out of trouble," she said.

"Yeah, yeah, yeah." I walked into the living room and hoisted my backpack onto my shoulder.

Dad was near the couch, fretting with the baggage tags on

his rolling suitcase. "I'll be in Chicago until Thursday. Take care of your mother."

My stomach clenched. And that was my job, why?

"Mom takes care of herself because she's a full-grown adult. A little warning would have been nice, though. Your schedule's getting harder to keep track of." I marched toward the door, not wanting to see his expression.

I didn't want him to go. It was partly because I wanted him at home, and partly that I needed the buffer between me and Mom. Mom wanted a cheerleader for a daughter, the type of girl she could try out new hairstyles on, someone she could shop with. Someone like Val.

Meanwhile, I had spent my first paycheck at the local salon, getting my hair chopped into a pixie cut and dyeing it black. Mom and I hadn't been the same since. For my mother, cutting off my long locks had been a tragedy, right up there with Hamlet and Othello.

I wasn't Val. I never would be, and I didn't understand why she couldn't accept me for who I was. At least when Dad was around, I wasn't the only one. She was determined to fit him into her little 'perfect husband' box. It may mean more time playing referee, but at least when he was with me, I felt like there was someone who understood, who was in my corner. But now that someone would be in Chicago until Thursday.

"If I could pass them up, don't you think I would?" Dad said, his voice sounding small.

He wouldn't. Not if it meant more time around her.

I wished they would just get divorced already. Except maybe that wouldn't make things any better. If I wasn't important enough to make him deal with Mom for me, maybe divorce would send Dad even further away. That thought made something in my chest shake.

A horn beeped outside. Adam was too polite for a honk. It sounded like he barely brushed the horn.

I shrugged and moved for the door, grateful for the distraction. "That's my ride. I'd better
go."

Dad lightly tapped my elbow to still me. "I'll be home soon."

"Yeah." I kissed him on the cheek. "Have a safe flight."

"I'll text you when I land. Love you."

"Love you, too."

Adam's old blue Honda Civic waited in front of the house. I took off at a gallop down the stairs, past the growing daffodils in our garden, across the front walk, and past my own personal birch tree. The birch tree was one of many in our town and the reason for its name, Birchwood Grove.

I slid into the backseat of the car where the fresh scent of roses engulfed me. Val's perfume filled the surrounding air almost anywhere she went.

The car was short one person.

"Where's Reeve?" I pulled the door shut behind me.

In the rearview mirror, Adam's dark eyes winced. Val, who was facing toward the back seat, looked nauseated, her perfect features twisted. Only then did I notice Nina huddled on her side of the car, her head pressed against the window opposite mine.

My heart clenched.

"Nina..." I brushed aside the curtain of Nina's dark, springy curls and peeked at her. She quickly swiped her eyes with the backs of her hands. "What happened?"

For a moment, she just sniffled. "Reeve broke up with me," she said. She pushed her hair back from her face. "Last night."

That. Dick.

My fists clenched at my sides, but I forced the reaction down. It wasn't the first time. It may not be the last. But rather than lash out, I focused on the real problem.

"What? Why didn't you call me?" I scooted closer to the girl who was always there for me and pulled her into my arms.

She rested her head on my shoulder, glancing up at me with her brown eyes. Nina was dazzlingly beautiful, even when she was just being casual. She had golden-brown skin, those curls, and cupid's bow lips. Even when she hid the curls in a bun and didn't bother to wear makeup, she was stunning. Today, however, she looked puffy and reddened. I hadn't seen her this distraught since junior high when Dad thought we might have to move out of town.

"I didn't tell anybody until today." Her tone edged with a defensiveness I recognized. She thought I was accusing her of telling Val before me.

"Yeah, but why?" I ran my fingers through her hair. "You decided you'd torture yourself a little before you shared?"

She pinched my leg, which I may have deserved. "No, bitch. I was gonna try to act like I didn't care."

"How's that working out for you?" Okay, my anger at Reeve was still in my brain's driver seat. I needed to calm down.

"C'mon, leave her alone," Val said. "Why do you have to be like that?"

I batted a dismissive hand her way. "Val, I think I know how to handle this. You're the one who said she needed me."

Val's face scrunched up, her features coming together into a somehow still dainty ball of anger. "Well, handle it nicer."

Adam laid a hand on her arm. "Val."

She retreated into her seat.

I gave Nina a little squeeze. "Did Reeve say what stupidity went through his head this time?"

"This time he means it. He said I'm too difficult." She forced herself to sit up and violently swiped away her tears. "I mean, what the fuck is that? He says I never want to do anything he wants to do, and I'm always acting like I don't need him. I never ask for help, and I do things without him. He got mad because I went to the movies with you without informing him first, Brynn. He's all, 'I only found out because Scott and I saw you from the bowling alley.' And when I told him that was because I knew he'd be shitty about me going, he started whining that he wanted to go bowling and I didn't want to. I don't *like* bowling." She sank back against the seat. "God, what an ass."

I stifled a laugh. It was always good to see Nina rebound after a moment of self-doubt, even if Reeve caused most of those moments. He was her blind spot, the only thing she didn't listen to me about, and it never ceased to make my blood boil. Despite how much it might hurt her to hear it, I tried to hammer the positivity of this break-up home. "Damn straight! He doesn't like your independence? He's a Dildo Baggins."

Trying to find my way back to you.

The words from the breakup song of the season slid from the radio speakers, filling the car with possibly the worst song that could have played at that moment. Adam shot forward, finger jamming the station search button. Val's hands fluttered madly as she tried to beat Adam to it and failed.

"Real covert, guys," I laughed. "Anyway, if that's his problem, what the hell do you need him for? You're doing everything right. You can only be with someone who loves you for who you are."

"Yup," Adam piped up from the front, his presence only visible by the black curls that stuck up over the top of the driver's seat headrest. "If he didn't like the real you, he was a waste of time."

"You see, that's what bothers me. Wasting my time." Nina had suffered from severe asthma since she was a baby. She had spent far too much time at Westchester General Hospital, and she took time-sucks very seriously.

"I honestly think you should take this as a lesson," Val said. "Maybe sometimes your personality can be too strong, and it scares people away. Find a middle ground. Something that works for both of you."

Something inside of me reared up, ready to attack. "Or, you

know, don't compromise who you are for an asshole. You could do that instead."

Val scowled. I loved Val, I really did, but sometimes I wanted to smack her in her stupid but adorable face. And she thought I was the one who was being insensitive?

"I hate this feeling." Nina sniffled. "I hate that he can get to me like this."

Seeing her cry made me want to cry, and I wasn't doing that in front of Val and Adam. I fished out a tissue from the pack in the front of my bookbag. "You just need some time. You're too strong to let him get you down for long."

"Right," Adam said. "He's obviously a prick. I'm surrounded by the three of you all the time and it doesn't unnerve me."

"Not even a little bit?" I stifled a laugh. Sometimes, when Adam was with the three of us, he looked helpless, as though desperate for a life preserver.

"Yeah, sure, but it has nothing to do with you all being independent. It has more to do with you guys being loud." He plugged his ear and winced, making sure we could see his expression in the rearview mirror.

Nina cracked a shaky smile, and the dark feeling in my chest lightened.

BY THE TIME we met up again that afternoon in mythology class, Nina looked more like herself, although the bags under her eyes were a dead giveaway to her earlier state. Still, it was a relief to see her smiling and goofing off with Val.

They were already sitting in their seats, so I took the desk beside them. It was a desk/chair combo, and my hips were a tight squeeze. I barely ever made it without banging the desk across the floor, a clatter that might as well be the "Brynn's got some junk in her trunk" shuffle. I wedged my ass into the seat and momentarily bemoaned the invention of the corset of school furniture.

A moment later when the late bell rang, Adam slid past Mr. Howard with a sheepish smile and a wave. He found the empty seat next to Val and settled in with his own extra noise as he rustled through his backpack and pushed his frameless glasses up his broad nose.

"Are you done, Mr. Hernandez?" Mr. Howard asked.

He winced. "Sorry."

Val squeezed his hand and tossed a sheet of her bouncy blonde curls over her shoulder.

"Good morning." Mr. Howard called the attention of the class. Slowly, the chatter around the room tapered off. He waited until it was completely silent, and our eyes were all on him. "There you are. Today, we're going to get started on that group project I promised you."

A collective groan rose from the students, myself included. Nobody liked group projects.

"Projects will be presented in June, which leaves you an entire month. I warned you to enjoy spring break because you'd be working hard when you returned." Mr. Howard's tone was awfully playful for a man handing out jail sentences. "I'll be posting the presentation schedule at the end of this month. The project will require groups of four—"

That was all I needed to hear. I grabbed Nina's hand. She grabbed Val's. Val's hand tightened around Adam's.

"What are we doing?" Val whispered. Adam smiled.

"I see some of you have already chosen your partners." Mr. Howard grinned. "That easy to wake you guys up, huh?"

Someone tapped my shoulder. Raphael.

Raphael was a decent looking boy in my class who intensely ordinary, at least to me. Nothing about him stood out. He blended in with the rest of his fellow castmates in the school play and barely managed to maintain a B average. His family had moved over the summer, but they let him stay with a family friend in Birchwood until he finished high school. And though he'd barely spoken with me before his reappearance, he'd spent every minute since senior year started trying to get me to go out with him. He was awful about it.

"Bree, drop them and come work with me?" he whispered, glancing between me and our group.

The assumption that I would drop my best friends to work with him was part of that *something off* about him. The other part?

"Brynn. You know I hate being called Bree."

I'd told him a million times, but he didn't seem to care. Only Nina got away with calling me Bree, and that was because she'd been using the nickname since we both learned to talk.

"But... weren't we supposed to hang out?" he asked.

No, I had never agreed to hang out with him. He'd creeptastically invented that in his own brain. Stifling a shudder, I put a finger to my lips and shushed him, just in time to realize I had no idea what our project was about.

"Break into groups and brainstorm topics. Exchange phone numbers and email addresses. Lay down the groundwork. After today, we won't be devoting class time to this project, so make sure you get it all covered."

I turned my desk toward the others. "Raphael was being Raphael. What's our project?"

Adam frowned. "He bothering you again?"

"Again?" I said. "When did he stop?"

"He can't take a hint," Nina said.

"That little worm," Val grumbled, her nose wrinkling in that adorable way it always did. "I've never liked him." Her nose unwrinkled and she perked up. "Doesn't anybody nice *ever* want to date you?"

"Val!" Adam scolded.

The words sliced through me, but I had bigger problems to

deal with. I didn't even need to look behind me to know Raphael was about to barge into the conversation. My hand snapped up like a stop sign. "No one need apply. I'm not on the market. I'm not interested in romance; I'm interested in the project."

Val gasped. "You're not... interested... in romance?"

"The project, Val! Can we focus on the project?"

"We're supposed to pick a region of mythology we learned about in class and find a topic we want to study further. We need to come up with a presentation we want to do and get his approval. Then present on our assigned day," Adam recapped for me.

"The Trojan War. We talked about the war itself, and, you know, the horse. Everybody talks about the horse. But what about the causes? How the war happened, who was involved. How it was really all Eris' fault." Val leaned back in her chair. "Greek mythology is my favorite."

Who could have guessed that Greek mythology would be Valentina Kokinos's favorite? It truly was a shock.

"We'll read up on it ourselves, then we'll make plans to meet up and decide what we want to do with it this weekend." Adam shrugged. "It won't be hard to find time to talk about this."

"We could do half during the slow shifts at Scoopy Doo," Nina said, referring to the ice cream shop where we all worked.

"That may be a no go," Val said. "I hear there's someone new starting this week. Greg or something. We're gonna have to train him."

"Craig," Adam said. "Sammy's gearing up for the summer rush."

"We'll manage, or we'll meet up after work," I said. "We'll play it by ear. Deal?"

We all agreed.

Once class ended and we were heading to lunch, I pushed aside my disgust with Val's current behavior. We had to talk.

Our previous after-school plans wouldn't mesh well with Nina's new situation, and the last thing I wanted was to remind Nina of the break-up. I looped an arm through Val's and pulled her back to walk with me.

"Prom dress shopping after school is a no then, huh?" I whispered.

"No way! I don't even know if she's going now." She shook her head, morose, as though missing prom was akin to a death sentence. "Why would she go to the prom by herself?"

I tried not to be offended. Offended was my standard state around Val. "I'm going to the prom by myself."

"Well, you're different." She patted my arm. "Besides, now you can go with her. But I'd let her mourn awhile first."

I took a deep breath and reminded myself that, whether or not I liked it, Val was Nina's foster sister, and I was stuck with her unless Nina said otherwise. This involved regular mental gymnastics to keep me from throwing the nearest heavy object at her.

Between my desire to get away from Val and Nina's insistence on locking herself in her room and listening to depressing music until she felt like herself again, I no longer had plans for the evening. After making Nina swear to call me if she needed me, and worrying that she totally wouldn't, I headed home hours before my nine o'clock curfew.

Mom would be surprised. I rarely walked in any earlier than 8:58 p.m. Things in the house were always too tense, and I'd rather avoid it as long as I could. Most days, Nina's parents fed me.

Once home, I kicked off my shoes and jogged up the stairs. "Mom! I'm home!"

No response, but a lot of shuffling and movement from upstairs. Had Mom gone to bed early? I hoped she wasn't coming down with something.

"Mom?"

She didn't respond. Dread hit the bottom of my stomach like a weight, and I swallowed against it. Pushing my fear aside, I approached her room and pressed my ear against the door.

"What do you want me to do, Chelsea? Sneak out the window?" A man's voice. Worse, I knew that voice. Not that there was much chance I wouldn't in a town as small as ours. It was Jesse, from the local antique shop. He came in for ice cream at Scoopy Doo once a week "as a reward for a particularly hard day of work." Like a kid who did well in school.

That room belonged to my mom and dad, and Jesse had absolutely no place anywhere near it. I snarled. "Mom, open the door now."

The paint made a sticking sound as the door cracked open. A few months ago, Mom and Dad put their war to rest, and the three of us repainted every room in the house. Mom even let me smear some on her nose.

That Mom was the same Mom whose head poked through the crack in the doorway. Innocent and youthful, years of tension disappeared from her face. She regarded me with wide eyes, a hesitant smile hovering on her lips. "Bree-baby, I can explain."

I wanted her to explain it all away. But she couldn't. There was only one explanation, and it was ugly and wrong. The darkness that had been biting at my heels since Nina had told me her news flared to life again, and I spoke my next words through teeth gritted hard enough to crack. "No, Mom. No, you can't. And Jesse? Get the hell out of my house. You can use the door, but you should use the window, like the weasel you are."

I escaped to my sanctuary, even as she called after me. It wasn't until I was alone that it all sank in. I collapsed onto my bed and breathed. And breathed. And kept forcing myself to breathe until it felt natural again.

I wished there was a way to forget the truth. The truth about love was Reeve breaking up with Nina after two years of dating, for her being exactly who she'd always been. The truth about love was Dad leaving on business trips and staying away from home as often as he could, desperate to avoid the woman he had married. The truth about love was Mom, after twenty years of marriage, getting caught banging an antiques dealer.

Nina had been in love. My parents had been in love. Now they all walked around like a vital piece of themselves was missing. Like the world had ended when their relationships did. And I was supposed to want that? I was supposed to go looking for pain?

The truth about love was it sucked. And I wanted no part of it.

CHAPTER TWO
SMOKE AND MIRRORS

I COULDN'T TELL my friends about Mom.

In Birchwood Grove, everybody knew everybody. For instance, I knew Adam well enough, the way anybody knows their neighbor. Adam's mother had been the town pediatrician, and when she passed away from cancer a year and a half ago, the entire town mourned. But nobody mourned like Adam. He walled himself off from the world. He had seemed lost. And then Val came to live with Nina.

Val had been forced to join a group of kids who already knew each other well enough to know what their worst subjects were, and which arcade games were their favorites. We'd been to each other's childhood birthday parties, and we'd all been in the same classes together since elementary school. We ran into each other's parents on Main Street, and I knew the ice cream order of every single one of their siblings.

When Adam shrank away, he'd become an outsider, and Val came from the outside. It only made sense that he'd become her welcoming committee, and in doing so, he remembered who he had been before losing his mom.

So I knew them, but not as well as I knew Nina. And Nina had her own crap to deal with, even though she claimed she needed a distraction. We knew each other better than we knew ourselves, and I would not give her another reason to feel bummed. It didn't seem right, even if it hurt to keep it from her.

If I could avoid everybody for a while, I'd have time to decide how to deal with it. The morning was easy. It wasn't uncommon for me to not want a ride to school. I liked the walk. It was a good time for me to listen to music and center myself. That worked well, since Adam wasn't available to drive us all the time. He and his father shared the car, and while his father was a freelancer and often worked from home, sometimes he needed the car for an appointment.

When I made it to school and saw Nina with her head stuffed in her locker, pulling down the pictures of Reeve she'd pasted there one by one, I made it my mission to help her instead of wallowing in my own issues. Nina looked like a sleep-deprived horror, or the Nina-equivalent of one, anyway. She needed my help more than I needed to mull over my own drama.

Nina, Val, and I had a shift at the ice cream shop to get through as well. We got in around three o'clock and the owner, Sammy Chase, greeted us as soon as the bell over the door jangled.

"Ladies!" Sammy shouted. "Thank goodness you're here. I've got to go." He yanked his apron over his head and tossed it to Nina. "You're on cake decorating duty today."

Nina grabbed it out of the air without a moment's hesitation, but stared blankly at Sammy. "Where are you rushing off to?"

"A date." He punctuated the words by jamming a meaty finger into the air. Sammy was a tall, thick man with burly arms. He wasn't fat, just large, and he took up most of the space behind the waist-high freezer that held all the scoopable flavors.

"Oh, look at that!" Val smiled, pearly white teeth gleaming. "Who knew our Sammy was a ladies' man?"

"What do you mean, who knew?" Sammy let out a low

rumble of a chuckle. "I knew." He danced his way toward the door, his sneakers squeaking on the white tiles.

"Please tell me you're changing out of that before you go?" Val called. I elbowed her.

Sammy made a face. "Obviously! You think I'm going on a date smelling like spoiled milk? Goodnight, ladies."

"Goodnight, Sammy," we called after him in chorus.

Val plucked her uniform shirt to her nose and sniffed it. "I don't smell like spoiled milk."

"Of course *you* don't. You always smell like roses. Besides, that smell only comes after a full shift." I was glad we had come in our uniforms since Sammy was in such a rush.

"I'm so proud of our Sammy," Val said as we headed to the back of the store to drop our backpacks off on the break room table. "Getting out into the dating world. I don't think he's gone on a date since I met him."

I straightened my hunter green polo and khakis and pulled the matching baseball cap over my head. While Val and Nina threaded their ponytails through the backs of their caps, I washed my hands.

"He and his wife got divorced, like, two years ago." Nina swiped a clean rag from the sink and wiped the table she used for cake decorating. She was the only other person besides Sammy allowed to work on them, because she was the only one whose cakes didn't look like a left-handed kindergartner decorated them, forced to use his right. "It was ugly. I'm not surprised he stayed away from the dating scene."

Val climbed onto the foot stool beside the huge metal monster in the middle of the back area. The soft ice cream machine was an outdated model, and as such, was far larger than it needed to be. "Please don't tell me you intend to steer clear from dating, too." She lifted the lid and peeked in. "We're good on vanilla, but chocolate will probably need to be refilled in about an hour."

The bell over the door rang as the entire after-school program of Birchwood Elementary entered. Nina cursed under her breath.

The next half hour went by in a blur of milkshake blending, sundae topping, cone swirling, and scoop stacking. The counter was a tight fit for all three of us, but we had the process down. We weaved between, under, and around each other. Nina reached over my back for the black cherries while I bent to scoop the mint chip. Val rolled a cone in sprinkles, while I reached over her to pass change to a customer.

It was the kind of fluidity I loved about the job once I'd mastered it. The three of us, while dissimilar, understood each other enough to finish each other's sentences——and each other's orders. Once we got into the zone, a peace settled over us, and my mind reveled in the opportunity to go blissfully blank.

Once things settled down, Val picked up on her previous question like she'd never stopped talking. That's how she was. A dog with a bone.

"Nina, you're not gonna swear off dating now, are you?"

Nina groaned. "I'll be in the back, decorating."

The back of the shop wasn't all that far from the front, but it was behind the ancient soft ice cream machine, so it was far enough away that she could tune us out. I didn't blame her.

"Why do you keep doing that?" I swiped sprinkles from the counter into my hand with a rag. "You're not helping Nina. They broke up yesterday. Yesterday, Val. That's barely any time at all."

She giggled, her dimples denting her cheeks. "Oh, Brynn, that's like a nanosecond in the grand scheme of things. All the more reason she should move on."

I raised an eyebrow.

"Life is so short for mortals."

"You've been reading too many vampire books, Val."

"There is no such thing as too many vampire books, Brynn."

She shrugged and nonchalantly pumped some hot fudge into a small cup. "You should love while you can. Before you know it, this mortal life is over."

I barely processed the sentiment, too distracted by the pool of fudge she'd created. "What are you doing?"

She grabbed a spoon and ate the fudge straight from the cup like that wasn't disgusting. "Fudge is wonderful. Love is *also* wonderful. You only get to experience it so many times in your life."

"Shouldn't you only experience it once?" I asked, leaning against the cash register and trying desperately not to think about how happy Mom looked with Jesse. Happy, despite the panic at being caught. I couldn't wrap my head around it.

"A person can love on so many levels, Brynn." She waved the spoon at me, mouth filled with fudge. "There are even different kinds of romantic love. Nina will love again. The sooner, the better."

"Not everybody wants to fall in love," I said. "Some people just want to live their lives."

"Yes, there are people who are aromantic, but that's not you, and it's not Nina." Another shrug. "I would know if it was."

"Naturally," I grumbled. "What don't you already know?"

"Am I wrong though?" she asked.

I mean, she wasn't, but that wasn't the point. When I heard Val waxing poetic about the virtues of love, all I saw were Nina's puffy eyes from yesterday morning, Mom guiltily peeking out of her bedroom, and it was a struggle not to punch her in her smiling, glowing face.

"What is your obsession with love, anyway?" A nasty edge crept into my tone. "You think because things are all lovey-dovey with Adam that love is perfect? You only get to be this happy for a limited time."

"Now that's simply not true," she said, her voice raising to match mine. "I've seen many couples get their happily ever after."

"Their happily ever after? For what, five minutes?"

"No, Brynn. I mean it. I've known couples who got to live—"

"You watched them die together, holding hands? Or are you just saying that because it's what you want to believe?"

She pressed her lips together into a thin line. "You'd be surprised." She gave herself a little shake, and the toothy smile returned to her face. "Love is a powerful thing."

"Yes," I said. "That we can agree on. Destructively powerful."

"Any power that can be used for destruction..." Val chirped.

What was she, a damn Disney princess? "Can be used for good too? Is that where that was going? Because that's not true. Two words: Atomic. Bomb."

She deflated. "Love can be painful, true, but it can also be wonderful. It creates. It builds. It nurtures. Most people aren't purposely destructive. The trick is to find the person who won't be destructive for you."

"There are plenty of shitty people in the world, Val. You're delusional." Reeve. Jesse. Mom. Even Dad sometimes. He could be shitty to Mom, at least. Sometimes, he could even be shitty to me when avoiding Mom.

"Delusional? No. I prefer to call it hopeful, Brynn, my dear." She patted my head and flounced off into the bathroom.

I made a good faith effort to shoot heat darts through the back of her head. Nina snorted, only barely glancing up as she smoothed whipped cream over the top of an ice cream cake with a spatula.

"You have to humor her." She pushed the spatula back into the mixing bowl to scoop up more whipped cream. "If I didn't, I'd have killed her by now. Can you imagine living with that and taking it seriously?"

No. No, I could not.

"Val's been through a lot. If she needs to believe in love to get her through it, or if she seems a little strange sometimes, who am I to question it?" She shrugged. "She's a pain sometimes, but she's a Lopez now."

I nodded. "We take care of our own." I may not be an actual Lopez, but I'd been an honorary one all my life.

"That's right," Nina grinned. "So stop trying to kill her with your imaginary laser eyes. I'm okay, promise."

I rested my chin on her shoulder as she continued to ice the cake without missing a beat. "But *are* you okay? About Reeve?"

The spatula dove into the bowl with a little more force. "I will be." She leaned her head against mine. "He's behind me now. I've got my eyes on the future."

My eyes were on the future, too, especially when I returned home that night to two fantastic bits of good luck after my recent streak of bad. First, my mother was out of the house which meant I didn't have to pretend she didn't exist. Second, there was an envelope sitting unopened, but waiting, on top of my desk.

It was from Hunter College, a school in the City University of New York system. I had applied because I wanted to go away for school——far enough away to live in a dorm, but not so far that I couldn't visit my parents regularly. Assuming I still wanted to after whatever clusterfuck was about to go down whenever I figured out what I was going to do about Mom.

My heart beat so hard it shook my rib cage, nervousness and excitement starting up a war within my chest. I tested the weight of the envelope in my hand, then tossed it onto the desk. It *thunked* down.

This kind of thing could drive a person nuts. I needed to open it.

I grabbed my phone. Moral support was necessary during times like these. I called mine and waited two rings before her voice greeted me from the other end.

"Yo," Nina simply said.

"I have it. It's on my desk and I have to open it to see what it says."

"I got mine too. I've been staring at it for the past ten minutes."

"We should open them together, right?" I asked.

There was a long pause on the other end. "Bree? What if we don't both make it in?"

"I'm sure we will. But don't worry. If we don't, we'll go to an upstate school and live our city dream in graduate school." It wasn't that I was more confident than her, it was that I'd already worried myself insane and had sampled the best coping techniques.

"Or, you know, we could just let each other go," Nina said.

I... what?

My heart clenched. Life without Nina would be like jelly without peanut butter. Absolutely unthinkable, and totally uncalled for. Was this Val talking? Because it certainly didn't sound like Nina.

Nina erupted into peels of genuine laughter. Her laugh was incongruous with her appearance——an inelegant guffaw that often led to snorting——and it immediately pulled me into its raucous melody. I couldn't fight my own laughter when she laughed that deeply.

"Did you think I was serious? Let's just do it! Rip off the band-aid!" she shrieked.

"One... two..." I readied myself, sliding my finger into the opening. "Three!"

I tore through the envelope and yanked the folded papers out, ignoring the slice of a paper cut. "Dear Ms. Stark, Congrat-ulations!" I squealed. I hadn't squealed in a long time. I honestly thought I was incapable of girlish squeals until that very moment.

"Yes! Me too!" A commotion on the other side of the phone

told me she had punched the air and accidentally knocked something over. "We're gonna be roommates, baby!"

My face ached from grinning. "We got one win this week!"

"Yes! And you know what?" Nina said, her tone sobering. "This is how we start over. The best is yet to come. I know it."

I hoped she was right. Either way, at least we'd be together.

Nina and I spoke for a little longer about school and what we would do once we got to the city. Then her parents came home, and she rushed to tell them, hanging up on me halfway through her mother's congratulatory hug.

She'd call me back later, if she remembered. Sometimes she didn't. Our conversations were fluid like that. Sometimes we'd call or text each other to say two things every hour. Sometimes we didn't hear from each other all day. But most days, we'd just stay on the phone together, eating in each other's ears and watching television.

My parents regularly thanked the heavens for a cell phone plan with unlimited minutes.

I unzipped my bookbag and hit the books, completing my Economics and Spanish homework before hearing my mother's car pull into the garage.

I needed to talk to her. I couldn't avoid her forever. And now, with the acceptance letter, I had a better way to start the conversation than "So, you're screwing the antiques guy while Dad's on a business trip. What's up with that?" Also, more respectful. Assuming I still had any respect left for her.

With a sigh, I dragged myself off my chair. I could do this. This was Mom. Even if we didn't always get along, she was still Mom. My heart rate kicked up even higher than it had been before I'd opened the letter. No, I couldn't panic. I had excellent news to share. How wrong could this go?

She walked into the house with several grocery bags in her hands, the flimsy plastic erupting in a chorus of rustling. A percussion line joined it as she tried to push the door closed behind her.

I stuffed the letter into my back pocket. "Here, let me get some of those."

"Thanks."

I helped her carry the bags into the kitchen and settled them on the counter. She grabbed one and started unpacking the items inside.

She was just going to continue about her business like she had nothing to say to me.

No apology. No justification. Nothing.

"You aren't going to say anything about yesterday?" I asked.

She stopped in the middle of sliding a jar of tomato sauce into the pantry and released a heavy sigh, her shoulders drooping. "I hoped we wouldn't need to discuss it."

"Seriously?" I wanted to scream. "It didn't occur to you I might have questions?"

She finished loading the pantry and turned toward me, hands on her hips. "We already had the birds-and-the-bees talk, so I think you're covered." She pursed her lips, an eyebrow raised. It was a challenge. She was daring me to keep pushing.

I could barely hear her past my surprise. And here I thought I'd gotten all my sarcasm and wit from my father. "Yeah, that part is shockingly not what I have questions about."

"Then what is it, Bree?" She threw her arms up in the air. "What do you want from me? Can't we just forget it happened?"

I smacked my hand on the counter, more for the grounding it would provide than any attempt at startling her into sanity. "Are you joking? No, I will never erase that mental picture from my head. Never. How am I supposed to look at Jesse when he comes into the shop? How am I supposed to look Dad in the eye?"

"You can't tell your father."

"What?" I couldn't have heard her correctly. "You don't want a divorce?"

"No. What made you think that?" Her mouth dropped open, just slightly, and then she seemed to realize that might be unsightly and sealed it up.

Pent up aggression zipped through me like a static charge, and I wanted to yank at my hair, wanted to throw the groceries at her one by one, but instead, I was left doing nothing, feeling helpless. "You slept with another man and just expect to keep living sourly ever after with a man you cheated on? Have you lost your mind?"

Mom took a deep breath. "Look, Bree, I understand you're upset, but you're ignoring an important truth. Your father and I may not get along, but we've built a life here, a routine. We're not in love anymore, but this household is a partnership. Besides, can you imagine what the neighbors would think if they found out—"

"What if they find out about Jesse? Do you even care about him, or is he just for fun?"

"Of course, I care about him," Mom snapped. "But I also care about you. You think I want you to come from a broken home?"

"It's already broken, Mom!" I yelled. "It's been broken for years!"

She flinched, and the words lingered in the air. Guilt, regret, and a sense of righteousness roiled in my stomach.

"You will not tell your father about this. Do you understand?"

I didn't answer. I didn't understand. I probably never would.

"I got into Hunter. I'm moving to the city with Nina in the fall. Soon, there won't be a home to break."

I stomped up the stairs into my room and slammed the door.

CHAPTER THREE
A DOSE OF REALISM

"HAVE YOU EVER HEARD VAL SNEEZE?" Nina asked Adam. "She sounds like something woodland creatures would flock to."

I laughed and bumped Adam with my elbow. "Dude, you're dating a Disney princess."

Adam wrapped his arm around Val and gave her a little squeeze.

We were hanging out after school in Nina's basement, which was a teenager's paradise, mostly because her parents were extremely cool. They believed in making life as enjoyable as they could for Nina and their foster kids. Currently, Val was their one and only foster child, but in the years I'd known them, there had been six others. Two of the older ones still came to visit during the holidays. Nina's mother was a partner at a big New York City law firm, and her father was a successful computer programmer, so their financial generosity stretched *pretty* far. Their lives hadn't been easy when they were young, and they did their best to alter that for the next generation.

For Nina, this meant a basement game room, complete with a 3-in-1 game table for pool, air hockey, and foosball. It also meant a magnetic dartboard on the wall, a fridge and cabinet stocked with all our favorite foods, a TV with a game system, and a comfy circular couch and a coffee table in the center of the room. It was the perfect hangout.

"Hey." Val snuggled up against Adam's arm. "Did you hear Nina and Brynn got into Hunter?"

"No, I hadn't." He smiled. "Congrats."

"You guys know Adam got a scholarship to NYU, right?" Val gloated. "He's going to be a doctor."

Adam's smile became a shy blush and a facial contortion, like he was trying to disappear into his neck. "I'm going for a pre-med major."

Like his mother. I wouldn't say it, though. Adam hadn't spoken about his mother since she'd died. He hadn't done more than acknowledge her existence to Val.

"That's awesome," Nina said.

"He's a genius," Val gushed. "And this is perfect. Now we can all move to the city together!"

Adam appeared to burrow into the couch cushions.

"Nice. What school did you get into, Val?" I asked.

An innocent question, but Val looked like I'd asked her to smell my armpit. "I didn't. I'm obviously going to be moving in with Adam."

Adam's eyebrows shot up. "So, um, Nina! Have you told your parents about college?"

"Yeah," she sighed. "Mom isn't happy that it's a public college, but the top schools wouldn't take me with all my absences."

Not only was Nina's asthma terrifying, but it also had the wonderful effect of keeping her out of school, often for significant lengths of time. Her B average was a miracle, given how much she missed. As for me, my family couldn't afford anything but the public option, and my grades weren't solid enough to land me a scholarship for somewhere more expensive.

"What did your mom say?" Nina asked me.

"I told her, but didn't really give her the chance to respond." I had somehow avoided thinking about it all day, but the mere mention of Mom brought our argument back in vivid detail. "We got into it last night."

Nina's eyes met mine. She opened her mouth, but quickly closed it. I was grateful for her self-restraint.

"Dad's coming home from his trip tonight," I said. "I'll talk to her more when I tell him."

He would be home soon, and I still hadn't decided what I was going to do. I could tell him, but Mom would be furious with me, and it would hurt Dad. Or I could choose not to tell him, but then I would face a lifetime of wishing I'd said something. Worse, I could see Mom using it as an excuse to bond, as though sharing a secret would cement our relationship rather than detonate it.

"Hey Brynn," Adam asked. "You okay?"

"Huh? Why?" My stomach lurched, and the room blurred around me in a swirl of color. A ten-ton weight lowered itself onto my chest.

"You just... um... look like you want to murder everything around you. That's all."

I tried to answer him, but my stomach bubbled, and the room pitched.

"I don't think that's her murder face," Nina said. "Her nostrils aren't twitching. That's her... oh no."

She hadn't even finished the sentence before I took off in a wobbling run, diving into the basement bathroom. A panicked urge rose within me, and I got my face over the toilet just in time to feed it my stomach's contents from what felt like the last two days. Nina's hand rubbed soothing circles on my back.

"Oh no, poor thing," Val said, in a tone that made me feel like a horse with a broken leg.

"I got her water and some paper towels," Adam announced.

Oh god. I flushed the toilet and slammed the lid down while he was still outside the room.

"Thanks," Nina said. She shoved a wad of paper towels in front of my face. "Clean up and sip some water."

I was mortified, and I half-wanted everyone to leave. But then I'd be alone, so I took the paper towels and water. When I was steadier, I glanced back at Nina. Her eyes were sharp with worry.

"Are you gonna throw up again?" She bumped me with her shoulder.

"No?" My breath hitched on exit, and the words scraped free from my throat.

She frowned. "Are you asking me or telling me?" Her authoritative but nasally tone was a perfect imitation of Ms. Arthur, the English teacher from our Birchwood Elementary days.

I cracked a smile, the pain in my chest easing slightly.

She knelt beside me, her perfectly plucked brows knitted in concern. "What's going on? Are you sick?"

"I don't think so. I think I'm just nervous," I admitted. I needed to tell them. I needed their advice.

"It's far, but it's not *that* far. Just an hour drive." Val pushed her way into the small room. "They won't take it too badly. Maybe they'll see it as you being responsible."

"Yeah, you have to grow up sometime, right?" Adam supplied, thankfully hanging out in the doorway.

"No, it's not about that." I leaned against the toilet, my head lolling back against the lid. "It's that…" I sucked in air. "My mom is having an affair."

Nina's eyes widened comically.

"Whoa," Adam said.

"Wait," Val said. "How do you know?"

"Val," Adam said, his voice growing stern.

"What?" she asked. "You can't just go around making accusations. What if it's all just a misunderstanding?"

My stomach lurched again. I threw the toilet open just in time, my stomach rebelling violently, hot tears pouring over my cheeks. If I didn't stop soon, my head was going to pop clean off my body.

"Val, shut up," Nina said.

"Yeah, I'm pretty sure she's sure," Adam said. "What can we do to help?"

I closed my eyes and let my head drop back against the cabinet behind me. It took a couple of swallows and quite a few deep breaths, but eventually my stomach steadied out. I rose and rinsed my face in the sink.

"Thanks Adam, but I don't know how you could help. And yes, Val, I'm sure. I walked in on her trying to sneak Jesse out of the house."

"The guy who runs the antique store?" Nina asked. "He's like fifteen years younger than her. At least."

"Hey, age is just a number," Val said. "Maybe she connects with something ageless in his soul."

Adam shot Val a look. "More like she connects with something ageless in his pants."

"Don't say that." She frowned.

"Anyway, she doesn't want me to tell Dad," I said. "She wants them to stay together for me."

"That makes zero sense." Nina rolled her eyes.

"Yeah, well, she's gonna be pissed if I tell him, and he comes back tonight. She'll find a way to spin it if I do it in front of her, so it has to be before he gets home. I don't know what I should do."

I looked to the others for an answer. I needed to decide now. His flight landed in an hour. But the more I thought about it, the sicker I felt.

"Where's he flying into?" Adam asked.

"Stewart Airport in Newburgh."

"I'll take you," Adam said. "Home or the airport. You can decide what to do during the drive."

"Really?" I hadn't expected that. I assumed I would have to

call Dad and have the conversation over the phone. But Adam was right. This had to happen face-to-face. "I would, but I'm supposed to be home at..."

"Pretty sure you're past violating curfew if you tell him." Nina let out a nervous giggle.

"I don't understand why you guys want to." Val's eyes were wide with alarm. "Sometimes there are good reasons for violating a marriage contract."

Adam looked at her as though he'd finally realized she was two scoops short of a sundae. "There are good times to cheat? That's what you're saying?"

The panic in Val's eyes doubled. "Not when things are going well, obviously. I mean... love is... there are things... sometimes... when..."

"God, Val, you're spinning your wheels so hard it's making my head hurt more than it already does," I groaned.

"Come on." He held out a hand to help me up. "Up you go."

I placed my hand in his and let him pull me to my feet, my legs still too shaky for me to stand on my own. "Thanks."

He nodded, shrugging off the gratitude. "Let's get you to the car." He motioned to the others to follow.

"We can't," Nina said. "Curfew."

Val shook her head. "But—"

"They won't let you date Adam if you break curfew with him," Nina said, motioning toward the staircase. "I would know. They did that with me and Reeve for a solid month." Her voice wobbled a little when she said his name.

Val looked from me to Adam. Then she placed her hands on his shoulders and pressed a kiss on his lips.

I glanced away. Watching them be all cute with each other made me feel like an intruder.

"You take care of my Bree, okay?"

"Of course." He patted me on the arm. "Ready?"

I wobbled a little, and the world tilted, but there was no way

I was being led up the stairs like a little old lady. "No, but we're short on time."

I cautiously moved up each step, while he walked behind me, hand hovering at the small of my back, eyebrows drawn tightly together.

"Relax," I said with feigned confidence. "I'm not gonna tumble down the stairs."

He laughed, a weird giggle that cut off sharply. His nervousness seemed to drift into me, and my stomach fluttered.

"You look like you might," he said.

I grumbled and willed the necessary strength into my legs. It didn't work, but I pretended it had and kept walking like I was fine.

We emerged in the middle of the hallway and immediately attracted the attention of Mr. Lopez, who always insisted we call him Roman.

"Hey, are you guys still hungry?" he called from the kitchen. "Round two of dinner is in the fridge."

My stomach burbled, and I groaned.

"No thank you," Adam called. "It's just me and Brynn." He closed the basement door behind us. "I'm gonna drive her home. She's not feeling too great."

All my tough guy defenses disappeared under Roman's stern fatherly gaze as he approached.

"I threw up."

"Have you kids been drinking?" Roman asked. "Be honest, there's no judgment from me. But you shouldn't be getting in the car if you—"

"No," I groaned. "I think it was something I ate at lunch. I'll be fine."

"Come on, Mr. Lopez," Adam said. "You know I wouldn't drive if I was drinking."

Roman clapped Adam on the back so hard Adam stumbled forward. The joy returned to Roman's face. "You're a good boy.

Always responsible." He looked to me. "If only Nina dated boys like him."

I smiled weakly. "We didn't realize what a jerk Reeve was soon enough. I'll beat the next guy up before he has a chance to hurt her."

Roman laughed, a hearty sound that made him clutch his rounded stomach. "Oh Bree, I love your fire. Anyway, you won't be beating up anybody in the shape you're in. Go home and get some rest. I'm going to go bug the girls and see if they want leftovers."

We exchanged our good nights and headed to the door.

Rain pelted me when I exited the house, and I threw the hood of my black sweatshirt over my head. Adam just kept his head down, his hands stuffed in his pockets. I was grateful to have a ride home. This was the kind of spring shower I should have anticipated, but I'd been too distracted to bother checking the weather.

He unlocked the car, and I dove in, annoyed by the smack of the heavy rainwater. Annoyed was all I could manage. Pain lanced through my head, starting between my eyes and spreading across my forehead like an invisible blood stain.

I didn't realize Adam had gotten in the car until he started it. I had never sat in the front seat. The dashboard filled the space with bright blue lights, and I stared into them, mesmerized.

"I should have stayed home," I whispered, more to myself than to Adam, who cast concerned glances my way as he drove. "I should have known I'd ruin everyone's night."

Adam pulled the car over. He said nothing until he had successfully parallel-parked, a task I noticed required a lot of concentration.

"You haven't ruined anyone's night."

"Really? Because the minute conversation turned to me, things got a little grim."

"You guys take care of each other," Adam said. "Sometimes

it's calming Val down about her bad hair day. Sometimes it's comforting Nina after breaking up with her boyfriend. Today, it's this."

"But never you. And here I've brought you into it. Threw your evening out the window," I whined, and my self-loathing level ratcheted up a notch.

"Brynn." His voice took on a hard edge. "Just because I don't tell you guys you're helping me, doesn't mean you aren't. Now, am I driving you to the airport or to your house? You don't have time to wallow before you decide."

Ouch. "The airport."

He pulled out of the spot and we continued on our way while I listened to the squeak of the windshield wipers against the glass, watched the pattern of the raindrops as they fell. Tears filled my eyes and I let them fall soundlessly, hoping Adam was too focused on the road to notice.

After a few minutes, Adam began to flip through music stations, darting past when a song was either too morose or too happy. Between that and the boring advertisements, he barely stopped flicking. It took about ten minutes before he gave up completely.

"It's gonna be okay, Brynn. You'll get through this."

"Don't," I groaned. "Don't say nice things to make me feel better. I don't need platitudes. I need to figure out what I should do."

Adam pursed his lips. "Well, okay, let's try to see things from their point of view. What if it were you? You're in a marriage for..."

"Twenty."

"... twenty years." He blew air out between his teeth. "Shit."

"Yeah, shit," I muttered, turning toward the window.

Adam stared ahead, tapped the steering wheel, chewed the inside of his cheek. "Sometimes people aren't happy with the person they're with. I mean, they care about them, but they aren't really happy. Or they're just happy for now. It doesn't make the relationship mean any less. It just means they aren't meant to be together forever."

"What does that have to do with anything?" I huffed. I didn't want to talk about this, and I no longer wanted to hear what Adam thought.

"I'm just saying, maybe your mom wasn't happy, and instead of leaving when she should have, she held on for too long, or they both did. Then they started resenting each other..." He trailed off, took a deep breath. "Maybe they should have broken up a long time ago, before things got bitter."

"Yeah, great. Maybe they should have broken up eighteen years ago." I rolled my eyes. "Then you wouldn't be stuck doing this with me."

He glared at me. "I don't remember saying I didn't want to."

"You didn't need to." I returned my attention to look out the windshield. More silence.

Adam sighed, weighty and forlorn. "I wish you wouldn't put words in my mouth. You do that to people a lot."

I side-eyed him. "Are you seriously going to pick a fight with me?"

"Would it help?" His voice raised slightly, then he seemed to shrink back from the conversation. "Look, Brynn. I'm not annoyed. I just... don't know how to help you. Your mother screwed up. Badly. Your father deserves to know. But I'm not sure you should be the one to tell him. Do you want to get stuck between them? About something like this?"

"No! But if I don't tell him, who? She won't. Do I just let him continue thinking everything's normal?" If I told him now, maybe they would talk to each other, work through it. If I didn't, how would I be able to live with myself? "I hate her for making me do this."

"Yeah." He sat back in the seat. "I don't blame you. We're almost there."

"I'm gonna text him and tell him to meet me outside. You probably want to head home?" The needy way I'd turned that into a question made me curse myself.

"And then you'll both take a cab home? After discussing something like that?" Adam frowned, shaking his head. "No way. I'll drive you."

"You really don't need to—"

"Shut up already and text him." There was no malice in his words, but his tone convinced me not to argue.

I took out my phone. And stared at it.

"Hey Dad…" Adam prompted once he'd pulled into a space in the airport's pickup area.

"Shut up." Why was I snapping at Adam? He was trying to help me. "Sorry. I'm—"

"Don't apologize. I get it. But you won't ever get that text just right," he said. "You'll never get any of this right enough. You'll relive it for a while, no matter what you do or say."

I glanced away from the phone to Adam, whose eyes glistened in the screen's glow. He looked away, playing with the air conditioning, and I knew he spoke from experience.

"Right." I nodded and returned my attention to writing the text.

Surprise! I'm here with a friend, picking you up, so don't catch a cab.

I waited for a moment before adding where he could find us. After about five minutes of me drumming on the dashboard, picking at the lint on my clothes, and apologizing for annoying the crap out of Adam, my dad texted back. I fumbled with my phone for a moment.

Wow, that's a great surprise! Thank you! I'm just waiting for my suitcase and I'll be right out.

I answered with a description of Adam's car so he could pick it out without me standing in the rain waiting for him. "He'll only be another minute or so. Jeez, he seems happy to be home."

Adam shot another glance my way. "You don't have to say anything. It's your call."

"But you think I should say something." It was unfair, looking to him for an answer about my private life. As if he deserved to bear the weight of being right or wrong.

He shook his head. "I do, but it isn't up to me."

"I know." I sighed, dropping my head against the rain-battered window.

"You should get in the back so you can sit next to him," Adam suggested.

"I don't want to leave you up here like you're my driver or something. It's insulting."

Adam tilted his head against the seat, a sleepy smile on his face. "And I'm the one people make fun of for being overly polite. Get back there."

I hesitated.

"You are hereby banned from my front seat!" he bellowed, stabbing a finger at the back of the car.

I scrambled over the console and into the backseat, playing along with his fake intimidation act, making a show of flopping onto the floor and scrambling upright. I popped up and glanced into the rearview mirror. His glasses had slipped halfway down his nose. His eyes met mine, crinkled at the corners, kind, and chocolate dark.

My phone chimed.

I tore my eyes away from Adam's to find a text from Dad. He was having trouble finding the car. For a moment, goofing around with Adam, I had forgotten all about why I was here.

"Good luck," Adam murmured.

I peeked outside. There was Dad, wheeling his suitcase behind him and struggling with the parking lot's uneven concrete and the rain still coming down in sheets. He held a newspaper over his head in a futile attempt to stay dry.

I waved him over, and he rushed my way. Adam popped the trunk, then opened his door and got out.

"Here," Adam yelled over the roar of the downpour. "Let me put that in the trunk for you. Get inside where it's dry."

Dad thanked him and lowered himself into the back of the car. He regarded me with a stern gaze. "You didn't say this friend was a boy."

"It's Adam. He's my only friend with a car. You know this."

He bumped me with his shoulder and laughed, then pulled me into a bear hug, his rain-soaked clothes dampening mine. Normally, I would playfully shove him away and complain, but he smelled like his woodsy cologne and a hint of airplane peanuts, and it was so damn good to see him. I wanted to lean on him, dump all this on him and let the adult take care of it. But first, I had to do the hard part.

Adam climbed into the car, tapping on his phone a few times before putting the car in drive. The rain had plastered his dark hair to his neck, curling at his collar.

"Well, thank you, Adam," Dad said, "for letting Brynn drag you all the way out here to pick me up." He ran a hand through his graying hair, shaking moisture free from the strands.

"It's no problem, really." Adam sounded distracted and uncomfortable, and I got the feeling he'd rather play the role of my driver than be a part of this conversation.

"And why, exactly, did you ask him to, Bree?" Dad asked. "Everything okay?"

My hands shook, and I folded them in my lap to keep them still. "How was your trip?"

Dad's eyes narrowed, but he answered the question anyway, despite the edge in his tone. "My trip was fine. The usual convention. Sit, listen to a few panels. Learn some new marketing options, et cetera. Nothing you'd care about."

"Great," I said. "I have news."

Adam's eyes shot up to the rearview mirror, and he gave his

head a little shake. Once again, proof he thought I was a complete moron.

"Oh?" Dad asked.

"I made it into Hunter College, and I'll be starting in the fall. Which means me and Nina will be moving to the city together."

Adam released a relieved burst of air, and it was a struggle not to roll my eyes.

"Oh. Wow. Well, that's great, honey," he said, befuddled. "I didn't know you were considering that as an option, but I guess I understand. At least you'll be going out there with Nina."

"And Val and Adam will be heading to the city too," I said. "So it's not like we'll be alone."

Adam drummed on the steering wheel.

"You three will take care of my little girl, right?" Dad laughed.

"We'll look out for her, of course," Adam said, "but you know she takes care of herself."

"True enough," Dad said.

Adam slowed the car to a stop. A glance out the window revealed a greasy spoon diner with lights that cut through the falling dark of the evening.

"Um, Adam?" I asked. "What are you doing?"

He turned in his seat, looking over his shoulder. "Looking out for his little girl." He smiled. "I'm going into that diner and getting myself a plate of fries. You're going to have the conversation you're here to have, and when you're ready, you'll text me, and I'll come out and drive you home."

"Bree?" Dad asked.

Adam leaned forward. "You're not gonna feel comfortable doing this while I'm here." He gave my arm a little squeeze. "I'll see you in a bit."

He got out of the car, leaving me with my father and my own unspoken words.

CHAPTER FOUR
BANDAID TORN

DAD BLINKED blue eyes that looked just like mine.

"I'm sorry you had to find out like this," I said. "I know you guys have had problems—"

A bitter laugh escaped him. "Problems? We hate each other."

Now it was my turn to blink owlishly.

"You can't act like you don't know."

I knew their relationship wasn't good, but hate? Hate was an ugly thing, and the admission made my insides feel shaky and wrong.

"I'm sorry." He shook his head, letting out air in a stream, like he was trying to get control over his breathing. "I'm sorry I'm being so abrupt. I had a bad feeling something like this was going on."

"And you didn't warn me?" I asked.

"I'm not the one that does my best to drag you into our arguments, sweetheart." Another huffed breath. "That's not very productive either, is it? Pointing fingers won't help you feel better. I just never believed she would risk you finding out this way. The affair itself? We're a mess. Anybody with eyes can see that, and I'm convinced she's not fooling the neighbors the way she thinks she is. But after everything she's said to me, I can't believe she'd risk you finding out about it."

"Why does that matter? I'm not the issue here. She ruined

your marriage!" I sounded desperate, and I didn't even know what I was desperate for. Not to be the messenger of bad news? Not to be the person who ruined Dad's life? Not to be hated by Mom for the rest of eternity? Not to be even more in the damn way?

More head shaking. "There wasn't a marriage left to ruin. We'd spoken about the possibility of divorce before. Several times."

"Then why didn't you do it?" All the memories of being curled up on my bed, plugging my ears, and wishing I could will away the sounds of their constant bickering came whirling back at me.

He hesitated.

"Come on, Dad. Someone should be the honest one."

His eyes slid closed. "She didn't think you could handle a divorce."

"She didn't think I could handle it?" I parroted back.

"Because you wear black all the time," he said. "We think you're depressed."

"Because I wear black."

"Well, *I* think it's because you avoid spending any time outside of your room, and on the weekends, when you don't work, you stay in bed all day. *She* only brings up the black."

"I'm not depressed. I'm just avoiding her! And avoiding you when you fight with her." I facepalmed so hard, the reverberating noise spread through the car. "Of course Mom would think wearing black is a symptom of depression. I don't want to compete with other people. I don't like being the center of attention. But I'm not depressed. And you know what? Things might be easier if I didn't live with parents that hate each other but think it's better to stick it out for me."

"Hmmmm... you might be right about that." Dad nodded in agreement. "We screwed up. We should have protected you from this. I'm sorry."

My heart squeezed and tears welled up again. "Okay. But now it's time to do something about it. You can't just keep on like this."

"I hear you. I do. Bree..." He pulled me into a tight hug, stroking my hair as he spoke. "I'll talk to her when we get home. We'll figure something out."

That didn't sound like reconciliation was likely, and a part of me was relieved. The other part was terrified of everything that might change.

We hugged for a moment, and I did what I'd been wanting to do since I'd caught Mom with Jesse——I let Dad take care of me.

He kissed the top of my head. "Why don't you call your friend and tell him it's safe to come out now." He dropped his face into his hands. "Christ, he knows everything that happened, doesn't he?"

My cheeks warmed. "I wasn't gonna say anything, but I was at Nina's and I was stressed, and my brain was flip-flopping about what I should do, and all the worrying made me throw up. So I told them."

"So Nina, Val, and Adam all know?" Dad said. I wonder if that's gonna spread. Val does like to talk..."

"Listen, I get that you don't want people knowing—"

"No." He ran his hands over his face. "No, it's perfect." He grinned. "Your mom's going to flip when she realizes it's starting to get around the neighborhood."

I glared at him. "So will I, Dad. Petty much?"

He frowned. "Sorry. You're right." He cleared his throat. "Text Adam. I'll send a message to Uncle Josh in case I need a couch to crash on tonight."

I pulled my phone out of my pocket to discover several messages from Mom. "Crap." I texted Adam to come outside, then texted Mom and told her I was with Dad.

Let her worry about that until we got home.

A moment later, Adam returned my text.

Favorite donut? Yours and your dad's.

I showed Dad. "Absolutely not." But there was a twinkle in his eye.

I answered for both of us.

Chocolate Glaze and Boston Cream. Thank you. I owe you.

You owe me NOOOOOTHHHHIIIIING.

I glanced up from my phone to find Dad watching me. "What?"

"Nothing." He smiled, a dimple cutting into his cheek. "I just blinked, and you're all grown up."

"Not really. Not yet." I punched him in the arm. "Don't go getting all mushy on me."

When Adam returned to the car, he passed back a paper bag filled with donuts, a couple of each flavor, wrapped in wax paper. "What did I miss?"

I shrugged. "It stopped raining."

Dad laughed out loud.

WHEN WE GOT HOME, Mom was sitting on the living room couch waiting for us. Her eyes were puffy and her blonde hair tousled, like she had tried to sleep but failed.

"Never do that to me again," she said, her voice flat.

I didn't answer. How was I supposed to know if she'd give me another reason to scare her or keep me from wanting to come home? I stomped up the stairs and slammed the door.

The yelling started before I even kicked off my sneakers.

"How could you risk exposing her to something like this?"

"Now you care? Why? It's not like you're the one who has to deal with how she reacts! You're too busy gallivanting around the country."

I lowered myself to the bed.

"On business! At least she has fun with me. You're too busy wishing she'd fit in some little box you picked out for her."

I wrapped my arms around my knees.

"Oh, sorry! I thought we were molding our child, not letting her do whatever the hell she pleases!"

And wished I could disappear.

"You are not the woman I married."

"I miss when you were fun!"

Dad's bellow and Mom's shriek blurred together into cacophonous noise. I clapped my hands over my ears.

A black hole started in my center and spread throughout my body, a violent force that crushed everything it came into contact with. I screamed into my pillow, kicking my mattress, sick to fucking death of every nasty word spoken in this house, of feeling like I should have done something to fix them, of how damn little I could actually do. The feeling of impotence dissolved into tears, cutting hot trails down my cheeks.

I couldn't do this. I couldn't listen to them. I needed a distraction. I picked up my phone and switched to my texting app. Adam's text from earlier was still open.

You owe me NOOOOOTHHHHIIIIING.

Nina was still dealing with her own problems. Before I stopped to think about it, I texted Adam what I would have normally sent to Nina.

Well, it seems that my life has gone from their quiet arguments, spoken through me, to loud arguments without me. Not sure that's an improvement, but, hey…

For a moment, I got no response. I wasn't sure what I expected.

Adam and I had never been more than acquaintances.

And then my phone buzzed. The message was an image of a cartoon boy hugging an adorable little monkey. Another buzz.

At least you don't have to do their dirty work anymore.

I wasn't sure I agreed, but I appreciated the sentiment.

How can I get your mind off the lunacy taking place in your household?

Somehow, that made me smile.

I don't know. Send me something funny?

Another pause. My parents' screaming voices muted to a low buzz as I waited.

He came through with a meme that made me snort despite the pain. For over an hour, we shot memes back and forth until it almost became a competition. I didn't remember drifting to sleep, but the next morning, I woke with swollen eyes, in the same clothes I'd worn the night before.

When I glanced at my phone, still beside me on the bed, I couldn't help but grin. An unread message waited for me.

Goodnight, Brynn.

CHAPTER FIVE
FREEZING OVER

SCHOOL WENT BY RELATIVELY FAST. I immersed myself in my work and, aside from catching Nina and Val up on what had transpired, forced myself not to think about it. It was in Dad's hands now, and he and Mom would figure it out. I would deal with whatever they decided.

By the time school ended, I had managed to fake the funk well enough that my mood improved. That was a very good thing, because the moment Val and I arrived for our shift at Scoopy Doo, we were reminded of what was in store for us.

The new employee, Craig, stood beside Sammy, their heads buried in the waist-high freezer. Sammy was talking him through the ingredients in each flavor. I couldn't imagine why Sammy would have him start on a Friday of all days. There was no way we'd have him weekend-ready by the end of the shift, even if he was God's gift to ice cream scoops.

As we made our way around the counter, Sammy tapped Craig on the shoulder, muttering something to him. They straightened and turned to face us.

Craig was cute, with shaggy blonde hair and freckles across his nose, and the minute I saw him I remembered why his name was so familiar. He was a junior at Birchwood High, and we had taken a required music class together. He had sung a pretty decent tenor, and I had warbled a questionable alto. I grinned at the sight of him.

"Hey man!" I reached out to shake his hand. "How are you?"

His eyebrows raised, and he held his hand out tentatively. "Do I know you?"

"Brynn. Stark. I was in chorus with you. I used to have brown hair. You know, before the dye bottle incident." Val's eyes darted back and forth between us.

"Oh!" His head ticked back a little. "Oh, Brynn! I totally didn't recognize you. The new look is...interesting."

It was...interesting...to everyone. The black clothes, the black hair, the complete lack of being on trend. It had been a year since I'd first decided to take the plunge and change my style. Everyone seemed thrown off by it because I used to try to fit in. I used to want to be one of those kids who styled themselves, sleek and perfect all the time. Some people, like Nina and Val, enjoyed it. I never did. It stressed me out. At some point in the middle of my parental debacle, I decided I didn't have enough stress space in me for a huge energy expenditure I didn't even enjoy. So I stopped.

My stomach twisted when my mind wandered to my parents.

Craig waited for a response with an odd look in his eyes.

"Thanks. I decided I no longer gave a shit what people thought of me. My hygiene exceeds expectations though, so at least I don't smell terrible."

Val audibly sighed.

"What?" I asked, as though I had no idea why she would be disappointed.

"I said something wrong, didn't I?" Craig looked to Sammy as though he could bail him out.

Sammy offered him a tight-lipped smile before looking at me. "Try not to scare away our summer worker, sweetie."

I saluted him. "Yes, sir." I marched past him in full military mode. Taking the turns sharply, I headed to the back and into the bathroom to change my clothes. The minute the door closed behind me, I deflated.

When I emerged in my uniform, Sammy was gone, but Val hovered nearby.

Yes, I know. I'm awful." I shrugged.

Val waved a dismissive hand in my direction. "No, he was a dick. 'Interesting?' Not the word he should have used."

I laughed. "So he should have lied and said I was stunning?"

Anger made her green eyes glow brighter. "Brynn, you are a beautiful girl. It's your attitude that sucks."

"I'm not in the mood for the 'why are you always acting like this' pep talk. Besides, there's a trainee waiting for me." I opened the bathroom door for her and waved my arm toward the entrance. "In you go."

I swore Val growled, but I'd never be able to prove it, and she'd charm eleven out of twelve jurors at the trial into saying no.

At the front counter, Craig awkwardly chatted with Mrs. Gorfeld. Because, of course, it wouldn't be one of the easy ones. Gorfeld always had a bug up her ass. She needed to rush back home to sit out on her porch and complain about the neighbors who talked too loudly as they passed, or something.

When Craig pulled away to prepare her order, I approached him.

"What did she want?"

"Um...a small strawberry shake, and a sundae with...um..." He bit his lip.

"It's fine," I said, voice as low as possible to avoid the customer from overhearing. "If they say they want a sundae, ask them the toppings as you're making it. Customers almost always change their mind or forget something anyway."

Craig nodded, the fear on his face lifting slightly.

I turned to the lady at the counter and switched on my smile. "Ma'am, I apologize in advance. I'm training our newest server, so it might take a little longer than usual today, but once I do, he'll be better prepared to serve you in the future."

The lady smiled back. "Just don't take all day."

Sigh. I waved Craig over to join me by the hard ice cream freezer. "Grab a small shake cup. I'm gonna make this and you're gonna watch me so we don't take up too much of the customer's time. We'll practice again later." I plopped one thick scoop of strawberry ice cream into the cup and jerked my head toward Craig so he would follow me to the milk refrigerator and the blender that were a little further in the back.

"Because she's a bitch," I muttered, loud enough for only Craig to hear.

He grinned. "Okay, so one scoop of hard ice cream?"

"Right. Two scoops for a large. A squirt of strawberry syrup. Then milk poured just over the ice cream line."

I felt eyes burning a hole in my back. I glanced over my shoulder and sure enough, Val was watching me teach Craig.

"Hey Val, why don't you make a sundae for our customer. She's low on time." I slowed the words down, just a little. Val nodded sharply and got to work.

"Okay, you hold down the button and you push this wand into the ice cream slowly, and it mixes it up." I started the machine, speaking louder to compensate for the whir of the mixer. "You control it. It does not control you. If you forget that, you'll be wearing it. Just take your time. It's gonna be hard at first, but eventually, you get it down to a science." I used the wand to show him how smooth the shake was. "See?"

"I think?" Craig said.

"You'll get it once you can actually do it on your own." I popped the lid down to cover the shake. "And be prepared to get a little messy."

I walked back up to the counter and my jaw dropped. A line of customers had formed all the way to the door. Val was whirring through them as fast as she could.

"Oh shit," Craig whispered.

I had to agree.

WE DIDN'T GET a break for another hour and a half. Craig did his best to help, but mostly he shadowed us, trying to catch on to what we were doing. Every time he tried on his own, he'd forget an integral part of the process—a standard issue on the first day.

"Now that it's quieter, maybe you should show Craig around the rest of the store?" Val said. "I'll go out and grab us dinner."

We gave Val our orders for Jack's, the diner on the corner. I took Craig to the back, showing him where we kept the straws, cake molds, and extra cups and lids. Across from them were two large freezers, where we stored our to-be-used tubs and our finished cakes. After that, I led him to the walk-in freezer.

The walk-in freezer was exactly what it sounded like—a large metal freezer designed like a walk-in closet. When I opened the door, the cold air rushed out, meeting the relative warmth of the store. I motioned Craig in, letting the door close behind us as I flipped the light switch.

Inside, four metal shelving units rested against the walls, holding boxes and various containers.

"Okay, this is where we store most of our toppings that aren't fresh fruit or a syrup," I said, my breath expelling in a cloud in front of me. "Chocolate chips and candy and frozen fruits. There are your mix bags. You've got vanilla and chocolate. We dump those into the soft ice cream machine." I turned to lead him back out. "All of the flavors use either chocolate or vanilla as a base. Then we add flavoring and toppings—" I tried the door handle. It didn't open. "—and freeze it..."

I tried the handle again, leaning my whole body into it. "Weird."

"Here, let me try it." Craig sidled past me, grabbed the handle, and slammed it with his shoulder. The door didn't budge, but Craig winced from the impact.

I knelt in front of the door handle to examine it. I couldn't see anything wrong with it. My stomach bottomed out.

"Could Val have locked it by accident?" Craig asked.

"It's not supposed to lock! There must be something wedged under the handle." I kicked the door. Pain ricocheted through my foot and my leg, and I screamed, channeling it into a name. "Val!" I rotated my ankle. "Well, that was a shit idea."

No answer.

Craig joined me, shaking the door as he shouted.

No answer.

He paled. The temperature in the freezer seemed to take a sharp drop. The tip of my nose started to numb.

"Val must have left already." I got out my phone and dropped down onto the nearest box. I called Val. No answer. I sent her a text. No read notification. It was stuck on delivered. Since when did Val not look at her phone? Most times, she checked it every other minute as if she expected the message to disappear if she didn't read it fast enough. "Looks like we're stuck here until Jack's cooks our burgers."

Craig shivered. "I feel like a burger...in a meat locker."

"It's okay, man," I said. "It's cold, but I'm sure we'll be fine for twenty minutes."

"It would have been nice if this place was a little bigger. More room to move around." Craig settled down on the box next to me. "What if the store gets robbed?"

"Yeah, I think Sammy will understand if that happens. Besides, I'd like to think nobody in Birchwood would do that." I squinted at the door handle, looking for something, a broken mechanism, a way to jimmy the latch. It was how I managed to keep myself far away from panic-land.

"That's kind of idealistic, but sure." Craig motioned at the space around him. "What else do you have to show me?"

I frowned at him. "I've shown you everything I can in here. Mix bags that feel about eighty pounds when you lift them? Check. Toppings? Check. We're sitting on a well-packaged box of cookie-crackers for ice cream sandwiches. We make those and keep them out front with the decorated cakes. Which are probably all gone, because you're right, we probably are getting robbed while I'm locked in this stupid freezer with you."

Craig frowned, sitting forward on the box, rocking in place slightly. "I don't think you like me."

I could not believe this. "So, what, this is a therapy session now?"

"See?" He jabbed a finger at me. "You don't like me."

I laughed. "I'm like this with everyone."

"Yeah?" His light eyes twinkled. "I guess that makes sense. You weren't like that in chorus. Guess it fits the whole new look."

"My look? And you're talking about me not liking you? The first thing out of your mouth was a comment about my 'look.'"

"I wasn't trying to be insulting," he said.

"You weren't trying not to be," I said. "My 'look' changed when I decided my outside should look more like my inside. It feels more authentic than dresses and makeup. To me, at least. So, what you tell me when you make a comment about it, is that you would rather I hide who I am with bright colors and perfectly styled hair, because my internal self makes you feel uncomfortable. Is that it?"

It could have been that my frustration about this topic was coming from somewhere else. Maybe. Possibly.

"I thought you said this wasn't a therapy session," Craig snapped.

He was right. "Fine, I'm sorry. I've just been getting that a lot lately. Shouldn't have taken it out on you." I glanced his way.

For a moment, air silently left his mouth in twisty white puffs. He nodded. "I hear that. I've got something similar going on."

"Yeah? What's that? There's nothing wrong about your look."

He smiled, his eyes warming, and my cheeks joined them as I realized how my words could be interpreted.

Well, at least I wasn't freezing anymore.

"Nah, not about that," he said. "I want to sing. Be the next Shawn Mendes or something. My mom and dad think that's an unreliable career, so they keep pushing me toward business school. I fought that, so they said if I didn't want business school, I could work in retail."

"Please tell me that's not how you wound up here," I said. "If this was an attempt to teach you to enjoy the workforce, you should definitely rebel."

"No, they knew I would hate it. But it's this or business school, so…"

"You're going to stay at a job you don't want to stick it to the man?" I grinned. "I don't know if it's worth all the shake-stained vomit-smelling uniform shirts in your future."

He scowled, but his teeth chattered, negating the effect. "What's that supposed to mean?"

"Just that retail sucks."

"Yeah? You sure you don't mean because I suck at this job?" he asked. "I know I'm supposed to be impressing you. But we're stuck in a freezer, and it isn't *my* fault, so I don't really care."

Could he be any more bristly? "It's not my fault either!"

"I can tell you think I suck at it."

"You need to focus more on trying to remember what I tell you. If your memory was any worse, you could throw your own surprise party."

Craig shot me a death glare, but I bumped him with my shoulder.

"You're fine! It's your first day! Literally everybody's first day is like this. Just remember whatever you can," I said. "You'll have another chance tomorrow."

"Brynn? Craig?" Val's voice just barely made it through the thick door.

We both whirled toward the sound, eyes eager. Jumping from our seats, we banged on the door, calling in unison for Val. The door pulled open, and there was Val, mouth dropped open, hand to her mouth, the picture of utter shock.

My eyes narrowed.

"We got locked in," Craig said sheepishly. "Brynn doesn't know how it happened. The handle looked like it was working fine and—"

"I am so sorry." Val replaced her shocked look with a broad smile. "Totally my fault! I went to refill the sprinkles and I must have accidentally bumped the rolling cart!" She eyed it tragically. "It was wedged under the door handle when I came in."

Craig visibly cheered. "Don't worry, Val. You're like our hero. You came and got us out."

"Are you two alright? It's awfully cold in there."

I gritted my chattering teeth. "Yeah, no frickin' kidding."

"Was there no way to stay warm? Could neither of you think of anything?" Val asked.

And that confirmed what I'd wondered the minute that door opened to her exaggerated face. I looked up at Craig, who awkwardly glanced between me and Val. "Why don't you go step outside? It's warmer out there."

"Okay, let's go," he said, motioning for me to come with him as he headed out. He stopped when he reached the front counter and saw I hadn't followed.

"You go ahead," I said. "I need to talk to Val."

"Oh, come on, Brynn." He bounded back over to me, then leaned in close. "It was a mistake."

"I'm not going to kill her," I said. "I just want to talk."

Craig's features twisted into a mask of concern. I motioned toward the door. Craig didn't budge.

"Fine! We'll go outside instead." I grabbed Val's wrist and dragged her out the door. She planted her feet, but I kept pulling. Her sneakers squeaked across the floor.

We burst through the door and out into the breezy spring air.

"What is the matter with you?" She yanked away from my grasp and shook her wrist out.

"What's the matter with me?" I snapped. "Did you do what I think you did?"

Val's gaze lingered on Craig, who stood at the front counter, idly swiping a wet rag across the counter in an effort to look busy. "I think we should go back inside…"

"If a customer comes, we'll spot them." I waved at the only entrance to the shop. "Did you lock me in the walk-in freezer with Craig, Val? Because if you did, so help me…"

"What on earth would make you think that?" She smiled, dimples pressing into her cheeks, her light eyes twinkling.

I fought to keep my eyes from popping out of my head. "You asked if we found ways to warm up while we were in there. Is that seriously all you think about?"

She shrugged. "Making an innuendo doesn't imply I—"

"You have spent the last week trying to make me believe in true love."

People were beginning to stare as they passed. Across the street, Tony Lin, star high school basketball player and purveyor of pizza at Emilio's, split his time between sweeping the storefront and staring at Val and me like we were about to catfight each other's clothes off.

When I spoke again, I lowered my voice. "Is that your idea of finding true love? Warming each other up in a freezer?"

She grinned, teeth gleaming. "I don't remember saying anything about true love."

Disgusting. "I'm not into making out with whoever's in a reasonable proximity."

Val snickered. "Relax, would you? It's not that big a deal. I was right outside. I wouldn't have let you freeze to death or anything."

"You wouldn't have let me freeze to death..." I let the words trail off. "Are you insane?"

"No, I'm not insane. I'm your friend." She glanced off to the side, like she couldn't look me in the eyes.

"Are you my friend, Val?" I snapped. "Or are you just Nina's sister?"

Val looked stricken, and for a moment, I almost felt bad. But then she painted over it with a sunshiney smile, and I remembered how infuriating she was all over again.

"I'm trying to pull you out of this bitter path you're on," she said, voice chirpy and saccharine. You don't like Craig, fine. You don't like how I pushed you together with Craig, also fine. But I'm just trying to help, so enlighten me."

A cloud filled my chest, leaving me feeling murky and wrong. "You think you can help me? You want to keep trying to set me up? Sure. Go ahead and try. I'm sure that'll work out great."

I stormed back into the store.

"That looked pleasant," Craig commented.

Resisting the urge to punch him in the face, I glanced back at Val. She didn't return for another few minutes. When she did, she didn't speak to me, only Craig. The rest of the afternoon passed in a tense silence, not unlike most days at home.

I STOMPED toward my front door, pushing off each step harder than normal, taking out my aggression on concrete instead of living flesh. Good thing, too, because living flesh was exactly what greeted me on the other side of the door—two blobs of it, shaped like Mom and Dad, each perched expectantly on opposite ends of the living room couch. Waiting. They were waiting for me.

I threw my ice cream stained cap to the floor as hard as I could manage. "You've gotta be frickin' kidding me. Will this shit day never end?"

"Bree!" Mom snapped.

"Mom, I caught you boinking the neighbor. I think we're past language restrictions."

"Brynn Stark. That's enough." Dad's eyes went hard, and I knew I'd better shut up. If he wasn't going to back me up, I didn't have a leg to stand on.

I sat down across from them on the loveseat, practically daring Mom to say something about the smell of old ice cream on her cushions. She just looked away.

"Brynn," Dad said in a tone he often used around me, but rarely did it hold such a solemn ache. It was his "time to get serious voice," and I instantly knew I was going to hate this conversation.

He took a deep breath, eyes rolling toward the ceiling as if someone would break through it, ready to supply him with whatever he needed to get through this conversation. "Your mother and I are getting a divorce."

I'd waited my entire life to hear those words, but the reality wasn't nearly as sweet as I'd imagined. Now that I was finally getting the divorce I had craved for my own peace of mind, all I could do was ache for the good old days I never had. And now never would.

Only one thing could save this.

"I want to live with Dad."

"Very nice, Bree," Mom said.

"I'm sorry. You're undeniably the better role model here," I deadpanned.

"I'm your mother." She stressed the word as though it forgave her of all her sins.

"I'm moving out." Dad spoke in a careful rhythm that made me feel like a cornered animal. "I'll be staying with your uncle Josh, and I'm not sure he's up for sharing his home with a teenager. It's probably bad enough he has to take me in."

My voice went shrill. "I'm nearly eighteen! I'll be leaving for school in the fall. It would only be a few months."

"And that's not a decision I can make for him," Dad said. "I understand what you want, but you need this time to work on repairing your relationship with your mother."

I couldn't believe what I was hearing. "I don't want to repair our relationship. How can you be so okay with this?"

For a moment, they both looked stricken, and I hated it.

Dad schooled his features until he appeared calm. "Bree, I need time to adjust, and you need to make things right with your mother before you leave. You're going to be going away to school for months without coming home and you've never spent any time away from her. Is this really how you want to leave things?"

"Yes." It was a stubborn growl, and maybe it wasn't completely true, but I couldn't fathom another few months of her hypocritical judgment. I couldn't stay with Mom. I couldn't even look at her. He sat up straighter, showing he would brook no further argument. "You'll stay here."

My throat burned, and I swallowed.

"Can I stay with Nina tonight?" I asked.

Dad looked at Mom. Mom looked away, her focus dropping to a faded stain on the living room rug.

"Yes. You can stay with Nina."

"Good." I didn't wait for their permission to leave. I hurried to my room before the fury building in my chest escaped.

I ARRIVED at the entrance to Nina's basement hideaway, my hair still wet from the shower, without telling her I was coming. It had been a short walk from my side of town to Nina's more well-off area. In that time, I'd managed to gain control over my emotions. I felt stronger, like I could dissect my emotions. I felt…

The door swung open to reveal Nina, looking at me with questions in her eyes. "Brynn? Are you okay?"

Behind her, I could see Val and Adam sitting on the couch. Val was doing her damnedest to look at anything but me, but Adam's eyes were fixed my way.

"What? Yeah. I'm good." The words were numb echoes.

Nina's eyebrows raised. "You've been standing outside for ten minutes without knocking. Adam spotted you but didn't think he should be the one to come out here and get you."

That burning feeling in the back of my throat resurfaced. "I…I didn't…I…" The tears started falling, and I pushed the heels of my hands against my eyes, trying to hold them back.

Nina wrapped an arm around my shoulders and ushered me in, kicking the door shut behind her. My friends formed a cocoon of comfort around me, even, surprisingly, Val.

In this way, at least, I was lucky.

CHAPTER SIX
GABE ON THE MENU

THE TWO WEEKS that followed were exhausting, but my circle saw me through. My father moved out with the help of Uncle Josh. My mother avoided me like I was a Better Homes & Gardens photoshoot, and her Feng Shui wasn't perfected yet. And I fumbled between home, school, work, and Nina's, avoiding all visible reminders of the nightmare at home.

But every evening, Mom expected me home.

"You live here until the end of August," she said. "Nina will have more than enough of you when school starts in the fall."

Which was why I was in my room, in my own bed, when the shrill ring of my phone broke through the relative peace of sleep. My body groaned for five more minutes, but the ringing wouldn't stop, so I picked it up, thoroughly planning to scream at whoever was on the other end.

"What?"

"Good morning, sleepyhead! We're having a barbecue today!" Val's upbeat tone greeted me on the other end of the line.

I pulled the phone away from my ear to look at the time. I had to squint to see past the sunlight streaming through the window. "It's 8:30 on a Saturday morning. Why are you calling me?"

"Be happy. I jumped on Nina's bed to inform her."

"You're a menace." I rolled over, turning my back to the rays of sunshine. "What's this about a barbecue?"

"That's the spirit!" Her voice was just a little too loud in my ear, like she thought she needed to yell for me to hear her. "The menfolk will cook the meat, and the womenfolk will serve and cater. Just like the good old days." A pause. "Well, not exactly. We won't have to hunt the animals ourselves, and I doubt Angie will allow us to drink floods of wine."

I groaned and smacked my head against the pillow. "Why do I continue to talk to you?"

"Because you love me," she said.

I didn't answer.

"You do and you know it. But seriously, this isn't about me. It's for Adam."

"We're having a barbecue for Adam?" I tried to imagine Adam wanting a barbecue.

Val sighed, sounding more impatient with me by the second. "Can you just come over around noon? Adam's family will be there. You can bring your mom if you want."

"She's working today." She was not working today. In the month since Dad had moved out, my relationship with Mom had only gotten more tense.

"Damn," Val said. "Well, can you puh-leeeeze make it? I'll owe you."

Something told me I didn't want that.

NINA'S HOUSE sat high atop a hill in the richer section of Birch-wood Grove, a two-story vision with sturdy stone walls of different shades, from a light tan to a deep brown. The top floor had a gorgeous bay window in the center, and airy curtains fluttered within.

I could smell the charcoal grill from the front door. I walked around the house, past the stone basement built into the hill, until I reached the open backyard.

Since Val was the one who invited me, I was cautious about turning the corner and walking in like I lived there, the way I usually would. Realizing my hesitance pissed me off. I'd been a welcome member of this household for years, and now I was cowering around corners, nervous about crossing from the driveway to the yard like I didn't belong there?

Hell no.

I turned the corner and observed the scene before me. The first table to come into view was straight ahead of me, on the far side of the deck. Nina's parents, Angie and Roman, sat there with Adam's father, William, each enjoying beers and plates of food.

On the deck corner nearest me, an unfamiliar guy taller than Val, Adam, and even Nina, smiled politely at something Val said. His hand pushed through hair that was short, black, curly, and shot through with an electric blue. Lean and a bit lanky, he looked about our age, but the naturally tanned skin of his arms was inked with swirly tattoos of black and red. Silver swirl plugs stretched his earlobes, and he spotted me before anyone else, his polite smile opening up into a true toothy grin.

Nina and Adam, whose backs were turned to me, followed Gabe's gaze to find me hesitating at the entrance.

"Brynn! Get over here, girl!" Nina waved me over.

I tried to merge with the scenery like a chameleon but failed like I always did. If only it was more than my imaginary superpower. Instead of a disappearing act, I gave them an awkward wave. "Hi guys! What's up?" I stepped out from around the corner and lost the shade from the roof. The sun beat down on my head once again, the black of my hair absorbing the heat.

"Brynn, I'd like you to meet my cousin, Gabriel Hernandez." Adam took my elbow and led me toward the new guy, depositing me in front of him. "Gabe, this is Brynn."

"Hey," Gabe said, gaze locking on to mine.

"Hey."

"It's nice to meet you."

"Yeah. You too."

Adam's eyes bounced between the two of us. "So... um... Gabe is staying with me and Dad until the end of the summer. He just wrapped up his freshman year at SVA."

SVA. The School of Visual Arts. Also in New York City.

"Oh, cool. What are you studying?" I swallowed hard.

"Cartooning," he said. "But it's not, like, kid cartoons. I'm working on this webcomic..."

Nina bumped my arm with hers and deposited a plastic cup filled with water in my hand. She fought down a smile. Beside her, Val wasn't even pretending to hide hers.

"Dude." It seemed unassuming, like everything Adam said, but there was a slight hint of urgency to it that drew our attention his way. He motioned toward the grill. The hot dogs and burgers were looking a little crispy.

Gabe swore and rushed to get them off the barbecue. They joined another set of burgers, hot dogs, and some grilled veggies on a plate beside the grill.

"Okay, that's enough of me putting you to work." Roman sidled up beside Gabe and turned off the grill. "Sit, enjoy the food. Thanks for your help, Gabriel."

Gabe nodded, his gaze sliding to his skull-covered red Vans.

I took that as my cue and grabbed a plate from the stack on a nearby folding table. I gathered the ingredients for a decent burger and a corn cob and headed over to the patio table beside the one where the adults gathered.

Gabe and Adam were still preparing their food when I sat next to Val and Nina.

"So, how do you like Gabe?" Val asked, her voice sharp.

I glanced at her before taking an undignified chomp out of my burger. "He's cool," I said through my food.

Nina laughed. "That's Brynn's way of telling you to back off."

I pointed from my eyes to hers. She got me.

"How cool *is* he?" Val asked.

Nina looked from me to Val. "She's not doing this with you."

The guys joined us at the table, Adam settling in beside Val, Gabe fitting himself into the space between Adam and me.

Gabe laughed. "You are not going to survive that plate." He pointed a fork at Nina's leaning tower of foodstuffs.

Nina had always eaten like her stomach had no end. We used to eat the same way. I expanded somewhat, developing thick thighs and a doughy tummy. She remained exactly the same. She said it was her asthma medication, but I'd met her Mom's side of the family. Genes definitely played a role.

Nina smiled her plotting smile. "You're probably right. But I don't know. I'm starving. Maybe I can."

Gabe's eyes narrowed, looking to each of us for a clue. I took another indelicate bite from my burger. Val poked at her veggies with her fork. Adam leaned his chair back to comment on his father's burger, just to avoid having to pick a side. Nobody was going to help the newbie, not even a blood relation.

"Okay," Gabe said. "Ten bucks says you won't go up for seconds."

Nina's eyes widened. "Seconds, huh? You ain't playin'." We shared a glance. "I'll take you up on that. However, I don't want your ten bucks. I will reserve the right to a payment of my choosing at a later date. Deal?"

Gabe speared a slice of grilled eggplant on the edge of his fork. "And what do I get if I win?"

Nina considered it, but looked to me for an answer.

"How about if you win—" Val started.

"Nothing," I cut her off. "You get the pleasure of knowing you were right."

He grinned. "Oh, do I?"

"Is that not enough?" I asked, eyes wide and innocent.

"How about..." His eyes tracked the surrounding space before they finally settled on me. "... I take my winnings from you? Same deal. Obviously, all requests on both sides should be within reason. Nothing crazy."

It sounded perfectly rational, but there was a glimmer of mischief in his eyes that sent an unfamiliar thrill right through me. "Deal."

His eyes lingered on mine for a moment before he spoke again. "So...Fall Out Boy." He pointed at my shirt. "Good band. Twenty-One Pilots is better, but FOB can still hang."

As we talked, Nina ate. And ate. And ate. Two hot dogs, a hamburger, corn on the cob, and a side of grilled veggies. She even cracked open a diet soda, which we all found somewhat ridiculous.

We took some time to get to know Gabe. I learned he had permanent ink stains on his fingers from his more intense art sessions, and I watched his confusion whenever Val's more energized, gushy side came out to play. He told us about what he was learning at SVA, and what it was like living on your own on campus. He prepped us for what we should actually bother bringing with us, and about the cooler places to hang out in the city.

He was open and friendly, and being around him seemed to unlock a side of Adam that we'd never seen. At school, Adam was pretty tightly wound, but here with Gabe, he was playful—roughhousing, telling raucous stories from when they were younger, and apparently less afraid of breaking limbs. He laughed more than usual.

I thought I'd already known Adam pretty well, but watching him with Gabe was proof that you could know part of someone, but there was often more to them than that.

"Hey, you're done!" Val's voice broke through my thoughts. She pointed at Nina's plate. "You win!"

"Oh, but no, she doesn't." Gabe waved a finger. "She has to go get seconds."

Nina turned a glare on him. "Okay, fine." She stomped over to the serving table and grabbed a grilled carrot, tossing it into the air and catching it in her mouth. "You happy? Seconds."

Gabe pushed back his chair. "I am outraged. Seconds consist of an entire plate."

"Not true," Nina argued. "I ate what was on my plate, and then I ate more. *Seconds*. You didn't say it had to be a certain amount."

Gabe sucked his teeth and crossed his arms, but not an ounce of his posturing was real. He was playing the bad guy, and it was kind of adorable. "Well, I still think you didn't win. But I didn't really win either, so what does that mean?"

"None of us win."

"Or we both win." A grin cut across his face, killing his villain act in seconds. "I guess that means I'm indebted to you, and Brynn——you're indebted to me."

"Don't get too happy about that," I said. "I'm not a cooperative person."

"Yeah, I wouldn't imagine you are."

I just smiled at him.

"So, who wants to go inside and play some air hockey?" Adam elbowed Gabe in his side. "You've gotta lose today somehow."

Gabe laughed. "I don't know if that's wise, man. I'm on a winning streak."

"I guess I'm gonna have to kick your ass then." Adam's eyebrows raised. "Kill your streak." He raced for the stairs. "Bet you can't get there first!"

Gabe raced after him, and with an amused look shared between the three of us, Val, Nina, and I followed.

"FAVORITE BOOK?" I asked Gabe.

Nina and Adam were playing their round of air hockey. Every conceivable team had played three times already, and this was the final set to determine the ultimate winner. Val had mysteriously disappeared, claiming she had to help the adults clean up.

That left me and Gabe curled up on the couch.

"Fifty Shades of Grey." He didn't even get the words out before he cracked up. "I'm sorry. Twilight. Okay, I'll stop now. The Dark Knight Returns. I do enjoy books, but I'm partial to comics. Remember, I'm a cartoonist."

"I guess that makes sense," I said, kicking off my sneakers and pulling my knees up to my chest. "Comics can have literary merit."

Gabe frowned. "You say that like you're giving them a gift. Oh, you can have some merit too, I guess."

"I don't mean it like that. I guess I don't read comics, really. Maybe, if I read The Dark Knight, you could read my favorite book?"

"And what's your favorite?" The smile returned to his face, and I was grateful to see it.

"The Perks of Being a Wallflower by Stephen Chbosky." Saying the words was like a summoning. I felt the weight of it in my hand, saw the pages slightly tattered from years of re-reads, smelled the print on the paper.

"You take good care of your books?" he asked.

"People who dog-ear pages are villains who must be persecuted."

"Worse if they do it to comics." Gabe nodded, stroking his chin. There was an uneven patch of stubble there I hadn't noticed before. "How about the next time I see you, I bring you a copy of my book, you bring me a copy of your book, and we see how we like them?"

"Cool," I said. This was... nice. It was good to meet someone new I could vibe with.

"Yes!" Nina shouted, doing a little victory dance around the air hockey table. "Looks like I'm the only winner today, Adam." She said his name like the bullies used to in elementary school. A Dumb. Because they were dicks and were jealous of Adam's intelligence. Adam had adopted it as an ironic nickname whenever he got two points off a perfect grade or something that was otherwise unfitting of his brilliance.

Gabe watched the interaction with a grin. "She's competitive."

"Yup," I said, popping the p.

"That was cheating, and you know it." Adam jabbed a finger in her direction. "Dad texted and distracted me." He stressed each word. "Gabe, we've gotta go."

Gabe frowned. "Aw, okay." He held a hand out to me. "It was very nice to meet you, Brynn."

"Nice to meet you, too." I slid my hand into his.

"I'll see you soon?"

"Yeah, definitely."

"Gabe," Adam groaned.

I shook my head. "You better go."

"Yeah, yeah."

Nina walked up with them, acting like an excellent hostess and showing everyone out. I stayed downstairs and waited for the girls to come back down. The night had been wonderful, just what I'd needed after such an awful couple of weeks. And Gabe was... easy to get along with. The kind of guy who had a winning smile and overwhelming charisma. The kind of guy I'd normally be wary of because it doesn't seem real, except Adam didn't hate him, so it couldn't be fake.

I liked him. Actually, I liked him a lot, but I couldn't shake the feeling he was missing some mystery quality I couldn't grasp, something that would make us a good fit.

I was sure Val had cooked this whole barbecue up just to introduce me to him, in the hopes I'd find the perfect person for me, but I wasn't sure there was anyone that fit that description. Even if there was, I would suffer through the inevitable break-up. I had decided not to look. Which Val couldn't seem to accept.

Val's light voice drifted down from the top of the stairs. She chatted with Nina, who laughed at whatever she was saying. I waited until she touched the foot of the stairs.

"I can see what you're doing, and I'm not falling for it."

Val stopped short, Nina careening into her.

"Damn it girl, move!" Nina snapped. "That's the kind of shit that causes car accidents."

Val snapped upright, like someone just shoved a stick up her ass. "Sorry Nina, Brynn seems to have something to say."

"Gabe. You brought him here on purpose."

Val stepped aside so Nina could get down the stairs. "Well, yes. I brought him here because he's staying with Adam, and I wanted him to meet everybody." She used a measured tone, like she was speaking to a kindergartner.

"That is not what I meant, and you know it," I snapped. "I thought we were beyond this crap after the incident with Craig."

"I have no idea—"

"Oh, can it, Val," Nina said. "She's right. You may have brought him here as a friendly gesture, but you were definitely looking to hook Brynn up."

"I wasn't against it," Val said.

I groaned. Nina plopped onto the couch beside me, exasperated.

"I know you think I'm trying to pester you into doing something you don't want to do, but that just means you don't understand the true importance of love."

I dropped my head against the back of the couch.

She ignored me and lowered herself onto the edge of the air hockey table, leaning forward like she was about to give me the secrets of the universe. "Love is the most powerful force in the world. Love can heal sickness and start wars. Believe me, I know." When she smiled, a little of her normal sparkle was gone.

"Oh, this again. Have you heard this, Nina? Val is an expert at love. She's seen it all, and she knows everything there is to know about it, because she's been exposed to it once or twice."

"What do you know about my life before I came here?" Val asked.

Nina and I exchanged glances.

"You're family," Nina said. "It only mattered if you wanted to tell us."

We'd always had the policy that Nina's foster siblings needed to be the ones to tell us information like this. We didn't want anyone to be treated differently because of their past. Worse, we didn't want to accidentally treat someone differently because we knew something they didn't want us to know. We just welcomed them into the family and went from there.

We always figured, if it was something essential, Angie and Roman would warn us. Still, we'd heard all kinds of terrible stories about what could happen in foster homes.

Val took a deep breath and released it slowly. "What I'm about to tell you is pretty deep. I would have told you sooner, but I didn't think you would believe me, and the last time someone found out, it didn't go well." She frowned. "That's putting it lightly, actually. There were torches involved. And pitchforks."

She was worrying me. "Val, whatever it is, you can tell us. You may drive me nuts, but you're a Lopez. That means you're family."

"Whether you like it or not, right?" She laughed, but it was harsh and sad. The youthful light seemed to vanish from Val's eyes, a deep frown morphing her features into a less carefree version of herself. "Okay, I'll tell you." For a moment, she stared at her shoes. Then she mumbled something.

"What?" I couldn't have heard that right. "Your name is Heidi?"

"You bought a nightie?" Nina said.

"You hid the body?"

"You're a righty?"

"I'm APHRODITE!"

I laughed. "Yeah, and I'm the Mad Hatter."

Val blinked. "You don't believe me?"

"Um...no." Nina sighed. "Val, what's this all about?"

"What do you mean?"

"You've been acting different lately," Nina said. "Running around the house like you've been dosed, talking about your mission. What's going on?"

Val was quiet for a moment. When she spoke, her voice was a low drone. "What's going on is Brynn. She told me she doesn't believe in love, and that is absolutely unacceptable to me. I hear more and more people saying they don't believe in love every day. If I don't get back to work, will there be any love left? And what if I don't want to get back to work? What if I want to stay here?"

Nina made the slightest move, a tiny nudge to my arm, and I felt the panic, the fear that our friend had completely lost it.

Val shook her head. "You think I'm insane."

"Val...you're claiming godhood," I said. "Can you really blame us?"

"Yes." Val stomped her foot, and the glasses on the coffee table shook. "Look, I don't just tell anyone this secret. And most of the time, people think I'm lying. Or they think I'm a witch and, well, the pitchforks. Or they think I'm joking. But I'm not. I'm not joking. I love Adam. And Nina treats me like family. And Brynn, you put up with my crap!" Her face flushed, like she had to force the truth out and it hurt. "I want to tell you guys. And I want you to believe me. Is that too much to ask?"

"Val," Nina said in a cautious, measured tone. "Maybe if you could provide us with some proof, we'd believe you. It's a bit difficult to swallow."

Val stared at us for one long, difficult moment, and I wasn't sure which I wanted more, for her to prove it, or for her to be completely batshit crazy. Neither option felt good.

"Close your eyes," she said.

Nina and I shared a look.

"Just blink, I promise I won't have time to kill you."

I blinked, but only after a strong eye-roll. The room filled with the scent of roses, so strong it was stifling. When I opened my eyes, Val's look had completely changed. She was taller, and she stood with her shoulders back and her chin jutted forward regally. A shimmering pink robe hung from her body and loose, honey-blonde curls adorned a head that had once held Val's tight platinum ringlets. An ethereal light emitted from her skin and her feet were delicately wrapped in gold sandals. Where Val was cute, with her button nose and youthful, rounder face, this woman was sharp cheekbones and a wry smile. The only thing that remained exactly as they had been were the sparkling green eyes and the dimples in her cheeks.

And then she opened her mouth. "Surprise bitches! I'm Aphrodite!"

Holy crap!

I didn't have words for this. She... was... a... what? Nina elbowed me hard.

"I am Aphrodite, the goddess of love, the very creator of its existence. I will take no other gifts of worship for my existence apart from your pursuit of true, unwavering, romantic love."

I blinked, and once again, she was Val, but somehow her entire posture had shifted into one of grandeur.

Aphrodite, the goddess of love, wanted *what*? "No, I don't think that will work."

"What?" Val slumped, her hands on her hips. She whined, "I'm a goddess! Worship!"

Now that she was more like my Val, I could muster a more Brynn-like response. "Nope. Sorry. Not interested."

"How do we even know you're Aphrodite?" Nina said. "You could be anything magical. Wouldn't mean you were really *her*."

"I'm the goddess of love *and* beauty. Hello? Have you seen me? Who else could I be?" Val motioned up and down her body.

"You've got to be kidding me." I grumbled. "Okay, okay. Let's say I believed this. Which would be a great big stretch, mind you. What does this mean? You said I was your problem because I don't believe in love. Is that why you're here? You appeared out of thin air because you sensed I needed some sort of godly guidance?"

"No." She crossed her arms over her chest and looked away from me.

"So, you just chose to show up here randomly and happened to find her?" Nina asked.

"No." She frowned. "Well, sort of."

"So you being my sister." Nina's voice got quieter now. "That was all just to get to Brynn?"

Val's lower lip trembled. "No, okay? No!" She stomped over and threw herself onto the couch beside us. "Father threw me out. No more Mount Olympus for me. And the longer I'm away, the harder it is to control my godly powers. And to shift into my godly form. About a century ago I got stuck wearing this face and body. I shifted that way once to fit into a town, and I got stuck."

"Like when my mom used to tell me to stop making faces, or I'd stay like that?" I asked, incredulous.

"I guess." She shrugged. "Kinda? Anyway, without being able to maintain my godly form for more than a minute or two at a time, I needed to do something to get by. By the thirties, they wouldn't let me take on honest work anymore. Child labor laws. I didn't even have a method to pay my way anymore."

"The nineteen-thirties?" Nina shook her head, eyes wide.

"So, I moved towns and changed tactics. I'd tell them the truth. I didn't know my mother, and my father was in another country. I didn't know how to reach him anymore. Then I'd embellish. Tell them the aunt I was staying with died. And get myself registered as a foster kid. It had worked for a while. I stayed in places until I aged out of the system, then drop out, forge new papers, lather, rinse repeat." She smiled. "Finding you guys was a happy accident. But now, I have real work to do. My kind of work."

"Work that involves making me fall in love," I reiterated.

"Yes. And yes, I know you don't want to. But hear me out? Roman and Angie are proof of true love." Val looked toward the stairs longingly.

"Are we sure they're so perfect?" I asked. "Everybody has their secrets."

"They're actually pretty perfect," Nina muttered. "They're really like that. Always have been."

"Fine. That's amazing, but they are relationship goals, and I'm not sure I want to take the chance that I'll either find a relationship like Roman and Angie's, or one more like my parents'."

"You can't be tricked into anything if you know what's coming," Val said. "I'll line some things up, use what's left of my Aphrodite mojo to get things cooking. If you aren't immediately into the guy after one date, you don't have to go out with him again. But Bree, baby, I'm so tired of seeing you down. You love your dad, but he moved out. You love your mom, but she's having a midlife crisis, or whatever is going on with her. Your friendship with Nina is the great love of your life, but you can have more."

For a moment, the three of us just stared at each other.

"I don't get it," I asked, looking down at my hands as I tried to process exactly what this meant. What all of this meant. If the Greek gods were real, were other gods real? Were they *the* gods? Did that mean I could meet Athena? Wisdom and war were way cooler things to be a goddess of than love. Wait. Did that mean Ares existed? Hades?

"What don't you get?" Val, no, *Aphrodite* asked.

"What are your powers? Like, what can you do?" I looked up to find her eyes glistening, the dimple in her cheek flickering as she lingered somewhere between sadness and joy.

"In my prime? I wielded love like a weapon, like armor. I used it to create beautiful things, but I also used it to... to harm. I think, maybe... I wasn't always so understanding of humanity. I think that's why Father threw me out. I made some messes, but I also did a lot of good." Her smile grew, and her eyes went distant, like she could see the pictures of past love in her head. "I did a lot of good."

Nina let out a weird little giggle. "This makes so much sense."

"It does?" It really didn't.

"Think about all the weird things she's done. Or said." Nina's eyes sparkled with mischief. "We already called her a Disney princess. But she's not a princess. She's a *myth*." She looked at Val. "Does Adam know about this?"

"No!" Val's eyes widened. "And we can't tell him. I never used my abilities on him. But would he believe that? Would you?"

I could see her point, but the idea of lying to him about something so huge... he wasn't just Val's boyfriend who I knew from around the neighborhood anymore. He was my friend.

"Please guys," Val said. "Maybe, when we move to New York, we can all talk about it. But first? Let's find Brynn a boyfriend. What do you say?"

Nina bumped her shoulder against mine. "She's Aphrodite. She wants to help you find love. Nobody else gets a matchmaker like Aphrodite."

"A matchmaker?" I grumbled. "So you're just going to set me up on dates until I find someone decent?"

"I've already begun." Val winked.

I wasn't convinced. "I could do that myself, if I wanted to."

"Again, Aphrodite," she chimed. "I have special skills and my instincts are better than yours."

"Come on Bree," Nina said. "It's just a couple of dates, right? If it doesn't work, what do you lose?"

Probably nothing. And I'd get Val to leave me alone until she found another pet project.

I dropped my head in my hands. Nina was right. Nobody got an opportunity like this. If I had any chance of finding someone who would be the Roman to my Angie, it would be through the goddess of love, right? "Ugh, fine!"

"But I'm serious, Brynn. Love is... wait a minute." Her eyes narrowed, and her head tilted. "Did you just... agree with me?"

I rolled my eyes. "Now I wish I could take—"

"No backsies!" Val shouted over me, and she rushed to me, taking my face in her hands. "You have no idea how fortunate you are about to be, Brynn, my love. Stick with me, and I. Will. Save. Your. Life."

CHAPTER SEVEN
FRILLS AND CHILLS

THE FOLLOWING WEEKEND, I stood in Val's bedroom, waiting to go on my first date. I still couldn't believe I was doing it willingly, but when a goddess arrived to teach you all about love, you took her up on the offer.

Or maybe you didn't, and I was making a really foolish decision. It was hard to say why, but I still showed up around four that Saturday, ready to see what Val had in store for me.

"Your date is for coffee and dessert at seven at Caffeine Nation," Val announced as Nina and I crowded into her room. "It's with Tony Lin, basketball player, the kid who works over at Emilio's Pizza."

Crap. "How'd you pull that off? Pretty sure I'm not his type," I said. *Like super attractive and a size six.*

"I told him the truth about you." She reached into her closet and pulled out a pink garment bag, which she laid gently atop the dusty rose comforter on her bed.

"You told him all about her winning personality?" Nina pinched my side.

"Bitch, I will cut you." I gnashed my teeth, making a show of just how winning I could be.

Nina giggled and Val ignored us, choosing instead to pull the equivalent of a carton's worth of makeup and hair products out of her dresser. "Of course not. I told him I knew you weren't a cheerleader, but you were seriously pretty when you cleaned up, which you would——for this date."

"Ouch," I said. "You meant the actual truth."

Nina grimaced.

Val rolled her eyes at me. "Was I supposed to lie? He's seen you. Now, take off your jacket. I'm going to get you date-ready and Tony Lin-worthy."

I sighed but did as directed, handing my leather jacket to Nina. "Here. Hold my dignity."

Nina snatched the jacket. "You shouldn't be doing this."

"What? People get dressed up for dates all the time."

"Whatever." Nina dropped onto the edge of the bed.

"You're the one who thought this was a good idea," I muttered.

"Yeah, I thought you would be going out on dates, not getting a makeover."

"Look." Val picked up a brush. "It's just dress-up. Tonight, she gets to become somebody else. And once she's got his attention, she can show him why she's so awesome."

"If he doesn't see that already..." Nina trailed off.

"How can he?" Val threw the brush onto the bed. It bounced off and hit the floor. "How can anybody see her when she's hiding?"

"Hey, I'm not hiding from anybody!"

"No? Your hair falls in your eyes. You don't wear any makeup except for that black eyeliner, which nobody can see because you're always looking at the floor. The all black clothes. That stupid black beanie."

"I haven't worn that beanie in weeks," I argued.

"It's nearly summer! Of course you haven't! You collapse in on yourself. Your posture is preposterous, and you never smile. You're not a tiny girl, and there are tons of clothes that would flatter your figure, but you're too busy hiding under baggy jeans and band t-shirts. It's a damn good thing Nina is your friend,

Bree, because if she wasn't, I wouldn't have even seen you under all that."

My stomach twisted. She spoke with such certainty that I temporarily forgot it was all bullshit. She cut into me in places I had never even known existed.

Nina stepped between us, her fists clenched at her sides, her chest heaving. "I don't care who you are, if you don't back the fuck off, we're gonna have a problem."

I almost told Nina to stop, that she was picking a fight with a god, but she knew that. And, if necessary, I would do the same for her.

Val blinked and took a step back, her beautiful face losing some of its glow. "I don't... I mean, I'm just being honest. I don't understand why you're so angry."

"Because you insulted my best friend?" Nina snapped. "I've known her all her life. There's no act with Bree. What you see is what you get."

"Love changes people," Val said patiently. "I can change you if you let me."

"Does anybody even have a choice when you get to them? When love changes them, do they even want to be changed?" Her voice got that choked quality it got when she fought back tears.

Val's eyes widened, her head snapping back like she'd just taken an actual hit. "Sometimes people need advice, even when they don't think they do. I can help people see their true inner beauty so they can revel in what I've created."

"What the hell do you know, anyway? You say you're a love expert, you created love, but where's the proof?"

Val's eyes glistened, and she swallowed hard. "I'm sorry he hurt you, Nina."

"Nina..." I tried. But once she got started, she wasn't easily stopped.

"Or has Adam finally said it? It's been seven months. When is all your expertise gonna get him to say those three words?"

Nina's verbal strike grazed me before it hit its mark.

Oh. I had assumed Adam and Val had exchanged those words a long time ago. I never imagined...

Val's lip quivered, and I cringed.

"I'll do it," I said. "It's fine, I want to."

Nina's eyes cut to me, sharp enough to slice. "What?"

I shrugged. "I'm not hiding, but it might be fun to try something different. Besides, Val is just trying to do something nice for me."

Nina stared at me for a moment. Her mouth opened like she was going to say something, but it snapped shut, her lips pursing. She dropped back down onto the bed. "Fine. Have at it."

Val's eyes darted around the room, as if searching for the excitement and determination she'd once had. When they settled back on me, some of her sparkle had dulled, but she was mostly back to her old self. She even managed a smile.

"First thing's first," she said. "I did a little shopping and found the perfect outfit for you." She unzipped the garment bag she'd placed on her bed, yanked some billowy fabric free from it, and unfurled it.

Flowers. Flowers all over. And a dress. I didn't *do* dresses.

Val's lips screwed up into a tiny pink pout. "Oh. You don't like it."

I shook my head.

"Sorry, Val." Nina boosted herself off the bed and walked toward me. "You had your chance but—"

"Wait." Val's arm shot out, stopping Nina. "I've got better."

"Better dresses?" I groaned. "You know I don't like dresses."

"Pffft. You think I really got you a dress?" Val laughed. "You've gotta aim high, right? Can you imagine if I got you to wear that? They'd give me the key to the city!"

"I don't understand. Why can't you just magic me into accepting all of your ideas?"

Val sighed. "That's not the way it works. I have charm. I can persuade. But I get tired really easily. It only lasts for a little while, and then I have to renew it. I think Father believed it was better that way."

"Jeez. And I thought *my* mom judged me." I laughed. "What exactly did you do to piss your dad off enough to turn you from a goddess into one of the peons?"

Her eyes skirted mine. "I... maybe... might have... a little... got myself kicked out of Olympus because one of my matches didn't work out the way I had foreseen."

"Like a bitter breakup?" I braced myself.

"Like the Trojan War."

Like the Trojan War?! "You know what you can do with your dress? You can stick it all the way up your—"

Val's finger flew up, and the words abruptly cut off. My mouth flopped open and closed, useless.

"I haven't lost all my abilities. Please don't forget that." She tilted her head, eyes wide and sweet, like she hadn't just effectively zipped my lips. "Anyway, what you were about to say would be very disrespectful to a goddess."

"Did you just..." Nina's eyes widened. "Give her her voice back, now."

Val laughed. "Come on, Nina. Don't be like that. I only took it away for a second." She snapped her fingers. "See?"

"I'm going to fucking choke you." I hadn't expected my voice to return, and its viciousness surprised me.

"You will do no such thing," Val said, completely unfazed. "Especially not once you see what I have picked out for you. You're going to look beautiful. And you're even going to like it."

THE FUNNY THING WAS, I did sort of like it.

Val dressed me in a loose-fitting pink tank and light blue capri-cut jeans. In case of a chill, she added a grey sweater that tied in the center. She tamed my normally shaggy black waves into a straight slicked style that curled under my ears and was held in place by a shimmery butterfly clip. The makeup she applied was light, keeping with the barely there style she knew I wanted, but it smoothed out my skin tone, hid the pimples that had sprouted along my chin, thanks to my soon-to-visit period, and made my blue eyes pop. Or at least that was what she told me.

Around my neck, she draped a silver rose quartz necklace from her personal collection. For my feet, she provided shoes that looked like ballet slippers, even tied like them, but boasted a kitten heel. I kind of loved them once I figured out how to walk in them. They weren't even uncomfortable.

And all that work had led to me sitting at a wobbly old wooden table by myself.

Tony had told Val he'd be there at seven. I glanced at my phone for the thousandth time. It was nearly eight. I tapped out another angry text to Val.

This is embarrassing. Has he written you back? And why didn't you give me his number?

I sipped at my cup of coffee. It was my second.

Laura Griffin was on a date with Murray Novak at a table across and down two from mine. Laura kept glancing at me over Murray's shoulder, her eyes sympathetic. That was better than Kurt Chambliss, who laughed at me, elbowing his friend in the side to make sure he saw me, too.

I couldn't wait to move to New York City, where nobody knew anybody, and I could fade in and out of a situation like this with nobody being the wiser.

My phone buzzed. Val.

He's not answering my calls. I'm so SO sorry, Brynn. He told me he'd be there.

Another text, this one from Nina.

Don't you wait for that boy another minute. Get out of there.

I swallowed the last gulp of my coffee and smacked down a five for the trouble.

"Bree, is that you?" Raphael Sanchez jogged out of the stock room wearing a dusty t-shirt, jeans, and a Caffeine Nation ball cap, complete with the dancing coffee bean logo. I'd forgotten he'd scored a job here.

"My name is Brynn, and you know that," I corrected. "You have the rest of your life to be an ass. Could you take the day off?" I hoped I projected fury, but it wasn't possible with my new look.

"I like this. It really suits you." Raphael looked me up and down, starting with my eyes, traveling down to my toes, and back up to my face, making all the necessary stops in between. He seemed to remember I'd asked him a question. "I can't take a day off. I just got this job."

It was like he didn't even hear me rejecting him. Amazing.

"Sorry I'm such a mess. I work in the back. Cleaning, fixing things. I'm good at that sort of thing. I only pop out to cover tables when someone's on break. But my shift's almost over." His eyes did a quick sweep around the shop. "Weren't we supposed to hang out?"

"Um...no," I said, "and no matter how many times you say we were, it won't become true."

I stormed out of the diner and didn't look back.

I didn't want to date Tony. I'd barely even exchanged a sentence with him. Yet, somehow, this whole thing left an empty feeling in my chest, like I'd missed out on something.

I walked down Main Street, past all the charming and familiar storefronts. My favorite thing about Birchwood Grove was this street. Scoopy Doo was at the end of the promenade, which meant I wouldn't be tortured with seeing any of my coworkers when I walked the opposite direction on my stood-up-walk-of-shame.

The Main Street shops transported Birchwood's residents to a bygone era, when all the businesses were owned by the towns-people. It was like stepping into a time machine. You felt good every time you bought something because you were helping your neighbor. That rich notion of community was what I would miss most when I moved to the city, even if I longed for anonymity.

As I admired the shops, I caught a view of myself in the reflection of the bakery window. There, with a backdrop of cookies and cakes I wished I could devour, was the truth nobody wanted to admit. I looked like a damn fool. What possessed me to listen to Val and dress like this?

Growling at my reflection made me look a little more like myself, but it also made the bakery worker shoot me a dirty look as she wiped a streak from her side of the window. Rolling my eyes, I stepped away from the window and continued down Main Street.

If it hadn't been getting late, I would have strolled off on a side street, so fewer people would have the opportunity to behold the physical manifestation of my declining judgement.

Even if I wanted to continue peering through store windows and feeling awful about myself, I couldn't. A movie had just let out at the theater, and a crowd milled around out front.

Wonderful. The Laws of Brynn Stark Mortification dictated that most of this crowd would be students from Birchwood High. For maximum regret, of course.

A giggle erupted from a group of girls, and my eyes drifted to them. The laugh came from Taylor Dallas, a tall redheaded cheerleader. Her hand was clamped over her mouth, her pointer finger aimed at me.

I tore my eyes away from her and nearly collided with someone. I put my hands out to steady myself, but so did he, and our hands awkwardly bumped together.

"Sorry," I muttered.

"Brynn?" *No. No way.*

My eyes lifted. There were Adam and Gabe, Adam in a plain t-shirt and jeans, and Gabe looking more punk than he had on our last meeting——blue-streaked black hair spiked, a black ring of eyeliner, studded cuffs on his wrists.

"And me without my copy of The Dark Knight." Gabe's eyes twinkled. "This is a different look for you."

"Yeah." My eyes drifted across the sidewalk, my head dipped low.

"It's lovely," Gabe said, although his voice rose in question.

"It looks ridiculous." Adam's lips were pressed into a thin line, his eyes hard. "What's with the frilly crap?"

What the hell made him think he had the right?

"Your girlfriend wears this frilly crap all the time, and you seem fine with it."

"Did Val dress you? This isn't you," he said sharply. "I've never seen you in anything but snarky t-shirts and jeans. What are you all dressed up for?"

"Dude, chill," Gabe chuckled. "You don't need to know that."

Adam went rigid. "Of course I don't. It's just weird, is all."

"Val set me up on a date."

"She did?" He looked at Adam, who shrugged.

"With Tony. At Caffeine Nation."

"And Tony didn't take you home?" Adam shook his head. "You deserve better than that."

"Tony didn't even pay for coffee," I muttered.

Gabe shrugged. "Maybe he thought you'd be offended."

"He didn't show," I blurted. "He stood me up." Gabe's face fell. Some annoyance leaked out of Adam's expression. "That's enough embarrassment for one day." I bowed deeply. "Have a good night, boys."

"Wait." Adam snagged my elbow as I moved past him, his touch gentle, fleeting. "We should walk you home. It's getting dark."

"He's right," Gabe said. "Dark here is darker than dark. I miss city streetlights."

One part of me wanted them to walk me home. I could use the company, and it was probably safer. Another part of me looked between the two of them and my heart ached. And the last part, the only part I was willing to acknowledge, spoke up. "It's not like it's midnight. It's not 'can't see your own hand in front of your face' dark."

"Brynn." I sometimes hated the way Adam said my name, like it was a warning or a grunt of frustration.

"What?" I countered. "Can't I live out this moment of forced humility alone?"

"Hey Bree!"

Raphael. Again.

"You need a ride home?"

I fought down a chill that crept its way slowly up my spine. "No thanks, man. I've already got one."

Adam nodded, one firm head bob. "Well chosen." He leaned forward and whispered, "My car is in the shop."

"I don't care."

"Suit yourself." Raphael's words had a hard edge to them. I'd heard it from him before. He had a case of the "nice guys," which meant he believed that, because he was nice to me, I needed to accept his offer to hang out with him.

They waited until the door slammed, the engine started, and Raphael's brake lights were in front of us before they started down the road.

"So, tell me how you ended up in this getup," Adam said.

"Dude," Gabe warned.

"Nah, I'm serious," Adam said. "This is not you in the slightest."

"It's not that dressy," I argued.

"It's sparkly. It's not your style," he shot back. "I know your style and I know *this* style. And it's kind of pissing me off that Val made you dress like her for your date."

Gabe just sighed.

"Val doesn't *make* me do anything. I agreed to it because she thought it would be a way to get Tony to take notice of me."

Adam gritted his teeth but swallowed whatever he'd been getting ready to say.

We continued walking for a bit before Gabe spoke up. "Listen, I'm not trying to be an asshole, and I really don't want to get in the middle of this mess, but am I the only one who thinks that, by dressing you up like herself, Val has implied that the person Tony really wants to date is...like...Val?"

Adam cleared his throat.

"What? No. It wasn't like that." I wanted to believe it wasn't. "Val's on some sort of weird mission to find me the love of my life. She's crazy, but she means well."

"Are you looking to find the love of your life, Brynn?" Gabe added extra bass to his voice, but it made him choke.

I laughed. "Quite to the contrary, actually. I'm not looking for anything. If I found something... worth it, I might consider. But this? I only went on this date to prove her wrong. Funny enough, I could have worn a burlap sack and proven the same thing."

"And what, exactly, do you think you proved?" Adam asked.

"That guys don't find me interesting." I shrugged.

"That's not true," Gabe said.

"Raphael finds you plenty interesting," Adam grumbled.

"No thank you," I said.

"On which one?" Gabe asked.

I rolled my eyes. "Oh shut up." But it did put a smile on my face.

He laughed. "What did I say?"

"Look, seriously, it doesn't bother me," I said. "I don't believe in the whole thing, anyway. Relationships suck the life out of you. No offense, Adam."

Adam shot me a dirty look.

"So you only did this to prove Val wrong?" Gabe said.

"And to get her to stop trying to hook me up all the time."

"All the time?" Adam asked.

"She locked me in the walk-in freezer with Craig, and..." The barbecue was another attempted hook-up, but there was no way I was admitting that in front of Gabe. "... there was one other time I will not discuss."

Gabe chuckled, and my stomach dropped. Did that mean he knew?

"The walk-in freezer? Craig? Are you kidding me?" Adam waved his arms around like a lunatic.

"Adam just realized Val is nuts," Gabe teased.

"Join the club, dude," I said.

We slowed down when we got to my front walkway, and just in time, because my adorable new shoes were apparently not meant for walking. My feet were aching.

"Listen, it's not a big deal. I knew how it would turn out. I'm just annoyed I wasted my evening."

Adam stopped between me and the walkway. "You're not nearly as cynical as you pretend to be. If you were, you never would have agreed to this farce." He squinted. "Is that a butterfly barrette in your hair?"

I glared at him.

"It's whimsical." Gabe's lips strained to hold back the grin spreading across his face.

I looked from Adam's scrutiny to Gabe's dancing eyes, and if I'd had a shovel, I would have dug myself an escape tunnel.

Adam took another step forward and pinched the barrette between two fingers, freeing it before running a gentle hand over my hair. He smoothed it, then tucked a wayward strand behind my ear. "The rest of this, I can live with if I must, but that thing is just intolerable."

I laughed, but it was an ugly, hitched sound, hindered by my sudden inability to breathe.

"Oh! I'm buzzing." Gabe yanked his phone out of the back pocket of his jeans and glanced at the screen. "I'm *clearly* getting a call that I really have to take *right this second*. I've gotta take this." I heard him walk a little way down the block.

Adam and I didn't look away from each other. Instead, he took another step closer, his eyes locked on mine, and rested his hands on my shoulders. "This isn't right," he said softly. "You don't need to change yourself, Brynn."

"I know." I didn't like how shaky I sounded.

"I'm serious. You're worth more than that. If some guy doesn't like you, it means he's gotta go. You're enough, no frills needed."

"I know that, too." I smiled.

He returned my smile, a fondness in his eyes I'd never seen directed toward me before. "I figured you did. I just wanted to make sure you knew you weren't alone there."

His hands slid down my arms, and I fought the urge to step in closer and...do what exactly? I didn't know. I was sinking into something dangerous and I wanted to take cover.

"I should go inside." I forced myself to take a step back.

Adam seemed to blink away whatever he'd been thinking a moment before. "Right. Right, you should."

"Say goodnight to Gabe for me."

"Yeah. Will do." He nodded jerkily.

"Goodnight, Adam."

"Goodnight, Brynn."

I walked toward the door and didn't look back, my heart

slamming against my ribs in sharp, painful jabs. Hopefully, I could sneak upstairs without dealing with Mom. My chances grew when I pushed open the front door and heard running water from the kitchen.

My heels clacked against the hardwood floor, and I winced with each step. Val was quickly becoming the bane of my existence; even the shoes she picked out for me were working against me.

The ghost of guilt squeezed at my chest. Maybe I shouldn't be thinking of Val as the enemy. Maybe I was worse.

"Bree, is that you?" The water running in the kitchen cut off and Mom rushed into the living room, her slippers slapping against the floor. She dried her hands on the towel she held like she was trying to beat it into submission. The minute she saw me, her eyes went wide, a bemused smile forming on her face.

"Oh sweetheart! You look so pretty!" She stepped closer, one hand floating over my face, my hair, but not touching me, as though afraid of spooking me. She finally settled on my chin, tipping my face up so she could get a better look.

"Thank you," I murmured. I wanted to sink through the floorboards and hide.

"What brought this on?" she asked.

"I'm stupid." I threw myself on the couch and yanked at the ribbon on one of the ballet slippers.

"Sit like a lady, Bree." She motioned at the way my legs were spread wide open.

"Who's gonna see me?"

"It's not about who will see you." Each word sounded like it was being hit with a hammer as it exited her mouth. Which was fitting because she was always figuratively beating me over the head with one thing or another. "It's about creating a habit."

I rolled my eyes and snapped my legs together. I wasn't even wearing a skirt. "I'm more comfortable sitting like that."

"You're more comfortable man-spreading?" Her well-groomed eyebrows jumped up her forehead.

"We should keep you away from the internet. It's not like I'm sitting in a crowded space, taking up all the seats. This is my couch." I spread my arms and fell back into the cushions.

"Why do you always have to be like this?" She sat beside me, back rigid, expression tense.

"Why do *you* always have to be like *this*?" I waved a hand at her, displaying her as Exhibit A.

"Can we have one conversation that does not devolve into sarcasm and witty banter?"

She wanted me to apologize, which was exactly why I wouldn't. "Um...no."

Her expression rapidly moved from tense to angry. It was a spectacular transition to witness, her eyebrows drawing together, face reddening. If she could see herself, she'd hate the way it made the lines around her lips deepen.

"What, exactly, do I have to do to get you to forgive me? It's been a month and you walk around here like you're morally superior."

I wanted to yell that I *was* morally superior, but I remembered the feeling I'd had standing so close to Adam, and suddenly it wasn't as cut and dry. That realization only served to further my desire to disappear into my room.

"You know how unhappy I was. I didn't mean to hurt anybody," she continued. "I just wanted to make sure it was going well with Jesse before I ended things with your father. In some ways, I think it was a stroke of luck that you walked in on us when you did. I didn't want you to find out that way, but I couldn't have told him myself. Which, I know, speaks well for me."

"So well."

"Your father made life difficult for me the past few years," she said. "He didn't understand why the way we're viewed by others is important. Truthfully, he pushed me into this and—"

"Are you ever planning on taking any responsibility?" I stood.

"I know my part in this."

"No, you don't." I clenched my fists to keep myself from shouting at her. "You keep saying 'if he was a better husband,' but if you were a better wife, you would have talked to Dad the minute you realized you wanted something with Jesse." I nearly choked on those words. "And if you were a better mother, you would work things out with Dad and get him to let me live there instead of the two of you forcing me to stay here in this— this stalemate. The only reason you want me here is because you need someone else to argue with now that Dad's gone."

"No!" she shouted over me. "You are my daughter, and you need my influence. Just look at how you're flourishing!"

"This?" I snapped. "This is not me flourishing. This is me forgetting who I am. And someone who really loved me would see that."

I stomped away, rushing up the stairs and into my room. I slammed the door and reveled in the reverberating noise.

At least until the reverberating noise in my head joined it.

Someone who really loved me would see that.

You're enough. No frills needed.

I felt sick. Adam and I had been talking a lot more since that night he'd driven me to the airport. Was I imagining that there was something between us? Sure, we were closer friends than we'd been, but were we more? I had to be imagining it, at least on his end. And even if I wasn't, nothing could come of it. If it did, that would make us no better than Mom and Jesse.

I plopped down on my bed and tried not to think about how close we'd been just a few minutes ago.

I needed to stay the hell away from Adam Hernandez.

CHAPTER EIGHT
INVESTIGATION

THE HARD ICE cream was a little too hard all day that Sunday. As Craig arrived to take over my shift, I was dipping a heated scoop into a tub and carving out enough slivers to fill a cup for Jesse, my mother's booty call, of all people. I had hoped he wouldn't try to talk to me, but he didn't seem to understand that would be a no-no.

"Your mother spoke to me about your argument last night."

I nearly dropped the scoop. Craig had been slowing to a stop beside me to say hello but changed direction. Instead, he walked toward the back at top speed, whistling all the way.

"I don't think this is the place to discuss this," I said, suddenly able to scoop the ice cream with ease. *Hulk, scoop!*

"I'm not trying to start anything," he continued, like I hadn't spoken. "I just think that if you cared about your mother, you wouldn't stress her out like this."

Sammy appeared behind me, but wisely stayed silent.

"You want to save her some stress?" I asked. "You're the reason for her stress. And you don't get to tell me how to handle my family."

Jesse frowned. "Well, as long as I'm dating your mother—"

"I'm gonna stop you right there." I handed him his ice cream. "You can have that free of charge." I pulled a five from my wallet and slapped it down on the counter. "Sam, I'm buying. Jesse, that means you're no longer a customer. Which means I can tell you to take your ice cream and get the hell out before you say anything stupider."

Jesse looked at Sammy.

Sammy shrugged. "You heard the lady. She's doing you a favor." Then to me, "Craig's here. Why don't you go to the back and get changed?" He pressed the five back into my hand and shooed me along.

I headed for the bathroom. Craig shot me a thumbs up and I grinned. He wasn't so bad, the more you got to know him. And he could make a large shake without wearing it now. Small shakes, however, were still a problem. They might always be...

I entered the bathroom, closed the door, and took several deep breaths. I rinsed my face; my cheeks burned, and I struggled to quell the fire. The moment I got home, I would have to deal with Mom's reaction to what I'd said to Jesse. How could I possibly mentally prepare for that?

My phone buzzed across the counter. Was she not even waiting until I got home?

Val never did a thing for our group project, and we're running low on time. I'm at the library now. Was here with Adam, but he left for work about ten minutes ago. Tag! You're it. Come meet me! I'm at one of the tables in the back.

Nina. She didn't realize how perfect her timing was, giving me a reason to avoid going home.

I pocketed my phone and stuffed my uniform into my bookbag before leaving the bathroom. Adam was sitting at the break table when I emerged, scrutinizing something on his phone. He pushed his hand through his wild curls, pulling the uniform cap over his head, then taking it off and adjusting it. I smiled at the self-conscious gesture.

He looked up and caught me. "What? It's hard to fit all this hair under here. You have it way easier."

"Think it's time for a cut?" I asked, though I hoped he

didn't. Though if he did, that would stop me from thinking about how soft his curls looked and how I wanted to slide my fingers through them. *Shit.*

"Nah. Dad will force me to get one before graduation, and we're only two months away, so..." He shrugged, then pushed himself to his feet. "I don't know. Do you think it looks messy?"

Why, why, why would he ask me?

"It might if you let it grow out until graduation," I said. "If you cut it now, there will still be something to cut by mid-June. Then you won't end up getting a forced military cut for graduation when your dad decides you need one whether or not you really do."

"You have a point. Oh, I got you something." Holding out a paper cup from Caffeine Nation, he cleared his throat. "This is me apologizing for giving you shit last night."

I took the cup from him. "Fantastic. So why'd you do it?"

He sighed. "Not gonna let me off easy, huh?" A shake of his head. "It wasn't you I was mad at. We should leave it at that. The point is, I'm sorry. For all of it."

All of it.

I nodded. "Apology accepted."

"Good. Did Nina text you?"

"Yep, I'm heading over there now."

"I don't understand why Val didn't do any of the work," he said, his shoulders slumping.

Little did he know, it made sense. "I think she planned to wing it. She... studied it before...so she knows the topic well."

He looked up at me, his eyes wide. "Yeah, well, we're all supposed to plan the presentation. She has no notes or anything, and now we're completely unprepared. I am *not* getting a failing grade because—"

I rested a hand on his shoulder, then remembered I shouldn't touch him. It would be too awkward to pull it away, so I left it there, hovering with only the slightest bit of contact.

"Nobody's going to let you fail, Adam. We know how important your grades are to you."

He searched my eyes for a moment, then swallowed and nodded. "I've worked my ass off."

"I know." I forced myself to step back. "Anyway, Nina's waiting for me."

"Right. Thank you." He gave an awkward little wave.

I said a quick goodnight to Craig and headed out the door.

The minute I was out of the store, I reached into my bag, found my headphones, and played some music, something with a pounding beat to get me out of my own head.

I hustled my way towards the library, the speed of the beat determining the bang of my boots on the concrete. I only got a block away before my music faded out and the rare sound of my ringtone played in my ears.

I clicked the button on my headphone wire. "Hello?"

"Um... hey," a familiar male voice answered. "Is this Brynn Stark?"

"Yes, it is," I answered cautiously. If I'd had my phone in my hand, I would have never picked up for a number I didn't immediately recognize.

"It's Tony. Tony Lin."

"Oh." I couldn't muster much more, no hello, no nothing.

"Yeah." He paused. "I'm sorry about yesterday. I forgot I had this thing to go to with my family and I couldn't get out of it. When Val set me up with you, I didn't think it was so important. But my mom insisted, and I didn't have your number. Val just gave it to me."

I wanted to point out that he could have called Val and told *her*, but why bother? We both knew he was lying. What good would it do to wave it in his face?

"It's fine." I couldn't care less. "Listen, I'm in front of the library. I have to work on a group project. Can I call you back another time?"

"Wait, what? Seriously? I call you and you can't talk?"

"Dude, I've gotta meet someone," I said. "You stand me up and then want to talk whenever you want? What's that about?"

"Yeah, I was right. I never should have agreed to the date to begin with," Tony said. "I always thought you were too fat and lazy, but Val convinced me. Val... she said I should..." He trailed off, like he'd gotten lost, and it finally clicked.

I wanted to smack my face into a wall. Val probably used whatever weird Aphrodite mojo she had to get him to forget his family plans. "Listen, I don't need anybody dating me to get to Val. Lose my number."

The phone went dead.

Predictable. Sighing, I yanked my headphones out and pushed through the doors to the library. I only had to wander for a short while before I spotted Nina by her hair, fanned out around her head, a gorgeous mane of curls. That generally meant she'd pushed it back with a headband and ran out of the house. Her face was hidden behind a stack of books.

"Hey there, gorgeous," I whispered once I was within earshot. "Is there room at this table for me?"

"Beautiful! Love of My Life!" Nina hooked an arm around my neck and planted a big kiss on my cheek. "Where have you been?"

"Scoopy Doopy Doo. I got a call from Tony on my way over. He tried to apologize for yesterday, then called me a fat ass when I couldn't talk to him because I was coming here. We hate him."

"Noted." Her face twisted into a sneer. "We don't *hate* Val, but we aren't happy with her."

"Yeah, even Adam's pissed off about her flaking."

"Not just that," Nina said. "I've been doing some research."

I screwed up my face, pretending to think very hard. "I think that's why we're here."

She smacked my arm. "Shut up, doof. That's not what I

mean." She waited for me to take the seat beside her. "The problem is, now I know more about her, and none of it is good.

We can start with how Val caused the Trojan War," Nina said. "It started with a god getting snubbed on a wedding invite. Eris, the goddess of discord, decided that was a good reason to throw an apple into the party. The apple had the words 'to the fairest' written on it. Aphrodite competed with Hera and Athena over the apple. Zeus appointed a man named Paris to judge the competition. Each goddess tried to bribe Paris so he would pick them. Aphrodite offered him the hand of her half-sister, the most beautiful mortal woman alive," Nina explained. "And she won."

"Helen of Troy." I rolled my eyes and sighed. "I don't get it. Why is she always messing with *other people*? Why not fix her own love life?" Even if the thought made my stomach flip, the question needed answering.

Nina blinked. "Maybe she can't?"

"Hm, maybe not."

Nina slid a book my way. "We should try to dig up whatever info we can."

I picked up the book and got started. Within the first ten minutes, I'd discovered something worth sharing. "Aphrodite was either Zeus' daughter, or she was born from the dissolved scrotum of the god Uranus after it was cut off by Cronos." I winced. "I'm hoping for Zeus as the father."

"We should bring her on Maury," Nina mumbled. "Zeus...you are not the father. Although I'm pretty sure it's Zeus, after the stories she told. Uranus isn't around in the Troy story. But Zeus is."

"Good point. It says here they forced her to marry an ugly god named Hephaestus, who she did not love, because he wouldn't be seen as a threat the way most men who were married to the most beautiful goddess ever would be." I read on and groaned. "She cheated on him and often."

"Well, that explains why she was so forgiving of your mom," Nina said.

I'd forgotten about that. A sick feeling of dread spread through me. I read on. "Known lovers include a man named Anchises, the god Adonis, and oh boy, Ares."

"Woah. She's got a thing with As, huh? I wonder if Adam realizes he's walking the same roads as the god of war."

Another stomach flip. "What if he's the jealous type?"

"Definitely not Adam," Nina deadpanned.

"Ares, not Adam!"

Nina shrugged. "It's been a while. Hopefully, he's over it. So who is this Anchises person? I've heard of the other two guys, but..."

I read ahead. "Oh wonderful! He was warned not to boast about their relationship, but he did anyway, so Zeus killed him with a thunderbolt. Adam's gonna get killed by a Greek god he doesn't even believe in."

More silence as we both read, looking for more Aphrodite facts.

"Holy crap," Nina said. "She once cursed a woman named Myrrha to be uncontrollably drawn to her own father because she claimed to be prettier than her." She looked a little green. "Then Aphrodite banged her son. Who Ares then killed out of jealousy."

"Dude." That was all I could manage. "Duuuuude."

"I know. I think I'm good on research for now." Nina snapped the book shut. "Shall we go?"

I nodded emphatically.

We left the library together.

"Adam told me he saw you yesterday," Nina said.

"Yeah." I stuffed my hands into my pockets. "With Gabe."

"How is Gabe?"

"He seemed pretty great."

Nina pursed her lips. "Cool." Silence. "You know, Adam got on my shit for letting you dress like Val."

"Adam seems to have a problem understanding people don't make me do things."

"I should have argued more against it."

I shook my head at Nina. She always did this. "You did everything you could have without annoying me the way Adam did last night. I had already made my choice."

"Yeah, he was furious," Nina said. "I'm nervous he's gonna take it up with Val. Before we found out about her, I would say he should. Now, I'm beginning to worry."

"I know. Me too."

For a moment, we walked in silence. "About Adam..." All I did was look at her, and her face fell. "No, Brynn. What the hell are you thinking? God, you look so guilty!"

"I don't know what you're talking about." I hated that she knew my innermost workings just by glancing in my direction.

"Brynn. That would have been wrong before we knew about Val. Now, it's dangerous."

"I'm not going to do anything about it, Nina. It's just there. I can't help it." We stopped where our paths split off: Nina's upper crust neighborhood to the left, my semi-middle-class neighborhood straight ahead. "I'm trying to fight it off."

"You have to. Besides, if Adam's the kind of guy who would cheat on Val for you, is that the kind of guy you want?"

"I don't think it's like that." A pounding pain drummed behind my eyelids.

"It better not be." She kissed me on the cheek. "Text me if you need anything. And be good."

"You be careful." I didn't like her going home to sleep in the room next door to the psycho goddess who cursed people to do horrible things, even if she swore she'd seen the error of her ways.

She shrugged and waved, hiking the purse she practically

lived out of up onto her shoulder. I tucked a piece of paper back into the haphazardly organized giant bag, then waved at her to proceed.

Once she was on her way, I pulled my phone from my pocket. I wanted to start up some music for the walk home, but a glance at the screen revealed I had a missed call from my uncle Josh. Dad had recently moved in with him, so I was used to getting calls from his house phone, but a call from his cell phone was odd.

My heart pounded with worry as I returned the call.

"Bree Bear! How are you?"

"Hey Uncle Josh. I'm good. Are you guys okay?"

"Yeah, we're good. Listen, your dad is on a business trip, but your mom called and left a message for him."

"What about?"

"She's mad you disrespected Buddy. She says your dad said he'd talk to you about it. I have no idea why…"

"You mean Jesse?" I giggled.

"Who?" That was Uncle Josh, forever irreverent.

"Yeah, I mouthed off at Jesse. I mouth off at everyone. Nothing new."

"Bree…you know that saying you do that all the time isn't an excuse to do that all the time."

"I learned it from watching you." I headed up my home's walkway and sat on the edge of the stoop. My stomach rumbled, hungry for dinner. When I got inside, I'd grab some food and take it upstairs. That way, I wouldn't subject myself to a dinner with Mom and *Buddy*.

"Don't blame me! Then she'll bother me about it!" he said in mock terror. "Listen, you're the one who's gotta live with her. If you keep moving forward, things will get easier. You'll start being able to accept their relationship and what happened with your parents. I was about your age when my parents split up. I get it. But it would be much easier for you if you—"

"Sit there and take it when he tells me how I should behave towards my mother? At my job?"

"Oh." A pause. "Your mother neglected to mention that part."

"Exactly. He's lucky I didn't spit in his ice cream."

Josh chuckled. "Ever done that to anyone?"

"I haven't, but Nina did once. The customer had said something nasty about me."

Another laugh. "Can always count on Nina to protect you when we're not around."

"Jesse should be glad it was just me and Sammy today."

"I'm getting your point, but again...you're the one who needs to live with your mother, and if that means dealing with Jesse, life will probably be way easier if you make your peace with both of them."

"What if I didn't have to live with her?" I asked. "What if I lived somewhere else?"

"Like when you go to college?"

"Like when I move in with you and Dad?" I said sweetly.

"Stop that," Josh said. "I can practically see the puppy dog eyes."

"If I'm whipping out the puppy dog stare, you've gotta know I'm serious."

Josh was quiet for a moment. "Your mother won't go for it. Your dad already tried, and she freaked out."

That wasn't what they'd told me when Dad left. They'd said they both agreed I should stay with Mom. "Well, it isn't working. I'm miserable. And if I keep having to see Jesse twice a week during my morning coffee, I'll poison his Mini-Wheats."

Josh sighed. "I don't think I can blame you. I'll talk to them. See what I can work out."

YEEEEEEEEEEESSSSSS. "That would be awesome, if you don't mind."

"Of course I mind!" he said. "I don't want to be anywhere

near that mess. But I know you won't stop bugging me until I give it a shot."

"You understand me, and this is why you're my favorite uncle."

"I'm your only uncle."

"I'm disconnecting before you change your mind."

"Don't expect me to work mira——"

"I love you Uncle Josh!!!!!!" I hung up.

I'd found a possible solution to one problem. I slumped against the stairs, remembering the other big problem that needed work.

After what I'd read today, if Val found out about my... somewhat complicated feelings for Adam, she could hurt either of us. I didn't want to believe she would, but I had to find a new place to direct my attention. To someone I actually enjoyed spending time with. Only one person came close. Even better, if Adam had any feelings for me, this would squash them.

I picked up my phone and texted Gabe.

Hi! It's Brynn. How would you feel about lunch tomorrow? Just you and me?

And as I got up to head into the house and await his answer, I swiped the tears from my eyes.

CHAPTER NINE
FALSE START

THE FOLLOWING SATURDAY, Gabe met me at Emilio's Pizzeria, because Tony Lin worked there. It was his idea, because he was still pissy about the way Tony had stood me up.

I wore a lace up black blouse with white jeans and my black boots that buckled up the sides. Just a little something more for Gabe, because I genuinely liked him.

I felt better about my decision when I spotted him strolling towards me. His hands were thrust into his pockets, tattoos on display, and my pulse quickened. Dating him wasn't the best idea, not with the way I felt about Adam, but his full smile, his twinkling eyes, that playful demeanor——it was all a good argument for moving forward. He was a cool guy, and I enjoyed talking to him. And he wasn't completely off limits.

"I'm a jerk," he announced as soon as he was within earshot. "I forgot The Dark Knight!"

"Well, I forgot Perks, so we're even."

He stopped in front of me, taking me in. "Yet another look. You are a girl of many faces."

"Same face. Same girl. Different clothes."

"Same girl. That's the most important part." He motioned toward the entrance.

I pushed the door open and stepped inside, handing it off to

Gabe. His eyes darted to my hand on the door, like I'd stolen his chance to be chivalrous.

"I can open my own doors, man."

He grinned. "I can see that."

Entering the diner, I claimed a spot in the back. "This is the best booth in the place. Nobody can see you eat."

"I like to sit at the window seats near the front." He slid into the booth.

"People walk past windows," I said.

He laughed. "Not a fan of people?"

"Never have been. Only a very precious few."

"So what's good here?" he asked.

"The pizza."

"Smart ass." But it didn't seem to bother him. "What do you want? I'll go order for you."

"The pizza." I winked to show him I was teasing. "A slice of the chicken and broccoli. And an iced tea, please."

"You got it." He got up to order, and I nearly laughed when I saw who was working the counter. Who else would take his order, if not Tony? Sometimes my life delivered delicious chunks of poetic justice.

Tony's eyes moved from Gabe to me, but he emotionlessly took Gabe's order and got to work. Inside, I was certain he was calculating the caliber of the bullet he'd dodged by not dating me, the girl who'd taken her latest date to her last date's work-place. That or Val's influence didn't stretch far, and he'd already forgotten he'd ever agreed to date me.

My phone vibrated, but I ignored it. I had told no one where I was or who I was with. I didn't want anyone to try to talk me out of it, prematurely celebrate it, or try to improve it. If I was going to date Gabe, I wanted it to be about dating Gabe.

Gabe crossed his arms and leaned against the counter, craning his head so he could watch Tony handle our food.

Finally, after a good five minutes, Tony slid the tray over to Gabe, this time with a petulant eye roll.

Gabe sidled up to our table and lowered our tray to the counter. He slid in on my side of the table, his hip bumping mine.

"This okay? I figured, if you don't like people seeing you eat, you probably don't want me seeing you eat."

"This works. Is that pineapple on your pizza?"

"Yeah...is that a problem?" He gave me a crooked smile.

"Of course not...as long as you don't mind being a degenerate cretin who ruins everything." I had a bite of my normal food.

"Wow, you don't mince words." He flashed me another smile around his pizza. "Mmm. Glorious."

Smashed up against my bag as we sat in the cramped space, I felt my phone vibrate again. I tried not to allow it to distract me.

"That's an abomination." I motioned towards his slice.

"You ever tried it?"

"Why?"

"You can't say you don't like something if you've never tasted it."

I rolled my eyes.

"C'mon." He turned the pizza toward me. "Have a bite."

I made a face.

"You can spit it into your napkin if you hate it."

"Because that would be so attractive," I said.

"Are you trying to be attractive?" His eyebrows raised.

I took a bite of the pizza. Sweet and savory mingled on my tongue in an alluring medley like nothing I'd ever tasted before. "Oh my God, this is delicious."

He waited, a smug smile on his face as I chewed. "So you like it?"

"I'm kind of shocked, to be honest."

"Can we be degenerate cretins together?" he asked.

My phone buzzed again from inside my bag. This time it was an incoming call.

I ignored it, my eyes still locked on Gabe's. I nodded, and he leaned in, his thigh warm against mine. He turned a little, dipping his head, and I moved to meet him. His breath tickled my lips, and he pressed his forehead against mine.

"This okay?" he asked.

I wanted to say yes. But I also wanted to say no. Gabe wasn't who I wanted, but he was also... kind of charming.

Another call.

"Do you need to get that?" He pulled back slightly. "It keeps ringing." His dark eyes held a mix of emotions, and I couldn't read if he was cool with it or not.

"I probably should." I surged forward and pressed my lips to his.

He tasted like oregano and sweet pineapple, and he returned the kiss, one finger grazing along my chin. My breath seemed to run away from me. I'd kissed boys before, but it was always awkward, and sometimes a little gross. This was soft and sweet, and I used the table for leverage to get closer.

Another. Damn. Phone. Call.

I broke away with a sigh of frustration. "I should get that."

"Yeah, you should." He frowned, the space between his eyebrows creased with concern.

I dug for my phone, fumbling and flustered. When I excavated it from the madness of papers and detritus, it had stopped ringing.

One missed call from Nina. A text from her. And then incessant calls from Val, and a text in all caps asking where the hell I was.

I rolled my eyes and flashed the phone at Gabe.

"Val is probably just freaking out, but Nina? You should call her." He scratched at the back of his head, offering me a mini shrug.

"Did you tell anyone we were hanging out today?"

"Only Adam."

My stomach dropped. "Oh yeah, what did he say?"

"He was cool about it." His eyes narrowed as if he expected a reaction. I would not give it to him.

Of course Adam was cool about Gabe dating me. Because Adam was just being nice to me and I was taking it all wrong. Going out with Gabe was the right thing to do.

"Which means Adam told Val." I didn't allow any change in my tone.

"And do you think, for a second, Val would interrupt us if it wasn't serious?" He shot me a knowing glance.

Shit. I needed to call Nina. Like, now.

The phone rang twice before Nina picked up. "Hey, there you are."

"What happened?"

"Why do you think something happened?"

"I *guessed* from the calls, I *know* from the sound of your voice."

"Damn it, Bree."

My laugh was strained with worry.

"Reeve called me."

Gabe tapped my shoulder, mouthing, "She okay?"

I made a so-so hand gesture. "What did *he* want?"

"He wants to get back together." She sounded almost robotic. "I'm thinking of saying yes."

"What?" That was the jolt I needed to break out of Gabe's spell.

"I don't know. I mean, I loved him so much. I never wanted to leave him, so maybe…"

A moment of weakness, one so bad it shook her foundation. This wasn't who she was, not by a long shot.

"Do you understand why I called so many times now?" Val screeched in the background.

I took a deep breath and looked to Gabe, who had taken to listening in.

"I borrowed Adam's car. I can give you a ride over there. She sounds like she can really use her friend."

I chewed on my lower lip. I shouldn't do this, but I had to.

"It's okay. Seriously. We'll rain check it."

"I'll be right over," I said to Nina. "We need to think about this and talk it through before making any decisions."

"Right," Nina said. "That's why I called you. He was so sweet on the phone, though. So apologetic."

I'm sure he was.

"It's... what he said before..." Her voice was thick with tears. "I'm so frickin' sick of crying!"

"Dude, I'll be there soon. Give me, like, twenty minutes."

"Okay. Thank you, babe."

"Of course! Anytime." I disconnected the call and looked at the phone for a beat. "You know how you asked me the other day if I was looking for the love of my life?"

Gabe laughed. "Yeah, but I was just messing with you."

"I know. But I met the love of my life in kindergarten. Yeah, a boyfriend is gonna be a different kind of relationship, but nobody beats Nina. Ever. She's like...my soulmate."

He avoided my gaze and plucked a piece of pineapple off his slice. "Can I tell you a secret a manlier man would never admit?"

"Shoot. Manly men are annoying anyway."

"That's like me and Adam. Cousins, yeah, but more like brothers. Is Nina okay?"

I ignored the squeeze in my heart, ignored that I had been cool with pitting them against each other just a few minutes before.

"She's having a crisis. A month ago, her boyfriend of two years broke up with her. He just called her, wanting to get back together. Are you sure you want to rush over there? I mean, you barely know her."

"I know her some," Gabe argued. He chewed his lower lip. "I've been over to see her and Val a few times with Adam when you were working. We've hung out while Val made moony eyes at Adam, and Adam was... well, Adam."

"Okay," I said, a little hesitantly. "If you're cool with it." I devoured my last bite of pizza. "C'mon. Let's go."

I grabbed my purse and my phone. He slid out of the booth and I followed. I moved for the tray, but Gabe placed a hand on my arm and shook his head. His hand slid down my arm, leaving chills in its wake, and he twined his fingers with mine. He shot me a wink, then tugged me playfully toward the front.

"Hey Tony," he called as his back pressed against the door. "Do you think we could get a clean-up on that back table?"

Tony shot him the finger. Gabe's smile could have powered Main Street. With unparalleled grace, he pushed back against the door and twirled me through it, waving to Tony as we left.

I giggled despite myself because it was a fucking fantastic bit of petty vengeance.

"I think Tony and I have a real affinity for each other," Gabe informed me as he led me toward the car, our hands still joined. "We'll be best friends before summer's through."

"Naturally." I laughed. "Again, thank you for not being pissed that I have to go."

"Hey, it's cool. Seriously. I get it better than you know."

The drive to Nina's was filled with small talk and silliness, but nothing with any depth. Gabe seemed to feel like I did. A little nervous. A little happy. And still not quite sure this fledgling relationship was the right thing for us.

Or maybe I was projecting my feelings onto him. I liked him. I found him attractive. But was that all I needed for us to cross the line into something more?

Thoughts spun through my head as we pulled up in front of

Nina's. Nina and Val sat on the front steps. The cognitive dissonance of spotting me in Adam's car with Gabe flashed over both of their faces.

Gabe untangled his hand from mine as we slid out of the car, awkwardly jamming it into his pocket like touching was suddenly off limits.

"Oh! Noooooo. I forgot!" Val's eyes lit up in a panic. "We should never have called you." She glanced over at Nina. "We should never have called her."

Nina's eyes were puffy and red, the skin around her nose wrecked from swiping at it with tissues. She offered Gabe and me a faint smile. "Sorry to interrupt."

"No, it's okay," Gabe said. "It seemed like you needed a friend——your best friend." He shifted on his feet. "I should go."

"No!" Nina grabbed for his arm, stopping him in his tracks. "Don't go. I won't keep her long. Just a few minutes or so. Besides, we're all friends, right?"

"Um... yeah. If you're cool with me being here, I'm cool with staying." A warm smile lit up his eyes.

I frowned as a weighty tension solidified between us. Ignoring it, I stepped toward Nina. She wrapped her arms around me and buried her face in my shoulder, which was impressive since she was a head taller than me, like she was a freakin' Amazon. "There you are."

I gave her a crushing hug and buried my face in her hair. "We've got stuff to talk about, huh?" Her dark curls, laced through with blonde streaks, practically swallowed my words.

"Lots," she muttered.

"Okay, in we go." I walked her around the building and all the way down the steps to her basement, with one arm wrapped around her waist. Val and Gabe followed behind.

I waited until she settled on the couch before speaking. Val sat on the other side of us. I lost track of Gabe, but Nina was more important at the moment.

"Catch me up."

"Well, Reeve called—" Val started, an edge of terror in her tone.

"Not you!" I cut her off. "Nina."

Val sat back against the couch cushions, pouting.

"He called me," she said in a wistful tone that almost sounded like happiness.

"And you answered." I frowned.

"Yeah, yeah." She waved a dismissive hand at me. "I answered. I didn't answer politely, but I answered."

"And what did he have to say for himself?"

"He said he missed me," Nina said. "And he was sorry that what he said upset me. And he never wanted us to break up. He thinks we should get back together but take it slow. He wants us to be sure we're right for each other."

"He's sorry that what he said upset you?" I growled. "That's not an apology! That's a complaint! 'Sorry you were so sensitive and got all upset for no reason and that I broke up with you. Wanna cuddle?' Nah, fuck that!"

Another weak smile. "You've got thoughts, I see."

"I could write a treatise on the thoughts I have right now! I don't just have thoughts. I have ideas. Opinions, even. And I'm not afraid to share them."

"You're not afraid of anything." Nina laughed.

"Now that's not exactly true, is it?" Val said. "Brynn's afraid of a few things." I scowled at her as her eyes tracked between me and Gabe. She leaned forward and whispered, "You don't want to come off as too strong. That's what got her into trouble with Reeve to begin with."

I made a face at her, a facial contortion that turned into a half-forced-smile, half-snarl. "As amusing as that comment was, Reeve's issue with strong women is just that——Reeve's issue.

Nobody should have to change themselves because their boyfriend can't handle who they are."

"But he wasn't always like that," Nina said. "I honestly don't get what happened, but I think he was talking out of his ass. We were together for two years. He waits until a couple of months before the end of the school year to break up with me with a bullshit excuse? It makes no sense."

"Look, Nina," Gabe piped up from the corner of the room where he'd settled on the floor. "This is what I'm getting from the very little I know about this whole thing." He stopped himself, frowning, then added a quick, "If you don't mind me saying, that is."

"Nah, it's cool. You can say." She slanted a nervous glance my way.

He shifted, switching his crossed legs over each other before settling back down. "Well, I've got two comments. One is the obvious one. You're strong and model-gorgeous, and it seems like that intimidates him."

Nina blushed hard and fought to hide a grin, but lost the battle.

"That alone would be a baffling reason to end a relationship, but that's not why he did it, if I had to guess." He chewed his full lower lip. "The senior trip is coming up in a couple of weeks, right?"

"Right," I said. "And prom is a couple of weeks after."

He made a thoughtful noise, his eyes moving between the three of us. I could practically hear the adding machine making calculations behind his eyes. Definitely Adam's cousin.

"He breaks up with you but makes up in time to party together on the senior trip, take you to prom, all the trappings of senior year. Because who else would you go with? He's stringing you along. But you're taking things slow. Which means he gets to have a summer fling, go away to college and hook up, and keep you on the hook, as long as you'll stick around for it. My conclusion? I could totally be wrong about his motivations here, but it seems like this Reeve guy is a giant douche canoe."

For a moment, we were all silent as we processed the possibility based on what we knew about Reeve.. And dammit...it did make a lot of sense.

"That's scary," Val said. "Like... evil genius level scary."

"And probably damn accurate," I noted. "Reeve has always seemed slippery." Reeve never understood why I didn't take to him, but I'd had the advantage of a front-row seat to all their break-ups, and his reasons always felt like excuses.

"Shit," Nina muttered. And then, after a beat, a little louder, "Shit! How could I be so stupid?" Tears leaked from the corners of her eyes, speeding up over the curves of her cheeks and then slowing to a stop near her chin.

"You wanted him to be who you thought he was." I wiped the tears from her face. "One day you'll find someone who really is exactly who you think, and he'll be worth it."

She groaned and punched the couch. She burst into tears, falling forward until her head was in my lap. She sobbed as I smoothed her hair gently, petting the mass of curls in the way that always calmed her.

Val slipped off the couch and knelt on the floor before us, taking one of Nina's hands in hers. "Oh, sweetie. I'm so sorry."

"You see, this is exactly what I did not want to do." The words broke through Nina's jagged cries. "Who the hell is this person and why is she crying over an asshole? This isn't like me." Her breath hitched.

"God, give yourself a break!" Gabe huffed, pushing himself to his feet. "A guy hurt your feelings and you're crying about it to your friends. So what?" He dropped in front of her, kneeling next to Val, and his gaze was hard as it landed on Nina.

We all froze, and my hackles rose. I practically hissed at him.

I should have never brought him in with me. Where the hell did he get off saying——

"Look, I get the need to throw as much bravado at this as you possibly can. But Adam told me a lot about you before I got here, and I learned even more when I arrived. The Nina he told me about was brilliant, thoughtful, and charismatic. She was the epitome of the loyal friend. What she absolutely was not is a robot. Feel what you're gonna feel. Get it out, because until you do, you're gonna keep needing to call your friends to ask them for the answers to questions you already know the answers to.

"It's not that anyone minds talking you through it. It's that you already know he's full of shit. That's why you were crying before we even got here." He leaned forward a little. "Sometimes, you have to be maudlin for a while before you can return to your previous outstanding state." He quirked a smile. "Until then, you've got friends for a reason, and it isn't for telling you what you already know. Brynn, Val, Adam, and me, if you'll have me. We're the people who are supposed to pick you up and dust you off, so you don't have to. You don't always have to feel tough as nails." He sat back a bit. "But that doesn't mean you aren't."

I glanced at Val and leaned forward to whisper in her ear. "Love," I scoffed. "This is what you want for me?"

Val didn't look away from Gabe and Nina as Nina thanked Gabe for the pep talk and slid her other hand in his, an acceptance of his pledge of friendship.

"Yes," she answered out of the corner of her mouth. "This is exactly what I want for you."

I couldn't tell if she was being sarcastic, or if I was missing something, but my stomach dropped at her answer.

BY THE TIME Nina calmed down, I was desperate to find something to lift her spirits. With Gabe and Val's aid, we settled on her favorite non-romantic comedy movie. As the credits rolled, Gabe stretched.

"Sorry guys, I've got to get out of here. I promised Uncle Will I'd run some errands with him, and I probably should have been back an hour ago." He launched himself to his feet, then leaned forward, pressing a kiss to Val's cheek. "G'night." Tenderly, he brushed an errant curl out of Nina's eyes. "Feeling any better?"

She smiled up at him with an appreciative glow. "A little, thanks."

"Good." He turned to me. "Brynn? Do you need a ride home? Or do you want to stick around?"

I slid off the couch, wincing at what I was about to say. "I should stick around for a bit longer. But I'll walk you out?"

"Cool."

The humidity outside was oppressive, my lungs immediately weighed down by the thick air. I made a note to tell Nina to stay inside. This would not be good for her asthma. Beside me, Gabe grunted and pulled at his damp shirt.

"Right?" I closed the door behind me so the grossness wouldn't get into the basement. "Hey, listen. I really want to thank you for everything you did today. You were incredible."

"Thanks Brynn." He shoved his hands into his pockets. "It was no problem, really. I've been where she's at. It sucks. And she's... she doesn't deserve to be treated like that."

"I agree." I smiled at him, but my eyes burned. Something felt wrong, like the chemistry that had been simmering between us earlier had fizzled. "Sorry about ruining our... hang out."

"It wasn't ruined," he said. "I really had a good time." A grimace. "No, not a good time watching Nina cry, that sounds awful. I had... a worthwhile time? I don't actually know what

I'm saying. Why am I single?" He scratched at his head, sending his spiky hair all askew.

"I think I get you." I just didn't really like what I was getting. Or maybe I did. Maybe the feeling I was getting——that Gabe liked me, but maybe liked Nina more——was a good thing. Gabe was a good guy. Nina deserved someone like him.

He leaned forward, his hands jamming so hard into his pockets that his jeans lowered a little, the waistband of his underwear peeking out over the top where his t-shirt pulled up with the shrug of his shoulders. Damn, he was hot. And that kiss... this was an absolute shame.

"Actually, I know exactly why I'm single. I just got through what Nina's going through now. It sucks." He stretched the last word out. "I'm not a genius detective, capable of determining shitty motives. Just a fellow victim."

Sometimes I looked at Gabe and all I could think was 'awwwwwwwww.' He might have been too cute for me.

"Well, whoever that was, she was an absolute fool." I pressed a kiss to his cheek, my fingers skimming the stubble along his jaw. It felt like breaking up, and my heart fell. "It was nice getting to know you better."

"Same here," he said. "And we should definitely try to have pizza together another time. So... rain check?"

"Absolutely." I had a feeling the next pizza date would be much more platonic, but I'd keep the door open, just in case.

CHAPTER TEN
PAINFUL MAGIC

THE NEXT MORNING, I walked to school. Not that Adam wasn't perfectly willing to pick me up after he picked up Nina and Val. I just wanted to sneak out of the house as early as possible so Mom wouldn't wonder why all of my recent fashionable progress had degraded to me wearing a t-shirt that said "The Book Was Better" with a pair of ripped black jeans.

I loved walking for long stretches. All I did these days was think. I needed time to listen to some music, open the hatch doors on my brain and let everything fall to the wind. So I plugged my earbuds in place and blasted the words of great lyrical poets into my cranium.

There was a pleasing breeze in the air, just enough to take the edge off the heat of the uncharacteristically warm spring. I walked through a few tree-lined side-streets, past house after house of colonials and Victorians and was about halfway through the largest stretch of my walk, before a nasally voice interrupted my peaceful travels.

"Brynn!"

I froze in place. Reeve.

I turned on my heel, and it was like the air turned solid around me, like I needed to push through stone walls just to stop myself from tackling him and punching him in the face.

Sometimes, my love for Nina was an actual force, holding me back from some of my meaner urges.

"Reeve." I greeted him, tension in my smile. "How amazing. We have the same classes, but you've never bothered to talk to me since the breakup. What could you possibly want?"

That was as courteous as he was going to get.

He muttered something under his breath, didn't even try to hide it, but then he scratched the back of his neck. At least he had the nerve to look chagrined. "You probably know I called Nina."

"Probably. I heard she called you back last night."

"Turned me down," he answered almost before I finished. His face reddened as he spoke. "She didn't want to get back together."

"Hm... maybe that's because you broke up with her for the fiftieth time." I turned and continued my trip toward school. "If you want to talk to me, you'd better follow. I'm not going to be late for class because your loser ass just assumed she'd take you back whenever you felt like it."

He rushed to catch up, jogging until he was walking side-by-side with me. "That wasn't it. I had some... complications. I was trying to figure things out. Like, where will I be at the end of the school year? You know? Do I want our relationship to last past high school? Forever? Like, I don't know."

"Does it matter?" I asked. "How about you stop overthinking things and stay with someone who makes you happy until they don't? I mean, weren't you happy with her?"

"Yeah." He hoisted his bookbag up onto his shoulders when it slid out of place. "I was happy. But she's moving to the city in the fall. I'm going out of state. So there's gonna be a long-distance thing. And I wasn't sure that was what I wanted."

"And now, suddenly, you are?" I asked, pleased by how bored I sounded. "What brought on that epiphany?"

"Well, Nina was so upset when I broke things off. And, well, so was I, of course. And I racked my brain trying to come up with something that would work for both of us. Maybe the key is like you said——go with the flow. We can stay together, but keep things open, keep them light, keep them—"

"—from being too committed so when you go off to college, you don't have to keep your dick in your pants," I finished for him.

He stopped short, and I turned to face him. "Yeah, that's right. We're on to you, putz."

He rolled his eyes at me. "Putz? How old are you?"

"I'm well read, and you're not denying anything."

Anger flashed in his eyes. "It isn't like that. You're the damn reason Nina acts this way. You're protective of her, like she's a child or your girlfriend, because you need a damn life of your own. And she starts to get the idea that behaving the way you do, all snark and false courage, is cool. No guy wants a girlfriend who would rather punch someone in the face than cuddle. And that's what you turned her into. A difficult bitch who thinks she's smarter and better than everybody else."

My throat tightened around my response, and I had to shove the words out into the world. "Why do you think we're friends in the first place? She was never very different from me. You just enjoyed seeing what you wanted to until you decided to head off for greener pastures. There was never any place for you in her life, because you never really took the time to get to know her. You were so busy bragging about your hot girlfriend, you never paid attention to anything else about her." I took off again, not bothering to look back. "So no, you anthropomorphized fart, I will not lead her down that road again. You're on your own."

I sped up my pace, leaving Reeve far behind so I wouldn't have to deal with him needling me all the way to school. I returned my earbuds to my ears and cranked the music up.

When I arrived at school, it was nearly half an hour before classes started. I'd hustled a lot faster than I'd intended, burning off my frustration as I moved.

Still, I heard Reeve's words in my head. That my behavior, my shitty outlook on life, had somehow screwed up his relationship with Nina, haunted me. Or rather, the idea that my cynical nature had inadvertently caused her any distress. I couldn't care less how Reeve felt.

I walked through the front doors, followed by Jake August, the star of the school's track team and Leanne Wilkes, the head of the yearbook committee. Both had been lingering on the front steps, chattering about something until my arrival seemed to remind them that school took place inside the doors, not outside.

"Brynn!" Leanne called. We'd known each other from two years of Spanish classes we'd taken together and her growing addiction to ice cream sandwiches. "Smile!" Before I knew it, her phone was snapping away despite my growl of protest.

"Thanks for the warning, Leanne!" I shouted as she retreated. That was way more likely to make it into the school yearbook than the flattering, posed photo Nina, Val, Adam, and I had taken in the lunchroom.

Reeve walked in behind me, and I ducked into the closest open door——the auditorium. The stage crew was putting up the sets for next week's production of *Bye Bye Birdie*. Craig was part of the stage crew and in the show itself. I headed down the aisle and past the rows of seats to say hello, and possibly to kill time until Reeve found his classroom... or walked into an empty elevator shaft. Whatever.

There were about ten kids working on various portions of the set, and I found Craig standing on a stepladder, hanging a sign that read "Sweet Apple, Ohio."

"Hey! No extracurriculars until you've perfected the cup control on your small shake!" I called to him.

He grinned. "Hey Brynn! What are you doing here?"

"Ah, nothing much." I sidled up to join him on stage. "Just killing time before class. I got here a little early."

"Hey, it's Bree!"

My eyes slammed shut, tension making my shoulders rise to my ears. Raphael. *Damn it!*

"Hi Raphael." I pointedly turned towards Craig. "So, you guys are almost ready for the show?"

"Yep," Craig said.

"Where are your friends?" Raphael looked around the auditorium.

"They aren't going to suddenly appear." I gazed pleadingly at Craig.

"Are you coming to see the play?" He scrambled to continue the conversation. "I do a mean Conrad Birdie."

"Sorry." I shrugged. "I know nothing about the show."

"Conrad is sorta like a fictional Elvis Presley." Craig stepped down the ladder once the sign was safely in place. Once on solid ground, he did an Elvis-worthy hip shift.

"Well, that sold it," I said. "Where can I get tickets?"

"I'll bring some to Scoopy Doo tonight. Do you think the others will want to come?" he asked, hope in his eyes.

"Well, that depends on who's working that night, but I'll ask Sammy for the day off, definitely," I said.

Raphael playfully punched Craig in the arm. Craig winced in annoyance. "You didn't tell me you were part of the Scoopy Doo gang!" He returned his attention to me. "Did Craig tell you who I'm playing in the show?"

"A sewer rat, maybe?"

"No, goof." Raphael just laughed, impervious to my attempts to make him go away. "I'm Mr. MacAfee, the main character's father."

"Congratulations?"

"I'll see if I can find a copy of the movie and we can watch it at my house before you see the show, so you know what we're talking about," he said. "My uncle will be away for the weekend, and we've been saying we would hang out for-eveeer."

"Um...no, I'm good." I winced. "I'd rather be surprised. And also, I'd rather eat rusty nails and pass them through my digestive tract."

Craig's eyes narrowed. "Hey Raph, aren't you supposed to be getting the props from 301?"

Room 301 was the classroom they used to work on the scenes that weren't currently being practiced in the auditorium. Hanging out with Craig at work often meant running lines and becoming an expert on our school's performing arts routine, even if I had nothing to do with it. Craig, as it turned out, was a cool dude, with moments of abrasiveness... but then, I'd just told Raphael I'd rather shit nails than hang out with him, so who was I to judge?

Raphael scowled. "Yeah, in a second, but first I need to ask Bree—"

Craig cut him off. "Except those props aren't going to move themselves, and Mr. G's gonna be on your ass if you don't get them."

"Why don't you go get the props?" Raphael grumbled.

"She'd just come with me," Craig said. "You get that, don't you?"

Raphael looked to me like he was waiting for me to argue. I shrugged and inched closer to Craig, and Raphael finally took the hint. He shot Craig the finger and stormed away to go do his actual job while Craig joined me in the aisle.

"Jeez, the guy can't take a hint. Sorry about him. He's a dick."

"Yep." I laughed. "That's why I've never gone out with him, despite him constantly asking."

"He's changed a lot since last year. Don't know what's wrong with him," he said. "It's funny, isn't it? It's always the ones you don't want that chase you.

"Funny, like a tragedy."

"He did have a point, though. You don't generally just come by to say hi. Why kill time in the auditorium of all places?"

I made a face. "I got into a nasty conversation with someone on the way here, and I needed a minute alone to clear my head before class. Which I didn't get by coming in here because I found you guys. But I wasn't just gonna ignore you."

Craig ruffled my hair. "You're growing as a person, Brynn. I hope you know that."

"Do that again and I'll kick you in the shins." I scowled.

"See? Growth! That kick would have been way higher a couple of weeks ago." He chuckled. "There's a staircase just outside the dressing rooms in the wings. It leads to the second floor and the lighting area. Nobody should go there for a while, so it's the place to think. Or cut class. Whatever you need."

I couldn't help but smile. "This is why I'm nice to you." I started for the dressing room.

"Whatever it is..." Craig said. "I hope you can work it out."

I turned back to him. "Thank you. You're growing as a person, too, you know."

His laughter followed me into the dull lighting of the wings. I easily found the staircase Craig had mentioned and settled down when I reached the top, right outside the lighting box.

I owed Craig; this was exactly what I was looking for.

Through the door's small square window, I saw people moving through the halls, making their way to a class or a locker, something or someone. Fast, excited paces, or lingering, dreadful steps. High school was different for everyone, but we all had one thing in common——it felt like the beginning of everything. It felt like if you made one wrong move, the rest of your life would be unstable.

I didn't know what I wanted to be when I grew up. I didn't know what job I would have, if I would get married, if I wanted kids. The only thing I knew was who I was, and the people I wanted around me would be those who would be there for me. People would want me, not some trumped up version of who I could be.

Reeve wanted Nina to be someone she wasn't, and I told her to stay away from him. Val wanted me to be someone I wasn't on dates, and I was letting her set me up and influence me. That had to stop. Even my move with Gabe was a misstep she had put in my head. I knew better than to follow Val's advice blindly.

"Hey." Adam's soft voice drifted through the hallway, and I remembered why I jumped whenever Val said I should. Because his voice sent my stomach flopping and my nerves fraying.

"Craig told me you were in here, hiding from Raphael. Again." I glanced up to find him leaning against the wall, arms crossed over his chest, a frown on his face. "Can I punch him?"

I offered a weak smile. "No. You really shouldn't."

He sighed and pushed himself off the wall. "Are you sure? I can just break his nose a little."

The smile widened, despite my brain screaming at me to resist. "That's not your style."

"You are right about that." He perched on the stairs beside me. "So, how did things go?"

"Things?" My eyes stayed focused on the door to the outside world, the halls of the high school emptying as the first class began. Adam had class, too. I knew I was too frustrated to sit in a classroom, but Adam wasn't like me. What was he doing?

"Your date? With Gabe?" Adam prodded. "He won't say, and it's weird because he tells me everything. Did one of you guys piss the other one off or something?"

"Craig told me I could come here for a little peace, and then he sent you after me? I thought we were cool." I huffed.

"That bad?" Adam winced.

"Things pretty much suck for me in general lately. Mom saw me dressed up for a couple of days and is now trying to push me to dress like the future homecoming queen. I escaped for school early so I didn't have to hear it, but I ran into Reeve and we had an argument. I come here to get a little peace and here you are asking me about a date I went on with someone el—" I cut myself off and prayed to every god I could think of that he didn't catch my slip. "With someone." Forget facepalms. It was all I could do not to punch myself in the head.

As usual, his dark eyes were inscrutable, his mouth a thin line. When he saw me looking at him, his eyebrows raised. He was still asking me the question, pretending like I hadn't said a word. I wanted to be angry at him, but this was his cousin and best friend. He was being protective. Like I had been with Nina.

I sighed. "I don't know. It went well, but not really a date? We spent time together…"

"But it wasn't a date?" he asked. "Gabe thought it was a date when he left to meet you."

"It was supposed to be a date," I explained. "I meant for it to be one."

"Then why wasn't it?"

"You're worse than Val. Who are you? Eros?" I rolled my eyes.

"Eros?" His eyes narrowed, head tilted. As usual, I was a specimen, something to be scrutinized under a microscope. It wasn't cruel, like an expression of judgment, but an expression of interest, an attempt at understanding something foreign to him.

The puzzled expression raised goosebumps on my arms, but I forced a laugh for his benefit. "Greek mythology? I thought you knew everything."

He frowned, pushing his glasses back up his nose. "I know who he is. I don't get why you compared me to him."

I wasn't touching that. "I meant to do the date thing with

Gabe, and we sorta did, but then Val called freaking out about Reeve. Gabe agreed I should go see what was up. He dropped me off there, but Nina said he shouldn't leave. It would only be a minute. That minute was three hours long. I'm surprised Val didn't mention it to you."

Adam stretched out across the stairs. Like he'd decided to stick around. "If I'd started hanging around you guys sooner, I would have warned you before Nina ended up with him. Reeve has always been a total bastard. And Val mentioned Reeve's phone call. She said she's rooting for them."

"What?" It was a near shriek. "We spent all last night talking Nina out of it!"

For a moment, Adam looked taken aback, but his recovery was speedy. "Well, you know how Val is. She has this idea of love being this incredible, magical thing. I wish she was right." He took off his glasses, wiping the lenses with his royal blue t-shirt. "But it's just people. Two, human, people. You put your heart on the line with this completely fallible person and wait to see what they do with it. That person either cherishes it or crushes it. And that's not magic. That's reality. You find a person you actually make sense with. Someone who listens to you and cares about you, and someone you can do the same for. After that, you just pray they aren't the one who crushes your heart." He glanced at me. "You see? No magic at all."

His nostrils flared, his intense gaze turned toward his sneakers. He poked a fingernail along the edges of his Chuck Taylors.

No magic at all? What was happening to me because of him was definitely magic, because there was no way in hell I would have allowed myself to get entangled in this mess if there wasn't some cosmic force at play.

Besides, Angie and Roman had magic.

"How did your parents meet?"

"Way to non sequitur." He chuckled, low and sad. "Dad had

just moved into town. His cousin lived close by, and he took him to Emilio's. Some of his cousin's friends were hanging out, and one of them was my mother..." He trailed off, still not looking up from his shoes, scratching at some imaginary mark on the canvas.

"No magic?" I asked.

Finally, his eyes met mine. "Why would you think that?"

His words were a gut punch. "I'm sorry, I didn't mean to sound like I was arguing Val's point, even if I wasn't sure what to believe. Playing devil's advocate, you know?"

"Well, there was plenty of magic. And you know what? When she died, that ended up hurting everyone too." He pushed himself to his feet and moved toward the door. "You know what, Brynn?" He turned to face me. "It doesn't matter what happens. Love hurts. The less involved you get, the better off you'll be."

"But...Val?" Because he was supposed to care about my friend.

He glanced away and swallowed hard. "Val is a sweet girl." When his eyes met mine again, they were pained. "Magic hurts more, ya know?"

"That doesn't come close to answering my question."

He smiled, but it didn't reach his eyes. "You call that a question?" This time, when he turned to leave, he didn't stop.

AFTER SCHOOL, we met up at the library. Or rather, Adam dragged Val to the library while Nina and I followed along. Our project was due at the end of the week, so we needed to wrap things up.

A tower of books once known as Nina emerged from the stacks. As she walked, the books tilted and dipped, and she struggled to keep them from toppling over. She lowered them to the table with great care, her hands steady, mouth twisted in concentration. "I want to use these for the research part of our presentation. I'm working on the bibliography. Everything we found for our research came from these."

Val flipped through the pages of research with great enthusiasm. "Oh, I didn't think they still talked about that one." She pointed out a paragraph to Adam. "I adore that story."

Adam looked puzzled. "You didn't think they still—"

"Which awful Aphrodite tidbit are you talking about, Val?" I cut him off to remind Val that most of Aphrodite's stories were not things to 'adore.'

"The one where she turned into a fish, of course," she said with a grin. "The change only lasted for a limited time, but they don't mention that."

Adam looked amused. "Is that so?"

"I mean, if she stayed a fish, how could she keep being a goddess?" She winked at him. "Anyway, being a fish would be delightful."

"Ohhhhh.... kay," Nina cut in, "so we've got the research done. What do we do about the presentation?"

"I know you're not looking at me," I answered. "I can't even cut a straight line."

"Yeah, I don't think artsy is the way to go. I mean, I could do artsy, but you three?"

"We could act something out?" Val asked. "Pretend to be Aphrodite and Helen?"

"If I pretend to be Aphrodite, I'm going to sound like a bitter jerk," I said. "Trust me. Besides, I don't think it's smart to make me speak in front of people."

"You're gonna have to say something in front of the class. It's a presentation." Adam leaned forward on the table.

"Why don't we play a fact game?" I asked. "I can do a Power-Point presentation and make it look like a game, and whenever someone gets the answer right, we can...do...something," I sputtered out.

Adam smirked at me. "Well, that was half of a decent idea. Who has the other half?"

"We could act out scenes to answer the questions," Val offered. "That way it's still creative and artistic, but not a play."

"We could take turns playing roles and being the host," Nina chimed in.

"Yes! That's brilliant," Adam said. "Nice work, Brynn." He gave my arm a light squeeze.

I covered the grin that overtook my face with faked excitement about the project. "We're gonna ace this thing."

I COULDN'T DECIDE. As I added my latest book acquisition, I considered the current state of my bookshelves. Should I keep them in size-order? The vivid purple of the new book's spine begged me to re-organize my books by color. This was a significant decision, indeed.

My cell phone rang, interrupting my careful planning. It was Dad, so I picked up right away.

"Bookcase: size-order or sorted by color?"

He laughed, a barky guffaw. "Hello to you too, Brynn. Color sorting sounds pretty. You could even decorate the room according to bookcase color quadrants."

"I wouldn't go quite that far until we find a place in New York," I answered, "but it's a brilliant idea."

"Good. So honey, how are you doing?" The words sounded strained. Whatever I answered, his response was bound to be something I didn't like.

"I'm fine," I said, perhaps a little too firmly.

"You're always fine. But your mother says you've been going to school early to avoid her. And Josh says you've been arguing with your mother's boyfriend." The last word dropped awkwardly, like he couldn't figure out if that was how he wanted to play it.

"Fine. I'm not okay," I said. "I mean, I'm safe. I'm just…"

"I'm unhappy, too, Brynn. It's going to be a difficult transition for all of us, for a long time."

"I know. I mean, I expected that. I just can't stop arguing with her. She's so damn difficult."

He chuckled a little. "You're telling me that?"

"Yeah, but it's not just that. Val is acting like a jerk, and Nina and her boyfriend broke up, and I'm incapable of normal human interaction without making people hate me."

"Now, I know that's not true."

"You clearly haven't seen me in a while because I've been a complete mess." I dropped my head into one hand. "Although I've never excelled at normal human interaction."

Dad's sigh was audible through the connection. "I think you just need a little time to adjust to everything."

"I need to reduce my stress," I said. "You know what would help?"

I could practically hear Dad smirk. "You need to try to make it work with your mother."

"I don't see how that's possible. I feel like I don't even know her."

"Tell me about it. Thing is, you can't just run away from your troubles. Any of them. The only way out of anything is through. You talk to Val. You comfort Nina. You deal with your mother. And eventually, you will find your way out of the stress. But until then, you won't get anywhere."

I released an exaggerated sigh. "This is why I should live with you. You give the best advice."

"Not always. I've been reflecting on some of my own decisions. The biggest lesson I learned? Avoidance is not helpful. It means you stay in bad situations for longer than you need to."

"So I should leave my bad situation?"

"That's what you took from that?"

"Fine, I'll try."

"Wonderful." I could hear the smile in his voice. "Trying is all I could ask for."

CHAPTER ELEVEN
MOVIES AND BONFIRES

JAUNTY MUSIC CAME from the massive television in Nina and Val's basement, the silliness of the scene we were watching prompting peals of laughter from our group. I wasn't sure whose idea it was to watch the latest Kevin Hart movie, but it was the perfect break from the recent angst in our lives. Val had planned this movie night a week ago, an opportunity to get everyone in a room together, just because.

It was also a nice opportunity to help me forget an entire week's worth of failed Val-inspired dates with a member of the soccer team, a skateboarder, and a college kid who believed his future was in parkour... but had nearly broken his face trying to show off for me.

Nina laid across the floor, her head propped up on her elbow. She stuffed her face with a slice of pizza that would never affect her flat tummy. Val and Adam sat shoulder to shoulder, Adam against the armrest, Val leaning away from him. They both laughed at the appropriate moments, but he seemed distracted, and she looked like she'd just eaten a lemon.

On the other side of Val, Gabe had one arm casually thrown across the back of the couch. It wasn't resting on my shoulder, though his fingertips brushed against it. I welcomed the distraction the movie provided, but remained worried about Val and Adam, confused by Gabe, and glad to see Nina laughing.

Val passed the bowl of popcorn to Gabe, who balanced it on the place where our thighs rested against each other. Our fingers brushed as we both reached into the bowl at the same time. Our eyes met.

"You can have the rest." He smiled, then dropped his eyes into the bowl. "Val devoured most of it, anyway."

"It's nervous eating!" Val snarled. "And Adam had plenty. It wasn't just me."

"God Val," Adam groused. "Does it have to be such a damn big deal?"

"Please don't do this." She made a disgusted noise and sank further into the couch cushions.

Adam rolled his shoulders.

"Thanks, Gabe." I winced. "You can have the rest. I'm good."

"Let's split it."

I spilled half of the remaining popcorn into his palm. He grinned. As he pulled his hand away, his eyes flickered to Nina, and the smile faltered.

We watched the remaining few minutes of the movie in silence. When the credits rolled, Val stood abruptly. "I've had enough. I'm going to get more snacks." She rushed upstairs before any of us could offer to go with her.

"Val, come on." Adam followed closely behind her.

Gabe yawned and stretched. "I've gotta pee. Be right back."

"Thanks for the announcement," Nina called after him.

"Hear ye, hear ye! I must empty my bladder!" I shouted.

Gabe shot us both the finger. Once he'd disappeared upstairs to use the bathroom, I turned to Nina.

"What the hell is going on between Val and Adam?" I hoped that didn't sound too eager. I was just super uncomfortable being around couples when they were fighting.

"Dude, the last time they argued like this, it was about Adam shutting down and not experiencing his emotions or some crazy psychobabble like that." Nina shifted until she was sitting upright, looking up at me where I was leaning forward on the couch. "That was right at the beginning of their relationship. Adam backed down because she was right. He was retreating into the bubble he created for himself when his mom died."

"So what caused this?"

"Well, they already haven't been on great terms lately, and I don't know why," she admitted. "But this time, it started when Raphael asked Adam if he'd seen you."

"Wait, what? This is about Raphael and me?"

"Adam had to go and be a dumbass and get furious and defensive. He even threatened Raphael. Said he'd kick his ass if he kept harassing you."

"Well, that was dumb. If he keeps harassing me, *I'll* kick his ass."

"Yeah, but Adam went into protective beast mode or whatever, and it ticked Val off." Then, softer, she added, "Didn't I tell you to be careful with him? Val's starting to figure out that something is going on between the two of you."

My heart did a strange little dance in my chest, and I felt winded. "But nothing is. It's completely one-sided."

"Tell that to pissy-pants, Raphael," Nina said. "He was terrified. And I've never seen Adam do something like that. It was wild."

"Shit. Adam has no idea what he's dealing with."

"Right." Nina picked up the remote and flipped through Netflix in search of our next movie. "Pissing off a teenage girl is one thing, but pissing off a goddess?"

I refused to think about it. Instead, I zoned out and stared ahead as Nina continued to scroll through the movie offerings.

"All our recommended movies are romances! Can't people just not get smoochy with each other?" Nina grumbled.

Val huffed as she came back down the stairs, arms filled with a bowl of fruit and a replenished bowl of popcorn. "Isn't that Brynn's line?"

"Eh, I'm not done with love," Nina said. "I just can't relate at the moment. Reeve is still a fresh blood stain."

"So morbid," I said. "I like it."

"I suppose you're right," Val said. "It's best that you stay out of the dating game for a while, while you take time to heal your heart."

"Or," Adam said, as he galloped down the stairs, "she could try to break away from Reeve instead of wallowing in the breakup. Forward momentum, always."

Val glared at him.

"What?" Adam glared back. "You're the one who wants everyone to fall in love, aren't you? I was trying to help."

"Not everyone," she muttered.

"Oh, that's an accolade you reserve for me?" I shouldn't have prodded her. She was in an awful mood.

"Not all the time," she said.

Gabe came down, carrying a pack of cookies and a bag of chips. "What are we talking about?"

"If Nina should get over Reeve or sit and stew," Adam said.

"Why are we discussing what Nina should do?" Gabe set the snacks down on the coffee table for community use. "We don't make decisions about her life by committee vote." His tone was amiable, but the words had weight.

He was right. We were meddling.

Val banged and slammed her way through cabinets, though I wasn't sure what she was looking for. She plopped onto her butt, defeated.

"What if I want to leave him in the past and move forward, but I'm having trouble?" Nina asked. "Then can we vote for help by committee?"

We all turned to look at her, and she smiled sheepishly.

"What's holding you back?" Adam asked, his voice gentle.

"We spent two years together. There are gifts he gave me everywhere. Pictures of us. Things that make me think about him, and it's not even him I miss. I'm just pissed that he's part of half of my high school memories."

"That's gonna take time to untangle," Gabe said. "And some of your memories will always be tied to him. He was a big part of your life."

Val glanced up at Nina, and her features softened, the anger fleeing her face.

"Oh, I don't doubt that," Nina said. "I just want some... I don't know. Closure isn't the right word. I've spoken to him. We've ended it. I halfway want to scream at him, but I'm also too damn exhausted for that."

"That's the one thing that's missing from this perfect teenage getaway." Gabe raised an eyebrow. "A punching bag, to let out some of the anger."

"Now that would be nice," Nina said.

Oh, idea! "Do you guys still have that fire pit from when we used to camp out in your backyard?"

I received four equally questioning looks.

"You want to build a fire, why?" Adam asked.

"We still have it..." Nina trailed off.

"You want to camp in our backyard why?" Val asked.

"I don't want to camp," I said, like my plan was perfectly obvious. "I want to burn Reeve's shit."

For a moment, they all just stared back at me.

"A boyfriend bonfire," Nina whispered.

"You can't find peace without first embracing the chaos," I said.

Val grimaced. "Romance is not war, Brynn."

We locked eyes. "Oh, but yes, it is."

"Aphrodite would disagree."

"Would that be before or after she fucked Ares?"

"Definitely after. Lesson learned and all that."

Adam and Gabe shared a look of discomfort.

"So, how do we do this?" Nina asked, eyes lighting up.

"I can go get some firewood from my shed back home," Adam offered. "That shouldn't take long. But you should get your father's permission first."

"I am not asking Roman if we can have a boyfriend bonfire," Val scoffed.

Gabe rolled his russet-colored eyes. "Well, no. You're asking to have a campfire. He doesn't need to know that the kindling will be a lot more than firewood."

"Fine, I'll talk to him," Val grumbled, turning her attention to me. "And what will you be doing?"

"Nina and I will be picking out said kindling."

It was nearly an hour before we were sitting in a circle around a blazing fire. I basked in the warmth it brought against the slight chill of the evening air. Piles of memories rested at our feet, ready to be thrown in. The disheveled collection mirrored our own state. Digging for memories and building the fire had been more difficult than any of us expected.

"Where do we begin?" Nina asked me. "This was your idea."

"Well, I read about it in a book," I said. "I know how that one went, but I don't know how ours should start."

Val gazed into the flickering licks of heat before us. "Tell us what you do know."

"Each time you throw a piece into the fire, you're supposed to reveal something connected to it. Preferably a negative memory."

A dog's bark echoed over to us from a few houses down, and Adam's head turned to follow the sound. "Wonder if they smell the smoke. Hope they aren't worried."

Val smiled fondly at him, their previous tension forgotten.

"What if some of these don't have a negative memory attached?" Nina asked.

"Then you share a good one. And you burn those away too," I said.

"Okay, who goes first?" Nina asked.

Adam moved to raise his hand but caught up in the playfulness, I wrapped an arm around his and yanked it back down.

"Me!" I shouted.

Adam glared at me, his cheeks rosy from the heat of the fire.

"Hey, all's fair in war and dibs." I picked up a tiny pink, stuffed bunny rabbit. "I think we both remember the memory surrounding this bad boy. Am I starting you off with an easy enough memory to burn?"

Nina nodded.

"Are you sure you're okay with this, honey?" Val leaned forward, resting a hand on Nina's knee.

I bit back a response. Suddenly, it was Val checking to make sure someone was okay before rushing in. Val reminding her she didn't have to if she didn't want to. Rather than just telling her what she expected of her. A different fire lit in my belly, my insides twisting as I watched her compete with me for Nina.

"Yeah." Nina looked to me, and I couldn't be sure what she saw, but whatever it was, there was steel in her gaze. "Yeah, we've got this."

"Bunny." I waved the ball of fluff in front of me. "Give us the reason."

"Reeve won that bunny for me during the carnival in Patterson," she said, her voice brittle. "But only because I was angry at him. He complained all the way there. He didn't want to go. Then he flirted with the ticket salesgirl. When I threatened to go home without him, he convinced me not to. Promised to win me something."

We shouted encouragements, and a smile flickered across her lips.

Gabe wrapped an arm around her. "You see? You've got this. Here's to new beginnings." He gave her a little squeeze, staring down at her, and she looked back at him, her smile deepening.

She didn't even look away from him before saying, "Bree? Throw it in the fire."

I saw the two of them together, and my stomach settled. Deep inside, I'd known where Gabe and I had gone wrong. This was confirmation. Nina needed to move on because she was developing feelings for someone else. And I was not the one Gabe wanted.

I smirked as I threw the fluffy pink bunny into the fire and watched it burn.

CHAPTER TWELVE
WHAT YOU'RE LOOKING FOR

AFTER WE'D GONE HOME that night, I texted Gabe and asked him to meet me at my house in the morning to walk me to school. It was a bold move, and one I was still questioning as I scrambled to get dressed and ready before he showed up. I had forgotten to ask Gabe not to ring the doorbell, and he hadn't responded when I sent him a last-minute text. If I didn't get outside before he showed up, Mom would have questions I didn't want to answer.

I swiped the toothpaste residue from my mouth and threw my clothes on. Applying deodorant at light speed, I nearly tripped over the rug outside the shower as I moved to grab my brush.

The doorbell rang before I could swipe it through my hair even once.

I closed my eyes against the sound, took a deep breath, and rushed to the door, hoping Mom had slept through the echoing *bings* and *bongs* of the bell.

I got to the stairs first, but Mom was a short distance behind me, hastily throwing on a robe. From inside her room, Jesse called after her, asking why she'd rushed out of bed.

I would have no choice but to open the door in front of her. If I tried to sneak out without telling her who was ringing our doorbell, she'd never allow me to leave the house again. I yanked the door open like I was pulling off a Band-Aid.

"Gooooood morning," Gabe crooned. He held out a cup of coffee for me, but I didn't have time to take it.

"Hey! Sorry about this." The words left in a rush, Mom reaching around me to pull the door open further.

"Good morning to you too." Mom's nose wrinkled as she took stock of Gabe. "Brynn, who is this and what is he doing here first thing in the morning?"

"This is Gabe," I said through gritted teeth. "He's Adam's cousin. Remember Adam?"

"Yes." She glared back at me. "That doesn't answer my other question."

"I'm helping him out with something, and I asked him to meet me here so we could discuss it on the walk to school." I left out that he didn't go to school with me and that I had gone on a date with him.

Gabe glanced between the two of us, shoulders hunched, his mouth stretched in a rictus of discomfort masquerading as a smile.

"You couldn't have let me know this when you made your plans so I wouldn't be woken up by the bell at seven in the morning?" Mom asked.

My nostrils flared, eyes narrowing as I struggled to hang onto the edge of the pot instead of diving into the scalding water. "Sorry. I forgot. Won't happen again. Can I leave for school now?"

"Of course you can," she said, "but I'll be calling Adam's father to discuss why it isn't appropriate for his nephew to come to your home at any hour, unannounced."

"It's not unannounced if I asked him to come, Mom."

"It's okay." Gabe grinned. "If you need to call him, I understand."

She offered Gabe a false smile. "Give her a moment." She

yanked me back inside and closed the door. Her voice became a hushed shout. "How many times do I have to tell you about the importance of appearances?"

"I've counted about seven hundred times but go for one more. You never can have too many."

"A boy, not just any boy, but a tattooed and pierced boy, picking you up at seven in the morning? Do you have any idea how that looks?" Mom snapped.

"Like I'm helping my friend with something?" I asked. "You keep calling Dad and Josh complaining about me like I'm doing something wrong. You know why I don't want to live here?" I stuffed my feet into my sneakers. "Stuff like this. Because of appearances." I grabbed my book bag. "Because, I mean, let's face it——the only reason you want me here is because you know how it will *look* to everyone else if I move in with Dad." My fingers wrapped around the doorknob. "You wouldn't want to get a bad reputation, would you?"

"Don't you dare walk out that door with that attitude." She grabbed for my arm, but I yanked it away.

"Watch me." I walked out the door and slammed it behind me. Closing my eyes, I took a deep, calming breath. She wouldn't follow me out here. She wouldn't want to start a scene.

"I got us coffee?" Gabe handed me the cup again, with a tense smile. This time I took it and we started down the road toward school. "Let me know if it's too sweet. Adam said I should fill the cup halfway with sugar and milk."

"That's about right." I took a sip and my eyes slid closed. I embraced the sugary boost of caffeine. "To me, black coffee tastes like watery dirt."

Gabe grimaced. "You certainly know how to make a point." He sipped from his own cup. "Mmm, black coffee."

I laughed. "Sorry. Hope I'm not ruining your coffee experience."

"Couldn't if you tried," he said. "So, I don't think your mother likes me."

"She doesn't know you. Please tell me you didn't hear that entire thing." I glanced at the cross street we were approaching, wondering if it was too late to lope into the forest and live the rest of my life in a tree hut.

"It sounded pretty brutal." He winced. "Sorry. I didn't see your text until after I heard you guys arguing."

I took another sip of my drink. "You know, Nina doesn't like coffee. She'll drink it after an all-night study session, but she hates every second of it. She's a tea person."

"Opposites attract, huh?" His eyes widened. "I mean you and Nina. Are opposite. And opposites attract. And that must be why you get along so well." He offered me a tight-lipped smile and a shrug.

"Whoa!" I couldn't help but grin. "Did you hurt yourself with all that backpedaling?"

He groaned, hanging his head in the hand that wasn't holding his coffee. "I don't know what you mean. Would you accept that as an answer?"

"Um...no." I bumped him with my shoulder. "It's fine. I'm on to you. You like Nina."

Gabe shook his head. "I'm an asshole. I know I am."

"No, you're not," I said. "You like who you like. You can't help that."

He shot me a sidelong glance. "You're not angry? I mean, we went out, I kissed you..."

"Yeah. My attention was divided too, if I'm being honest." I took another long sip.

Gabe laughed. "Yeah, your great love affair with Tony, right?"

"Oh yeah," I said. "The love triangle with Tony and Raphael, and I'm stuck in the middle. It's one for the ages. They're gonna make an epic movie about it."

"Yes, Tony and Raphael." Gabe nodded. "They're the ones in your love triangle."

I said nothing.

"Right. You're not here to talk about that. You're here to talk about Nina."

"And you," I corrected. "Nina and you. And what that means."

"Well, can we talk about what it doesn't mean first?" He stopped walking and turned to face me, taking my hand in his. "What it doesn't mean is that you're somehow less awesome, because the minute I met you, I liked you. I think you're a great person. A strong, smart, ass-kicking kinda person. And I'm so hyped to have met you and to hang out with you. And at first, I thought we could see if there'd be more. But I noticed... something... that made me back up a bit. Nothing bad about you or anything. But when I did, Nina came into view and she was just... some people are incredible. And some people are incredible for you. You know?"

"I do." And I did. I knew exactly what he meant. "I just wanted you to know that I think you'd be good for her."

"Whoa! That's huge coming from you," Gabe said. "Best friend blessings are hard, especially from one as—"

"Please don't finish that sentence."

"I was going to say badass."

"I was expecting bitchy, but okay, we'll go with that."

He smiled. "But really, I don't know. She's still broken up about Reeve. And I wouldn't even know where to begin. She's so..."

"What was it you said the other day? Model gorgeous? I'd bet that's intimidating. But I'm intimidating and you went out with me, so you'll be fine."

"You asked me! I didn't have to ask you! And it's not that she's intimidating. It's just that rejection... I don't know how to explain it. When I first started talking to you, it was a friendly thing. And I figured it could go either way. With her, I'm more sure of what I want. Friends, but more too. I'm pretty sure I'll be rejected."

"She'd be nice about it."

"I'd rather she not have to be nice about rejecting me, so I'll just stay quietly over here."

I released a weighty sigh. "You're adorable. I'm gonna find a way to make this happen for you."

He stared straight ahead. "Maybe." For a moment, we walked in silence. "So, what are you reading now?"

With the sun shining down around us and surrounded by the scent of growing flowers from the gardens we walked past, I spent the rest of our walk discussing my love for reading with my newly designated friend.

SCHOOL WAS its usual boring self. As the end of the year approached, we were just killing time until final projects and exams. Our mythology group met up in the library for a couple of hours after class and wrapped up the presentation. Once we were satisfied with what we'd produced, Nina headed off to her shift at Scoopy Doo. That left me, Adam, and Val standing in front of the library, wondering what to do next.

Three was a crowd. Especially this particular set.

"So... um... I'm gonna head home." I gestured awkwardly toward my house.

"Wait, what?" Val brightened immediately, and I got the dreadful feeling she had an idea. "I thought we could all go out to Jack's. Get a burger or something."

Adam winced, but Val didn't seem to notice.

"Um... I don't know..."

"Aww, come on," she said. "It's been far too long since we've spent quality time without Nina between us."

Adam's eyes darted around, searching in vain for an exit from this conversation. I could see why. If he encouraged me to go, she'd see it as him wanting to spend time with me. If he encouraged me to leave, it meant he was uncomfortable spending time with me. The poor guy didn't have to like me for Val to assume he did, and that was just as bad.

This was the perfect opportunity to show her we were just friends.

"You know what, yeah. I'm starving." I fished my phone out from my messenger bag. "Mom was expecting me home for dinner, but she was a real bitch when Gabe picked me up this morning, and I don't want to get the extended third degree over dinner with her and Jesse. I'll text her so I can't be accused of not letting her know I'm alive."

"Did I give him your coffee order right?" Adam asked, then swallowed hard. "I had to ask Nina, but we all know she doesn't know anything about coffee."

"Yeah, thanks," I said. "Smart move, asking Nina."

He totally hadn't. He'd brought me coffee before.

"C'mon," Val said. "Jack's is waiting! I want to get there before the dinner rush gets moving." She waved us along, clapping her hands.

Jack's was a quaint 50s style diner that looked like a giant jukebox. The outside was lined with a reflective metal cut through the center by tubes of red lighting. When I pushed open the door, a flood of music met my ears, the notes of Elvis Presley's Jailhouse Rock moving my hips.

I passed the door off to Adam and Val, mouthing the lyrics as I went. Adam's lips quirked in a smile. Val rolled her eyes at me.

Glass cases containing records lined the walls of the diner on one side while vintage advertisements for Coca-Cola and Chevrolet on the other. The black-and-white tiled floors were shiny enough to catch my reflection. We walked past the robin's egg blue counter, where a few kids from school were already perched, placing their orders for ice cream floats and egg creams. If our entire group was here, we would have chosen one of the large record-styled tables in the back, but instead, we chose a tight booth against the right wall.

I slid across the red and gray vinyl, making myself cozy against the wall beside the stand containing the dessert menu and the tabletop jukebox that held napkins and condiments. Adam sat across from me, his arm immediately lifting from the back of the seat so it could wrap around Val.

Millie Charleston, another girl in our graduating year, approached, wearing a frown along with her uniform, a pink dress with a white apron and a silly little hat. I genuinely felt bad for her. "Hey guys. Can I get you something to drink?"

"Chocolate milkshake, please," I said.

Val frowned at me. "Water with lemon."

Adam's eyes moved from Val to me and back again. "A Coke. Thanks."

"Sure thing." Millie slouched away, scribbling on her pad as she left.

Adam pushed his glasses up his nose, opened his menu, and stared at it.

"You should try to order light," Val said. "Men these days are not interested in any cushion."

My heart stuttered at the slice of her words, anger sparking within me. "And who the fuck do you think I'm trying to impress?" Still, my hands betrayed me, moving to straighten my shirt to ensure it didn't tuck into any of my curves.

"Obviously you aren't," Val said, her tone bright, "but that doesn't mean you shouldn't be."

"I think I'll have a bacon double cheeseburger," I announced. "What are you guys getting?"

Adam's mouth twitched. "That sounds greasy. I'm in."

Val sighed, her entire body slumping. "I'll get a Waldorf

chicken salad." She glanced around, eyes settling on someone at the counter. "Oh, Vinny! Hey! Come sit with us!"

"Wait, what?" I asked, panic filling me. *Crap.* I had walked right into this.

Vinny August was another athlete, a kid from the school swim team. Long and wiry, he had a lean muscular body and sharp facial features. His carrot-colored hair was buzzed short, and his dark eyes were a little too far apart. Everyone at school said he swam like a fish. I wondered if his fishy eyes helped.

"Vinny! How are you?" she cooed, waving him over.

He rushed to her side like a puppy waiting for a treat.

Adam shot me a sidelong glance and let out a long, slow sigh.

"Why don't you have a seat?" She flipped her long blonde curls over her shoulder. "You know Adam."

"Hey, bro." Vinny's voice deepened for Adam's benefit. He offered his fist.

Adam's fist met his in a lackadaisical bump.

If Val noticed, she didn't react. "And this is Bree."

"Brynn," Adam muttered.

No, Adam! What are you doing?

Val flinched. "What?"

"You know she doesn't like being called Bree," Adam said. "When you introduce her that way, it's like you're trying to piss her off."

"Fine," Val said tersely. "My apologies. Vinny, this is Brynn. Brynn, Vinny."

"Yo." I forced a smile, even as my insides danced in terror. What was going on with Adam? Was Val right about him? About us?

Shit.

Vinny barely nodded before returning his attention to Val, asking her about their environmental science class and a potential future in marine biology I hadn't heard about before this very conversation. He didn't bother to sit down, just hovered over the table.

"Oh yes, I love dolphins," she said, and I watched her in awe as she leaned into him. "We should do everything in our power to protect them. They *are* more intelligent than we are."

Something brushed my hand under the table, something soft, papery. I looked up at Adam, who pulled his hands up from under the table, sliding a napkin onto the surface. He rested his elbow atop it, then waited a beat, pretending he was enthralled by Val's sudden treatise on the tragedies of Sea World. He nodded emphatically, even as he slid the napkin over to my side of the table.

I grabbed it with my elbow and slipped it into my lap. Written in Adam's pointed scrawl were the words, "She's at it again. Get out while you still can. I'll do what I can to cover you."

My eyes shot up to Adam, then to Val and Vinny still engrossed in conversation. Adam scrunched his nose, his eyes taking on a stern quality. I could practically hear the admonishment——*Don't be an idiot. Stop staring at me and go.*

My knees wobbled as I rose to my feet, stuffing the napkin in my pocket. "Excuse me. I need the r-restroom." The words tumbled out of my mouth, quick enough that there was barely space between them. I rushed out of the booth and made a beeline for the bathroom. Anyone who noticed would think I'd come down with raging diarrhea or something, but I couldn't make myself care.

Locking the bathroom door, I pressed my back against the tiled walls and sucked in huge gulps of air. It wasn't the potential date that had my heart crashing against my ribs with the strength of a battering ram. It was Adam. Sharing a secret with Adam. The idea that Adam was facilitating my escape. Adam in general.

I slid my phone out of my pocket. The napkin tumbled out. I snatched it up off the floor so I could flush it down the toilet.

Except it was blank. I flipped it over, panic rising in my chest. *No, no, no, no!*

If the napkin wasn't with me, it was somewhere at the table. I texted Adam in a rush.

Didn't take it like I thought. Find that napkin!

I hesitated before hitting send, my stomach twisting, bile rising in my throat. If Val saw the text, it was probably ambiguous enough that we could find a way around it. But if Val saw the napkin, we were both fucked. I hit send before I could doubt myself. Then I called Dad.

The phone rang twice before he picked up. "Hey kiddo, what's up?"

"So, you know how you always said that if I needed help, I should call you and not fear judgment?"

Dad took a deep, steadying breath, though I don't think he meant for me to hear it. "Yes. Where can I find you?"

"I need a quick extraction from Jack's."

"You read too many spy novels." I heard the jingle of keys on the other end of the line.

"I read too much of everything."

"What on earth could be going on at Jack's that you need extracting from?"

"It's not an emergency, but if I don't get out of here, someone is getting punched in the face. I'm hiding in the bathroom so I don't get thrown in juvie by the end of the night."

"Seriously?" he asked.

"Seriously."

"Your uncle is gonna love this. I'm on my way."

"Cool. Thanks. I love you." I hung up, then took another deep breath. The phone rang, and I immediately grabbed it, knowing it could only be Adam or Dad. "Hello?"

"Hey! Have you decided yet?" an unfamiliar voice on the end of the line said.

I pressed the phone closer to my ear, as though that would tell me who it was. "Um... depends on what I'm deciding."

"When we're gonna hang out." Raphael. *Again. Again, again.*

"Are you fucking kidding me? How the hell did you get my phone number?" I snapped, struggling to sound angry but quiet, before someone outside heard and came to check on me.

No doubt about it, this guy was a bona fide stalker.

"What do you mean?" Raphael asked. "Val said you felt bad about how you acted the other day. That you wanted to hang out with me, you just had to decide on a date. She gave me your number so we could smooth things over."

But she doesn't even like you! She's hated you from the minute she met you!

I really needed to learn how one went about killing a god. I wasn't sure how much I meant that, but at that moment, it felt like a lot.

"Listen, I don't know where she got her information from, but Val is wrong." I wanted to be as mean as usual, but I just couldn't muster it. "I'm not interested in dating."

"Not right now?" he asked, and I winced at the hopeful note in his voice.

"Not at all. Sorry. It's not about you. It's...it's me." I hit the back of my head against the wall. What the hell was I saying?

"Sorry I bothered you." He sounded miserable.

"It's okay," I said. "See you at school?"

"Sure!" He seemed to do a complete one-eighty, sounding delighted as he hung up.

I'd given him hope. I shouldn't have. There was no hope for any of us.

Except maybe Nina and Gabe.

Thank goodness Dad wasn't far away. My phone rang about fifteen minutes after my hasty retreat. Val was probably wondering what was taking so long, but fifteen minutes was a reasonable amount of time for a stomach explosion. A bad one, anyway.

After telling Dad I'd meet him outside, I unlocked the door and cracked it open. Nobody was looking my way, so I snuck out the back door of the restaurant to the dumpster area. The odor of old food rotting in the summer sun mingled with the body odor of whoever had dumped it out crashed into me with the physical force of a brick wall. Between my nerves and the smell, it was a miracle I kept anything in my stomach. Holding my nose, I jogged around a stack of boxes and a few garbage bags and found my way out around the side to Dad's car. I hopped into the passenger seat and fell back against it, relieved.

"You're the best." I shook my head. "I have not had a good day."

Even though he wouldn't stop frowning at me, it was great to see him. He'd changed since he used to live with us. His hair was a little disheveled, and he'd grown a five o'clock shadow. He wore a t-shirt, shorts, and loafers. I'd never seen him dress so casually, and it made me smile. For too long, Mom's mission to keep everyone tightly buttoned up had worked far too well on him. This was who he really was——a bit more like me.

"Are you going to tell me why you spent the last fifteen minutes hiding in a diner bathroom? Because that seems important," he said.

"If you drive me somewhere else, I swear, I'll fill you in."

"Deal." He started the car, and we took off. "Wanna go to the docks?"

We went for walks near the docks all the time when I was younger. We'd get ice cream at Scoopy and take it to the docks, sit and watch the boats drifting along the water, the heat of the sun kissing our cheeks.

"That sounds incredible."

"Great." He rolled the car to a stop at a red light and gazed at me expectantly.

I sighed. "I was hanging out with Val and Adam, and Val called over this guy from school. I don't know him well, but I could tell Val was trying to set me up. Val is always trying to set me up."

"Hm."

"And then Adam slides me this napkin, and it says that the guy, Vinny, is a real jerk and I should sneak out. That he'd deal with Val."

"The cloak and dagger act was necessary? Why not walk out? Tell Val to stop trying to set you up and leave?"

"Let's just say I can't piss her off. It will upset the... um... political balance?"

"Well, you're a dreadful liar, but I won't push if you don't want to answer." He pulled the car into the parking lot just before the dockyard. "Besides, we're here."

We exited the car, and I circled around to his side. He wrapped me up in a big hug, lifting me off my feet. He smelled like burritos, which was probably what he and Josh considered dinner. I was so happy to hug him, I didn't duck away when he jokingly breathed spicy breath at me and declared it stinky.

"You've been hanging around your brother too much." I laughed.

"C'mon." Dad wrapped an arm around my shoulder. "Let's chat."

We passed the town's boating club, our feet clacking against the wooden planks. The wind blew in off the water, carrying the fresh scent of the mountain air, my hair blowing away from my face. The sun was beginning to lower in the sky, still about an hour away from sunset.

We walked until we reached the railing along the water where the docks ended and the space for viewing and admiring the Hudson River began. I stepped onto the lower metal railing and bent over the higher one, balancing on my stomach like I'd been doing since I was a child. It was beautiful—-the blue lapping waves, the space where they met the horizon, the sailboats gliding smoothly along the water, following the trails the air mapped out for them.

Dad leaned over the rail beside me. I tousled his hair.

"Cut it out," he teased. "If you keep that up, it will all fall out."

He was being silly. There wasn't a thin spot in sight. Gray, on the other hand...

"So what's the deal?" he asked. "You seem so stressed out lately."

"Well, let's see." I spat it out as quickly as possible. "Val is trying to set me up on all the dates because she wants me to want to 'find love.' I wanted to date Adam's cousin, Gabe, but he likes Nina. It was clear, like a smack in the face. So I asked him to walk with me to school so we could discuss it. When he showed up at the door, Mom flipped because he has tattoos and piercings, and then she embarrassed me. Then I went to school and I have this group project I'm working on, and I'm just trying to get through the rest of senior year, and I haven't even gone shopping for prom yet. And this loser is hitting on me, and Adam wants to beat him up. And then Val tried to hook me up with another loser, and I escaped, and now I'm here."

"Whoa," Dad chuckled. "That was a mouthful."

"I'm tired of all the things, man." I was still trying to catch my breath, and not because of how fast I'd spat it all out.

"I want to play the protective father here, but I also want you to have a normal life. I've gotta ask. Why don't you want to date?"

"Because I don't want to." It was a childish answer, but it should be enough.

"You see, I would accept that if you hadn't told me you had

wanted to date Adam's cousin, but you set him up with Nina instead? That seems like self-sabotage, don't you think?"

"That's not a done deal yet," I corrected, "and it's hard to self-sabotage when the guy you're with can't stop looking at your best friend, and she's trying like hell not to look back. It's just common sense to step out of the way."

"Yes, I suppose you're right." He gazed out over the water. "But there's nobody else you want to date?"

"None of the dim bulbs or the gorgeous athletes Val would set me up with." I shrugged. "And they don't really want to date me either."

Dad's gaze was a weight on my shoulders, but I wouldn't look back. I leaned forward, sucking in the scent of the river water, rich and earthy, like the purity of nature in a soft steam. I didn't want to know what he was thinking, and I lost myself on the breeze for a moment, my eyes sliding closed.

"You know, you're beautiful, Brynn." He broke the silence. "Inside and out."

"I regret a lot of things, Dad. Starting this conversation is at the top of that list."

"You mean you don't find this enjoyable?" He flashed me a wry grin.

"Pleasant as proctology!"

"Whatever. I'm trying to have a serious conversation with you."

"And I'm trying to subtly avoid it!" I leaned forward on the rail, kicking my feet out behind me before landing back in place.

He rolled his eyes, a chuckle escaping. "Listen, I'm not sure what upsets me more——you having Val set you up on dates, or you not believing people want to date you."

I sighed. "I know for a fact she's convincing them to date me. Besides, she wants me to find true love, but she's never gonna pull it off."

"And why not?" he asked. "Never mind that you're unlikely

to find the love of your life at eighteen. Push that aside. Why are you so sure she'll fail?"

I stared at the waves as they flirted with the mossy rocks down below, moving closer only to run away. "She's looking for a certain type of guy for me. She's gotten close, but not for the reasons she thinks."

"So tell her." He bumped my shoulder with his.

Those waves sure were pretty.

"But you can't, because then she'll know," he answered for me. "If she knows what you're looking for, she'll know where he is. And who he's with."

A chill ran down my spine, and my body went rigid.

"Your friend is trying to set you up with every guy in the senior class—"

I held up a finger. "Some in the junior class."

"—and the only one you want is her boyfriend? Jeez, Brynn."

I glared at him. "It wasn't a choice. If anything, you guys are to blame. Because I didn't think about him like this before that ride to the damn airport, and now I'm a flipping mess. And my life is a flipping mess, and I'm censoring myself because I'm telling *you* this, and now I sound like the television version of *The Breakfast Club*. 'Flip you!' 'Flip you, too!'"

Dad stared back at me, blinking hard.

"And now I sound insane." I dropped my head in my hands, hard enough for my knuckles to hurt where they bumped into the railing.

"But only a smidge more insane than usual." He placed a comforting hand on my back.

"How do I get out of this?" I choked out, tears prickling behind my eyes.

"Out of feeling this way?" He shrugged. "Write it down. You used to do that when you were a kid. It helped to release some of the pressure when you were feeling overwhelmed."

"Not what I meant, but thanks. How do I get myself out of this situation I've tripped into?"

"You don't. You live with it. Love doesn't go away. Not without time. Even when people are awful, the only thing that changes love is time."

"Like with you and Mom?" I muttered.

"Yes," he said, hesitant. "Like that."

"You see!" I looked up, Dad's face blurry through the tears, my chest a yawning ache. "I don't want to hate Adam. And I don't want to ruin my friendship with Val. I just... I don't know. This sucks."

Dad jumped off the railing and grabbed my hand, yanking me down from my perch. He tugged me to him, wrapping me in a warm hug. I rested my cheek against the soft cotton of his shirt, and he rested his somewhat pointy chin on the top of my head.

"Brynn, it's going to be okay," he whispered, pressing a kiss to my hair. "You're gonna get through this, and you're gonna come out of it okay. You'll see. Even if things go wrong. You're tough as hell. There's nothing you can't handle. And you're loved, so there's nothing you'll need to handle alone. I promise you that."

I wrapped my arms around his waist and cried, tears soaking into his shirt until the brilliant oranges, reds, and purples of the setting sun captured my attention. We watched the sun go down together, my head on his shoulder, his arm around mine, as colorful fingers stretched across the sky.

When the sun dipped below the horizon, Dad said, "Come on. Let's take you home before your mother panics."

The car ride home was quiet, a companionable silence. It wasn't loaded with the weight of judgment like Mom's silences tended to be. It was far too short though, and before I knew it, we pulled up in front of our little birch tree.

"Goodnight Daddy." I hated how small my voice sounded

almost as much as I hated how much I missed seeing him every day.

"Goodnight sweetheart." He wiped at the tracks of my tears with his fingers. I was still me, so I smacked at his hands to get him to stop, and he grinned. "See? Tough as hell."

I shot him a watery smile. "Sometimes." I turned towards the door, but something stopped me. "Do you feel like you made it out of everything okay?"

"Believe it or not, Bug, I still believe in love. I think that means I made it out okay. The only thing I believe in more than love is you."

I returned home with a warm feeling in my chest, and a seed of hope in my heart.

CHAPTER THIRTEEN
BELEIF AND REGRET

DAD'S WORDS kept playing in my mind.

Believe it or not, Bug, I still believe in love.

I was twisted up in my sheets, adjusting my pillow for the fortieth time in search of a comfortable position. He may still believe in love, but I believed in sleep.

You can survive without love. Sleep, not so much.

I banged my head against the pillow a few times. Not that I didn't believe in love. What choice did I have when Aphro-frickin-dite lived in my best friend's extra bedroom?

The buzz of my phone broke through my thoughts, rattling across the top of my bedside table. I glared at it, baffled. Nobody ever called me this late. I reached over and snatched it up.

Adam.

My heart stuttered in my chest. I shouldn't pick up. No good could come from it. I glanced at the time. Two in the morning. So late. I answered.

"Hello?"

"Hey." He sounded tired but alright, and I felt my raging heartbeat slow at the familiar sound of his voice. "I hope you're not asleep yet. Didn't mean to wake you."

I snorted, and I could hear Mom in my ear, telling me how ladylike I sounded. "What is this sleep thing you speak of?"

"That good, huh?" He chuckled.

"Frickin' wonderful."

For a moment, there was nothing but the hum of the crackling connection. "Wanna talk about it?"

I sighed.

"No then," he said. "I saw your text. Did you walk home?"

"I called my dad," I said. "He took me out to the docks so he could ask me why I needed to escape from a diner bathroom..."

A pause. "I'm getting a picture of why you're awake. How's he doing?"

"Eh. Better than me, if that makes sense."

"You've gotta give yourself ti—"

"Anyway." I shot up to a seated position, already tired of this line of conversation. "I got home okay."

"Good." Another pause. The crackling sound of wind pushed through the cell phone's speaker. He was outside. Why would he be outside at two in the morning? "Can I make a suggestion?"

"You could try," I said, trying to douse my worry with snark. "I may not listen."

"That's a given." I could almost picture his dark eyes rolling upward as if pleading with the heavens for an answer to my behavior. "I think you should learn to drive."

"No can do. I'm saving up money for our apartment in the city. I don't have enough to pay for driving lessons too. Mom isn't going to teach me, and I barely see Dad anymore."

"I could teach you, if you want," he said, his words accompanied by the sound of movement.

"Where are you, Adam?" I was getting worried.

"There's a place I go when I need to think," he said. "I'm sitting on top of my car, looking at the world from the top of a mountain trail."

"That sounds amazing." My eyes closed as the image played behind my eyelids.

"It is." His deep breath was ringed with static. "If you're going to keep going on these dates, you should learn how to drive, so you can get home. Without me, without Gabe, without your dad. It's not safe to have to wait for someone to bail you out. Some of the guys in this town talk a lot of bold crap. I don't know how much of it is true, and how much of it is grand-standing for the wrong audience, but I'd prefer knowing you had a way out of a situation you wanted out of. Just in case."

"Adam." I stifled a giggle. "You seem to forget that I don't have a car, which means I'm missing a considerable part of this equation."

"You can borrow mine, or you can steal the guy's. Whatev-er," he said dismissively, like stealing a car would be perfectly acceptable. "I'd just rather have you knowing than not knowing."

"We're actually real friends now, aren't we?" I teased, strug-gling not to stress the word friends. *Just friends. That's it.* "Like, on our own, without buffers."

"I always thought we got along well."

"Well enough," I agreed, "but offering your car up as a sacri-fice means a lot."

He coughed. "I taught Gabe to drive. And it wouldn't be a sacrifice."

"See? Friends."

He chuckled, and then the light of the conversation dimmed into silence. I tried not to read into it. It was probably nothing.

Then finally, "I didn't think you wanted me around. You never indicated you did."

"I didn't know you," I said. "I never had anything against you. I just...don't 'people' well."

A thoughtful hum. "Well, we probably should have been friends a long time ago, because I'm shit at people-ing too."

I smiled. "Adam... I know why I'm still awake, but why are you?"

He sighed, and there was rustling at the other end of the line. "I broke up with Val."

I gasped, then internally kicked myself for the overreaction. Except it wasn't an overreaction. Val was a goddess. You didn't break up with a goddess.

"I know," he said. "If you'd asked me a few months ago, I wouldn't have expected it to end so... abruptly. I just... I think by the time I broke up with her, she wanted me to."

How much of this had to do with that damn napkin?

I knew what I was supposed to feel, and I did, but I also didn't. I was angry at him for hurting her, but I was scared for him. I was sad that Val was alone, but...

"You know, I think you're wrong about that. I don't think there's anything you could have said that would have made her want to break up with you." I hated saying it. Something coiled in my gut, my stomach twisting.

"You should've heard the things she said before I broke it off. Anyway, it sucks, but Brynn, I just couldn't be with her anymore. And it would have been shitty for me to stay when mostly she just pisses me off."

"Did she find the napkin?" I needed to know how much of this was my fault. For their sake and for my own self-preservation.

"She did. But that was a small part of it."

"But Adam—"

"Stop!" he snapped. "This is not why I called you. I can't hear this from you of all people. Please." The last word was desperate, but lower, his voice almost fading out before he said it, and I imagined it slipped free from his lips without his knowledge, an escapee from the steel trap Adam sometimes seemed to be.

My heart ached for him, for Val.

Despite the way I felt about him, I'd never wanted this. For two of my friends to be left hurting... there was no good in this. Nobody won.

I swallowed against the growing lump in my throat. "So,

what did you call me for?" It was a gentle question, but the words immediately sounded like a complaint, so I rushed to follow it up with, "How can I help you?"

I was met with contemplative silence. "Could you... could you just... make me laugh?"

His sorrowful voice pained me, but I did my best. I conjured up a stupid joke Dad used to tell me. "What did the duck say when he bought a tube of lipstick?"

Adam groaned. "Oh boy."

"Put it on my bill. Ha! Get it?"

He chuckled. "A four-year-old would get that joke."

"Awesome, cuz that's when I learned it."

That earned a rare but genuine laugh from him. It was warm and rich, and as I slid into my bed and laid my head on my pillow, I decided there couldn't be a better sound to fall asleep to.

"Okay, okay, here's another one. What do you call a pig that does karate?"

MY MUSCLES ACHED as I scooped a heaping cup full of Maple Walnut ice cream for Luanne Burkhart, the head cashier at the grocery store. The tub of ice cream had frozen more solid than usual, and it gave me a workout, but I finished scooping just in time to catch Val walking in for her shift.

'Walk' might not have been the right word.

'Barreled in' might have been a little more accurate.

Nina followed shortly thereafter, dragging her feet. Her eyes were glued to the floor, her face twisted in a frown, and her shoulders drooped. It didn't look like anybody had gotten sleep last night, and I wasn't surprised.

I handed Ms. Burkhart her ice cream, collected her money, and wished her a good day, then rushed to Nina.

"Is she okay?" I asked.

Nina shook her head. "You spoke to Adam?" I didn't like the note of accusation in her tone.

"Yeah, he called me last night," I admitted. "He only told me that he broke up with her. Did Val say why?"

Nina's eyes narrowed. "Why? Are you looking for an answer that benefits you?"

I flinched. I shouldn't be getting this from Nina. "No. I'm worried about her. They're both my friends."

Nina sighed. "Look, I'm sorry. I just..." Another sigh. "He told her he broke up with her because she was too obsessed with trying to hook you up, and that he didn't like all the extra male attention it brought her. And that sounds like such crap to me. Did you say anything to him? Does he know?"

"I didn't say anything to him," I said. "I promised I wouldn't."

Nina pinched the bridge of her nose. "Okay. But this still isn't good, Brynn. She found the napkin from yesterday. And the butterfly barrette from the night you were supposed to meet up with Tony. He told her he foiled her plans to help you. She thinks he foiled her plans because he doesn't want you to fall in love with anybody else."

"That's crazy," I said firmly.

"But it means he's single," Nina said. "I would stay away.

The problem with knowing someone all your life was they knew what created you, the building blocks you hid from the world. Once you've bared your childhood soul for a person, they know you more than anyone should ever have the right to. They see you in ways you can't see, in ways you wish weren't there.

And she was right. I should be careful.

"Noted," I whispered, as Val approached the front, trading spots with Nina.

"Hey Val," I said.

"Hey yourself." Half an annoyed statement, half an absent blurt.

"Nina told me what happened." *Lies, lies, lies.*

"Yeah." She stared out at the storefront window, watching the people outside as they passed.

"For whatever it's worth, I regret the role I played in it." I had to apologize. My heart was a weight, dragging me down into the depths of guilt and regret.

Val's entire expression, her entire stance, was tight like someone had yanked on her pull strings. "Why are you apologizing, Brynn? It's not like you stole my boyfriend."

"Of course I didn't!" I winced at the speedy response.

"Right." She smiled, but it was more a terrifying baring of her teeth than anything resembling a sign of joy. "So you wouldn't mind another date, then?"

"Another d-date?" I stumbled over the words. My face went numb as I took in the disdain on hers. She was going to smite me and, damn it, she'd have a good reason. "With who?"

"Murray Novak." Her smile grew. "He'll be meeting you at the bakery for a treat and a movie after your shift."

Murray Novak was a strange creature. Like Adam, he was incredibly intelligent, well on track to become the salutatorian to Adam's valedictorian. Unlike Adam, however, he looked the part of a total nerd. Straight dark hair slicked to one side, devoid of any personality. Glasses with thick lenses and heavy black frames that hid his eyes. Still, he was relatively popular. We hadn't shared more than an occasional greeting, but I would've assumed his appearance would have prevented him from dating. Instead, it was said he was quite the ladies' man.

"Um... I'm not really date-ready." I looked down at my uniform.

"I brought you a change of clothes from the sleepover drawer..." She eyed me warily, as if waiting for me to disappoint her.

I forced a smile, wishing I didn't know I looked so damn

guilty. "Are you sure you didn't just pick out new clothes for me? Some frilly dress?"

"Nope. Just your regular old bum-ware." She blew me a kiss, a mocking imitation of the way our friendship had been.

An odd sort of sadness rose within me. Val and I were friends, yes, but that friendship was contentious at best. Still, now that I was responsible for hurting her, even though it had never been intentional, I found myself desperate to fix it.

"Great." I smiled. "I'm in."

For a moment, Val's eyes widened. Her mouth dropped open slightly and snapped shut. She clapped her hands and squealed, hopping in place. "Oh, that's wonderful! Murray is actually a really great guy, and I think he's more your type." She wrapped an arm around me, and I tried not to flinch. "I know I've been barking up the wrong tree with the jocks, and Craig and Gabe were too artsy. You need a man with a brain."

"I have a brain," Craig snapped as he walked to the front of the store in his street clothes. It had been our shift, and he had been in the back organizing toppings when Nina and Val had come in.

"So you keep telling us." Val winked and swiped at a smudge of chocolate ice cream on his nose. "Didn't you use the mirror when you changed?"

"You've been spending far too much time with Brynn," he said. "I expect the sass from her. You, not so much."

Val's smile lost a bit of its light. "Yes, Brynn and I share many things."

Nina wrapped an arm around my waist, and I returned the favor. "Go get changed." The frustration from earlier was gone. She was rescuing me from Val.

I gave her hip a squeeze before pulling away to get ready for my surprise date. I could endure this if it made Val understand I wasn't swooping in to steal Adam away from her.

I made my way to the bathroom and found my clothes neatly

stacked on the metal rack where toiletries were stored. I did my best to clean up before I headed out.

I wanted to look presentable when I met Murray. I shouldn't have grumbled about Val's mission. She was only trying to do something nice for me, and by agreeing to go on this date, I had really cheered her up.

My phone vibrated in my pocket.

RAPHAEL, THE MERRY STALKER

Right. That's what always pissed me off about Val.

I would rather be pecked to death by woodpeckers than answer that phone call. I hit ignore.

Bonnie's Bakes was just a few stores down, and I could already see Murray waiting outside for me. He had brushed his hair back from his face, though he still wore his glasses, and he was way more casual looking than usual in a t-shirt and jeans. Despite that, he looked more like a company CEO on his summer outing in the Hamptons than a high school senior.

"Hi Murray!" I waved, a genuine smile on my face. He'd never given me a reason to dislike him, so I could at least make an effort.

"Hey Brynn," he said. "I'm impressed you actually came to meet with me. I know some people can be intimidated by my package."

That required a double take. "Your... your what?"

"I'm the total package, you know? I've got brains and looks. It can be intimidating for some people."

Swallowing the urge to laugh, I leaned forward until he was within whispering distance. "Um... Murray... when you say, 'intimidated by your package' that actually means 'intimidated by your dick.'"

I pulled back in time to see his eyes widen. "Oh. No. I didn't mean to say that. That would be horribly vulgar to say to a girl. I haven't even fed you yet."

"Really, Murray?"

"Well, I should buy you dinner first at least, right?"

"Oh God, I'm going to need pastries to get through this."

Murray screwed up his lips. "Does that mean something I don't know about, too?"

"Let's go get some baked goods." I opened the door and ushered him to go in first. "How about we drop the whole 'Val has influenced me to want to bag Brynn' thing and just hang out? How does that sound?"

Murray stopped walking so fast, I bumped into his back.

"Sorry," he muttered. "What are you talking about?"

"It's what Val's been doing to me for the last two months. Approaching people, wowing them with her charm, and getting them to date me to win points with her, despite the lack of logic involved there." I walked to the counter, perusing the selection of cookies, decorated cupcakes, and inventively iced cakes.

"Actually...um...you've got me wrong," Murray said, falling in beside me to peer into the glass cabinets. "Val never approached me. I heard she was looking to set you up because that beastly atrocity, Vinny August, whined about it. I approached her."

Well, he was just full of surprises, wasn't he?

"So, nobody convinced you to go out with me?" I hated how shocked I sounded.

He made an undignified noise in response. "No, I've admired you since junior high." He rocked on his heels. "You're just so... self-sufficient... bold..."

"Bitchy?" I supplied.

He laughed, hiccup-y and genuine. "We'll say self-assured. I wasn't sure you'd be interested if I requested a moment of your time."

"How can I help you?" Bridget Danner, Bonnie's daughter, was operating the front counter. She was a few years older than me and had stayed behind to help her parents run their shop. Baking was in her blood.

I couldn't imagine how she could stay in this town past

college, but I admired that she'd found a career she could live with. I still wasn't sure what that would be for me.

"Good afternoon," Murray greeted. "I will have the chocolate eclair and a cappuccino, and for the lady..."

"The chocolate mousse cupcake, please." It looked glorious. "And a French vanilla cappuccino. Thank you."

Bridget offered a faint smile. "Sure thing."

As she gathered our requests, I tried for small talk, something that was normally a weakness of mine. I had nothing else to say to Murray at the moment, but I did have something to say to Bridget.

"Hey Bridget, how is business?"

"Huh?" she asked idly, as she took the baked treats out of the display cabinet. "Yeah, it's doing great. It's always a little weak in the summer. People are more interested in ice cream than they are in cupcakes." She shot me a wink. "But this is the place for specialty pastries, so it never really gets slow."

I glanced around. Four of the five tables along the other wall of the store were already filled with people, and there was a line forming behind us, waiting to order.

"Good, I'm glad to hear that."

"Thanks, Brynn," she said. Bridget had been in my art class in freshman year, and we'd talked now and then. "Hey, you're graduating this year, right?"

"Yep."

"What are you planning to do after that?"

"Going to Hunter College. In the city."

"Any idea on your major yet?" She set our cappuccinos down on a tray in front of us.

"Not yet, but I'm working on it. I'll let you know when I figure it out."

Murray paid for the food and took the tray from the counter. Bridget and I wished each other well, and Murray led me to the only spare table available.

The table was a small black marble circular slab, erected on a single center leg of shiny metal. The two matching chairs were similar, the metal coming up in an arch in the back, the seat a black vinyl pad that mimicked the appearance of marble.

Once we were seated, Murray brought his hands together in one prim clap. "Let's dive into these sumptuous treats."

I leaned forward, my eyes narrowed. "Do you just talk like that to impress me?" He looked startled, eyes widening. "Talk like what?"

"Never mind." I had to admit, he was kind of adorable. Not like Adam adorable, or even Gabe adorable, but the kind of adorable where you wanted to ruffle his hair and teach him how to understand humanity. Another oddball. I gave him a thumbs up. "You're good."

Delicately, so as not to disturb the icing, I peeled the paper off the base of the cupcake. I felt Murray's eyes on me, but I ignored it. If he could be weird, I could cherish the art behind the cupcake I was about to eat.

"So," Murray said, chewing through a mouthful of chocolate eclair. "No idea what you want to do in college?"

"Not really. You?"

"Economics," he stated with an utter confidence I envied. "Then I'm going for my MBA. There's a desk at my father's company waiting for me."

Mom would say he was a catch. I looked away.

"You should major in English. You always have a great mastery of the texts in class." He chuckled. "You score even higher than I do."

I smiled and bit into my cupcake. "You've still got me beat in math."

"Of course I do." He winked. "But your strengths are elsewhere."

I stuck my tongue out at him, ignoring the fact that there was still half-eaten cupcake on it.

Murray's lips curled in disgust, but there was a trace of humor in his eyes, and I realized that though he had clear faults, he really liked me, despite my tendency towards being uncouth.

We finished our snacks, sipped our drinks, and traded views and theories: the state of literature today (he believed the time of enduring literature was gone, I believed art had taken a different turn, and some works of today had equal or greater value than the classics), politics (he leaned conservative, I was as liberal as they came), the annoyingness of the senior camping trip (he thought it was a nice idea, I thought it was totally unnecessary), the relevance of the Kardashians (we both agreed on that one——they were inane).

Despite our differences, our debates were fun, not tense. We respected each other's opinions. Talking to him was surprisingly interesting.

Murray glanced at his watch, then threaded a hand through his hair, a motion that made him look slightly less uptight. He set his palms flat on the table and pushed his chair back. "We should get going. We're going to miss the movie."

"What are we going to see?" I cleared our table.

"*Betrayal*. It's a suspense thriller. Val suggested it."

I nearly flinched. It wasn't like I could back out of the movie. That would be like admitting I'd done something wrong when I hadn't.

I had never encouraged Adam or tried anything with him. I wasn't even sure Adam felt anything in return. There was certainly no betrayal on my part.

Still, my shoulders sagged. "Okay. Sounds good."

As we left the bakery, I aimed a brief wave at Bridget. She returned it, and we left the store and re-entered the somewhat sticky evening air.

We headed to the movie theater. A few steps into the walk, Murray stopped and turned to face me, eyes alight with mischief.

"So, how are you feeling about this?" He motioned between us.

"I'm thinking you're a cool dude. We should be friends." A definitive nod punctuated my sentence.

"C'mon, you know there's a thing between us. You feel it, I feel it. We would be outstanding together." He leaned in toward me, his eyes flicking to my lips.

I leaned too——back and away from him. "I'm sure we could. But I don't feel it. I really don't. I'm sorry."

He looked like I'd slapped him. Then he recovered with a dazzling, brilliant smile. "We still have time. We haven't even gotten to the movie."

I had to laugh. "You haven't even walked me to my door yet, and you're already trying to suck face with me. Try anything at the movies, and I'll remove your tongue."

"I love a tough girl." He waggled his eyebrows. "You've only served to further inflame my attraction to you."

I rolled my eyes and took off in the direction of the theater. "Do you take classes in this shit?"

"Are there classes?" He seemed hopeful.

I jerked my head toward the entrance. "C'mon already. If I miss the previews, I'll be mad. They're my favorite part."

His face twisted into a frown. "The movie isn't your favorite part?"

"The movies are great, but there's the anticipation of waiting for it to start, and the potential in the previews that makes it more fun." I shrugged, feeling foolish.

He nodded, his eyes lighting. "Like foreplay."

"I would leave, but you're harmless, and you already paid for the ticket." I turned toward the theater.

Once we were seated and waiting for the movie to begin, I checked my cell. There was one missed text from Val.

How's your date going?

He just referred to movie previews as foreplay, and this is all your fault.

By the time the previews started, I received her response.

I certainly hope so!

Stifling a growl, I typed "How to repel a goddess" into my browser app. The search yielded nothing of use.

CHAPTER FOURTEEN
ALL ABOUT PRESENTATION

"HEY, I called you over the weekend," Raphael said with a pout the minute my foot crossed the threshold of mythology class on Monday.

My entire body tensed, and I longed for the year before when he barely spared me a passing glance.

"Yeah, I know. I watched the phone ring." I plopped down in my seat at a table with Nina, Val, and Adam——now officially the most awkward table around, despite the fact that Val and Adam were trying to stay friends.

"Things were hectic yesterday," Val chimed in. "We were making the final arrangements for our presentation."

"But even if we weren't…"

Val smacked my arm. Nina rolled her eyes. Adam let his head drop to the table, his fists clenched.

"Raphael," I said, my eyes wide and innocent, "I knew from the moment I met you that I wanted to spend the rest of my life avoiding the *hell* out of you. You inspire my inner murderer."

He winked at me. Like that was a good thing.

Pointedly, I turned back to my group. "Okay, are we ready?"

"I believe so," Adam said. "We have our facts straight, right?"

"Yes." Nina straightened her bowtie. She wore black pants, a white halter faux-tuxedo shirt with a bow tie, and black pumps. "All ready to play game show host."

I glanced to Adam to find him already looking at me, waiting for my answer. "I'm ready to be Athena-" I picked up my toy sword- "Eris, the goddess of discord-" I held up the apple I had spray-painted gold- "and King Menelaus of Sparta-" I motioned to my crown- "so I can fight Adam's Paris over Helen, my prize."

"I still think you should have played the Trojan Horse," Val said. "You know, coming in looking all innocent, and then 'surprise bitch,' everything goes to hell."

I glared at her. "Do you feel prepared for your two roles? 'Bitch just like you named Aphrodite,' and 'Bitch just like you named Helen'? Not much acting there, is there?"

"I'm just thrilled about my roles as Paris, Zeus, and my favorite for comic genius, Hera," Adam said, his flat expression directed towards Val. "Thanks for that, by the way."

Val winked at him and he glared in response.

I leaned toward Nina. "This is gonna go well."

I worried, but it didn't go that badly. Our fellow students were unenthused, but I did get a thumbs up from Murray for my role as Athena. That was pretty cool, even if he had to remind me afterward that he found my tough side sexy. Nina swatted at him and chased him down the hall, which got us all laughing.

There were a couple of thinly veiled jokes by Val announcing she was on the market, or sniping at Adam, but he seemed unfazed, and worse, unburdened, which made me wince for her. She could be a pain in the ass, but the way Adam seemed completely unaffected irked me, especially because it wasn't true. When he'd called me, there was pain in his voice. It had hurt him to break up with her, even if it had been his idea. But he was too proud to let her see it bothered him.

In the end, our teacher appreciated our work, and that was all that mattered——the presentation, not the way our friendships had splintered and shifted since we'd started planning it.

"BRYNN, YOUR PHONE IS FLASHING," Nina said as we were preparing to leave school that afternoon. She would know better than I would, since my phone was in my back pocket.

I finished packing my unneeded books in my locker and yanked my phone out to find a voicemail from my mother. I played it, despite the dread settling in my heart.

"Bree, this is your mother." Mom's voice was sharp as a knife in my side. "Since you've been running out before I'm awake in the morning and refusing to speak with me or even eat dinner with me, I figured a voicemail was the best way to reach you. Tonight, I need you to come home for dinner or you will not be going on the senior trip next week."

I wanted to argue back, as if she could hear me, as if this wasn't a voicemail left a while ago. I was so done with all of this, and it was just one thing after another, and I was just so overwhelmed, and I couldn't think of a single way to stop any of it without losing all of it, and I just...

"God, I'm so tired of her crap!" I slammed the locker door.

"Easy there, brute." Val rolled her eyes. "The entire hallway doesn't need to hear your life issues."

"Could you fucking not?"

"Val," Adam cut in. "You don't even know why—"

"Shut up!" Tears sprang to my eyes. "Could you just shut up?" I whirled on him. "Do you think I need *you* to defend me to Val? *You?*"

He looked stricken, his mouth parted as though to speak, though he just stood there, staring at me like an idiot.

"You're making it worse!"

"Brynn," Val spoke out of the side of her mouth, her gaze floating from one part of the hall to the other. "I'm sorry. Just let this go. People are staring."

Nina closed her eyes and shook her head. She knew where

this was going. And because she knew me so well, because she was the only person who really fucking got me, she stepped back and let me lose it.

Because I really needed to lose it.

"Do you think I give a single fuck who is staring?" My voice went deep, and an odd calm washed over me. I looked past Adam, out into the after-school crowd in the hallway. They were all watching, waiting to see what happened. Vultures, waiting to jump on the dead carcasses left behind. I smiled at them, waved, then shot them the finger. I was far past caring.

Adam stepped toward me like I was a feral animal, hands held out. "I think we all need to go outside and off school grounds before we have this conversation."

I waved him off. "I'm not having any conversation. I just want you to know that I don't need your help." I took a step closer, locking eyes with him so there would be no mistake. "I've got this. All of it. You can ask Nina. There isn't anything I can't handle. I don't need anything from you."

He took a sharp breath. "Not even a ride to the airport?"

He didn't say it loudly, he didn't yell it, but the words hung in the air long after he said them. I couldn't look at the others, only at him, at the way his eyes widened. That *oh shit* look on his face.

I walked away before the anger and frustration and futility took over, before the tears burning in my eyes spilled over onto my cheeks where I could no longer pretend they weren't there.

"Brynn!" he called after me.

"She needs to be alone. Let her." Nina. Bless her, she really was the best.

I walked all the way home with that righteous anger brewing. When I arrived at my front walk, I couldn't remember the journey there. My brain was a fog of anxiety and fury, and I couldn't see or feel anything through it. Numb with rage. And it scared me.

I didn't even bother checking for Mom when I walked in. I was pretty sure she was at work, but it didn't matter.

The adrenaline surge wore down and my limbs shook from its loss. I was weak and exhausted, so I did what I always did. I climbed into bed with my latest book. I tried to lose myself in the story, tried to immerse myself and pretend nothing else was real, nothing else was true; everything in the world existed in its pages.

But life *was* real, and it was true, and I couldn't run from it, not even by throwing myself into a book. When I tried, my mind kept whirring in the background, forcing me to re-read whole lines, paragraphs, pages. A half-hour later, I'd only gotten through three pages. I threw the book down on my bed and jumped to my feet, pacing from wall to wall in a room that felt inexplicably alien.

I had decorated this room when I was in elementary school, and in the years since, I hadn't bothered to re-do it. Posters of old pop stars plastered the bubblegum pink walls. There was a freaking unicorn on my dresser, and my jewelry was housed in a wooden box with a ballerina on top that twirled when you wound it.

I had asked a few times in the past to redecorate, but Mom made me feel bad for not wanting to be her little girl anymore. So I kept ballerina jewelry boxes, unicorn statues, pink walls, and framed family portraits. All to keep a fragile peace that wasn't even my responsibility.

When she stopped buying my clothes for me, my appearance became the only thing I could control. That and my desk, where I could still be me. Where emo and electropop artist pictures and memes about my love for reading peppered the cork board behind my computer. Where a picture of me and Nina was in the center, and on the outskirts were pictures of me, Nina, and Val, one of Adam and Gabe, and finally, replacing a picture of our group with Reeve, a recent picture of our group with Gabe.

My space.

Dad had told me to write when I felt like this.

I sat in the chair. I woke my computer out of sleep mode. I opened my word processing software.

And I wrote.

I poured out every thought, every feeling, every last overwhelmed emotion I had until I'd filled ten pages with everything I'd been through over the last few months. It felt good, it felt true, it felt like writing away my rage.

By the time Mom knocked on my door to call me down to dinner, I was drained, but I was back to myself.

Dinner was chicken parmesan and spaghetti, and my particular plate was served at the table... across from Jesse. He was sitting in my father's chair.

A toned-down version of my previous rage surged to the surface.

"I had assumed this would be a family dinner." I slid into my chair. "As in you and me, and not the guy who works at the antique store."

Mom ignored me and set a plate in front of Jesse. The rich scent of Mom's pasta sauce lingered, and my stomach ached with hunger——until one look at Jesse and his slick blonde hair and Ken doll smile had it twisting with nausea.

"Why are you glaring at me?" Jesse frowned. "Cut that out. You'll get wrinkles."

Where did Mom find an idiot as vain as her? "I'm hoping you'll spontaneously combust."

"Brynn!" Mom scolded.

"I'm your mother's boyfriend, Brynn." The normal whine of his voice took on a sternness that made my blood pop and spit beneath my skin.

"Stop talking to me like a parent, Jesse. You're what? Twenty-four?"

"Twenty-nine, actually." He squirmed a little.

"I don't understand why you hate him so much," Mom said, settling in her own chair. "But it had better stop being an issue."

"It's not that I hate him, Mom." My tone softened, and I offered him a sweet smile. "It's just that, if he was on fire, and I had a gallon of water, I'd drink the water."

"Do you not realize you're disrespecting Chelsea with your attitude?" Jesse asked. "This isn't about me. You're hurting her. Is that what you want?"

"You care what I want? That's adorable, coming from you. None of you care what I want." I sliced into my chicken parm violently, vaguely surprised Mom would give me a knife when I was in this condition.

"Listen," Mom said. "I get why you're upset, and I'd like to offer an olive branch."

I stopped savagely destroying my meal. "I'm listening."

"Your father and I have agreed to let you move in with him."

I ate a piece of chicken, waiting patiently for the other shoe to drop. I couldn't taste the normally delicious meal. My nervousness had stolen my taste buds.

"But—"

"I knew there was a but."

"But I expect you to stop bad-mouthing Jesse and me to everybody who will listen. And I expect you to continue to come here and visit, not try to hide from me like you have been." She put her fork down on the table. "I understand that you don't agree with my choices, but I asked you to stay here, hoping we could put that behind us and learn to get along again. It's clear you're too stubborn to let it go without a fight. So I give up. I can see you won't start accepting this until you get your way."

"It's not me being stubborn," I argued.

"It is. Because rather than work through this with me, you're ready to cut and run. You've already made me the villain of your novel. And I'll admit I've done some things to deserve it. But that's not why you want to stay with your father. You're choosing him because your father is the simpler choice. And of course he is. He's more like you." She said the words like an accusation, tinged in disgust and disapproval.

"That's better than what he could be like," I said. "More like you."

"You do realize the only reason I haven't grounded you is because I feel bad for how you found out about this mess, don't you?" she asked. "Because if I wanted to, you'd have had the book thrown at you long ago."

"You can throw it," I said. "But I won't be following your rules."

"And even when you've gotten your way, you continue. You know, in the city, you're going to have to deal with people who don't agree with you. You'll have to agree with people who judge you in college. It's best you learn now how to live with that. But no. You won't learn to push through this. Instead, you insist on acting out."

"Because you don't even like me!" I shouted, finally toppling under the weight of the past few weeks. "Why would you force me to stay here when you can't stand who I've grown up to be? I am not some perky little princess, and I am not concerned about dining etiquette, so really, the only reason I can think of for you torturing me is so you can get your way! You put your foot down because, on principle alone, your daughter needs to live with her mother. It doesn't matter if you actually want me here!" I pushed my chair back and drew in a miserable breath that sounded more like a whine.

"Well," Mom said, straightening her hair in a sorry attempt to appear composed. "I certainly don't like you when you act like this."

I marched upstairs without a second glance her way, terrified she would stop me, that she would see the grief written on my face. Slamming the door behind me, I rushed around my room, filling my already over-stuffed bookbag with a change of clothing, my laptop, newest book, toothbrush, hairbrush, and necessary device chargers. Lastly, I tucked my cell phone and my wallet in my pockets and threw on a pair of sunglasses.

I did not look back at Mom as I headed for the door. I didn't bother trying to figure out what she was saying to Jesse in hushed tones of frustration. I slammed the door behind me when I left.

Mom didn't call after me. She didn't ask me where I was going. She never even called my cell phone to make sure I was safe. She didn't care. She didn't want to know.

With my sunglasses covering my eyes, nobody could tell how crushed I was. As long as I kept wiping the tears off my chin, as long as I kept my lips from quivering, nobody would even know I was broken.

It was about a forty-five-minute walk to my destination, and I didn't look at anyone, and I didn't tell anyone where I was going. I considered telling Nina, but she'd just try to get Roman and Angie to drive me, and I couldn't sit in a car with anyone in the condition I was in, even if it would get me there half an hour sooner.

Or, worse, she could call Gabe and Adam, and I really didn't want that.

So, I walked until I wound up on the front stoop of a ranch-style house on the outskirts of town. Pulling my sunglasses from my face, I found them filmy, marked with my tears. I hung them from the front of my shirt and rang the bell.

A corresponding electric buzz filled the inside of the house, and only a moment later, the wooden door opened with a tell-tale squeal, alerting everyone within a block radius that it could use some oil on its hinges.

"Brynn?" Dad's eyes were wide with worry, and he threw open the screen door between us. "Are you okay?"

The tears came fresh once again, and I let them, a sob tearing from my throat. "Can I stay here tonight?"

Dad was already nodding, taking my arm and gently guiding me into the house. "What happened, baby?"

"I've had a seriously awful day."

I walked into the living room. Uncle Josh was already on his feet, game controller dangling from his hand, his brows pressed together, and a fiercely protective look in his light eyes.

"Whose ass do I have to kick?"

I shook my head, still not able to make words happen, nothing more than whimpers and sobs escaping. Dad led me to the couch and sat me down, cradling me in his arms, and I punched the couch with my free hand because I felt so damn weak and I hated it.

I hated crying, and I hated emotions.

"Hey, Couch Pete-ato never did anything to you." Josh waved at the couch with a wry smile.

I couldn't help but let out a wet, snot-filled laugh at that.

"Are you going to tell us what happened?" he prodded.

"Josh, let her catch her breath," Dad said.

He waited a beat before saying, "Did she catch it yet?"

I could tell Dad was about to scream at him, but I finally squeaked out, "I got into a huge fight with Mom."

Anger flashed in Josh's eyes. "You call her, or I will."

Dad gave me a gentle squeeze before he stepped away, pulling his phone from his pocket.

Josh lowered himself onto the couch beside me, watching me with careful, analytical eyes. Though one would never guess based on personality alone, Josh was a freelance journalist with an edge toward hard-hitting investigative pieces——which had disillusioned him enough that he hated almost everyone. It was difficult to find a heartwarming story in this world. Most of the more interesting stories were also terrible statements on the human condition.

He placed a hand on my shoulder and gave it a squeeze. "You

know, I always wanted you to come here. Don't tell your dad I told you."

That sent me sputtering into tears again. Cool Uncle Josh had always been there for me, but I'd grown up and, at some point, had stopped wanting to need him. But here he was, backing my father up, ready to kick the ass of whoever had dared to harm me.

I smiled through my tears. Josh had no real horse in this race. He just wanted me to be happy. I settled in and told him the day's stories, from top to bottom, even as Dad shouted at Mom through the phone.

Once Dad got off the phone, he and Josh ushered me to their second guest bedroom, which consisted of a bed, a dresser, and a closet. Josh had purchased the house when Grandma was still alive, so she could come up from Florida to visit, and he could have space for my aunt, Rebecca, who lived in Virginia, in case of a large family gathering. Because despite his caustic sarcasm, Josh was all about family. They were the only people he enjoyed.

"Go ahead and dress it up however you want," Josh said. "It's yours."

"You're the best!" I planted a kiss on his cheek.

"We'll take care of getting your stuff from your mom's house." Dad's face fell. "Brynn, I'm really sorry I didn't do this earlier. I wanted to try to get you to fix things with her, but I only made it worse."

"It's okay." I sighed, dropping my heavy bookbag onto the floor. "I get what you were doing, but you forgot... I'm an unstable element."

Dad smirked. "Instability goes both ways, kid. You could have been really crazy and forgiven her."

I rolled my eyes so hard I could see my frontal lobe.

"Anyway, go. Unpack, get some rest. Let us know if you need anything. I'll drive you to school in the morning."

They left me to my own devices for the rest of the night. The walls in the house were thin and I could hear them whispering to each other, sharing perspectives on what had happened to me today.

I tuned them out, slid out my laptop, and picked up on the document I had typed earlier. Though I had calmed, I began typing once again, to pour my emotions onto the page just so I could shake them out of me.

And then my phone vibrated. I had forgotten it was in my pocket. I yanked it out and found three texts from Adam waiting for me.

An hour ago.

I'm sorry.

45 minutes ago.

I'm so sorry.

15 minutes ago.

That was the WORST thing I could have said. I was angry at you, but there's no excuse.

My heart squeezed painfully. I wrote him back.

Hey. I swear I wasn't ignoring you. My meltdown didn't end at school. Things are just finally settling down.

I had barely hit send before my phone rang. Adam, of course. I picked up.

"Hey."

"Hey. You okay?"

"Not really. It's been a rough few days. But, on the plus side, my mom sorta kicked me out, so I'm at my dad's house."

"Shit," Adam said. "You seem better now, though?"

"Better," I said. "Although don't expect me to ask you for help again for a while."

"Damn it," he growled. "I'm an asshole."

"I shouldn't have been acting like I could handle everything on my own," I said. "I can't. I walked to my dad's house and collapsed on his couch and made him and my uncle Josh mop up the puddle I became."

"I'm so sorry, Brynn. I wish there was something I could do."

"There is always something you can do. It involves listening to me. Talking to me when I need it. But letting me fight my own battles. You never had to step in between Val and me." I swallowed past the lump in my throat. "I feel like I messed things up for you."

"You didn't," he said. "I'm not going to get into it now, because this isn't about me, but we were already going down that route. She would talk about moving to the city with us, and I would cringe. Not because I, like, hated her or anything. But because I didn't know how to tell her I didn't want her to up and move to be with me. Because maybe soon we wouldn't be together, you know?"

"I get it."

"I'll try to be better at just listening and not trying to fix things," Adam said. "I already messaged Nina to let her know you're okay. She was concerned. So was Val, honestly. But nobody wanted to be the one to call if you needed space. Nina said you get like that."

"I do." I smiled, genuinely touched that they were all so worried about me. "Thank you for telling her." I paused. "I can't imagine what people must think. I walked two places in a complete daze, one while crying, the other while fuming angry. I had a meltdown in school, a screaming match with Mom, and a sob fest here. That must have looked awesome."

"So?"

I snorted a laugh. "You know my mother is all about presentation."

"I don't give a crap what people thought. I care about how you feel."

My heart skipped a beat, and I almost wanted to punch myself for how lame I'd become.

"I feel like I've gone a round or two with a bear," I admitted. "But I'll be okay. Make me laugh?"

I heard jumbled words in the background. "Yeah, sure. Wait, hold on." Then, away from the phone, he said, "Yes, it's Brynn. I'm trying to, but you're interrupting me. Yes, I told Nina. Yeah. Seriously?" A frustrated sigh and he returned to the phone. "Sorry. Gabe was worried about you, too. Apparently, Nina called him earlier."

Another smile. "That's sweet." And then my crafty brain started spinning out an idea. "So Nina is talking to Gabe on the phone now?"

Adam paused. "Oh no. Not you, too."

"Oh, come on, you have to know already."

"But you're not supposed to set people up. That's what Val does, and you hate that." He whined. He actually whined.

"Okay, it is one thing to set up two people who genuinely like each other, and another to threaten to turn someone into a toad if they don't go on a date with someone they don't like and mean it."

"Val threatened to turn you into a toad?"

"That's off-topic," I said, waving off the question. "My point is, Gabe and Nina like each other."

"Yeah, but I don't know if either of them are ready to take that step yet," Adam said.

"Gabe wants to take that step. And if Nina wants to, then it isn't up to us, is it?"

Adam sighed. "And what if they break up because they aren't ready? They're both recovering from really bad relationships and——"

"Okay, okay, stop," I cut him off. "You know Gabe. You know Nina. Are they the type to treat each other like utter crap and never speak to each other or us again if it turns out it just wasn't the right time?"

A pause. "Probably not."

"Chill. I've got an idea. It's gonna take a few calls to execute, but I think it might work. And I think even you would approve."

"Why Brynn, you sound positively jolly." I could hear the smile in Adam's voice, the way it warmed, the playful lilt. "Quite the metamorphosis in such a short time."

Wait... was he flirting? My thoughts tangled. Had he always been flirting?

"Um... well... I..."

"Give me the pitch, and we'll knock down the obstacles together, should I decide that it's doable with minimum damage."

"I'm getting our best friends to date, not marching into battle."

"Isn't that bound to be the same thing?"

"Love isn't war, Adam."

"That depends on who you ask."

And just like that, here I was, having faith in love.

"Your plan?" Adam asked, just when I thought he would bail.

I closed my laptop and set it aside, then flicked the light switch off. Without the man-made illumination, the moonlight was free to slip through my windows, blanketing everything in its pale glow.

"My plan is to surround them with good company... and work from there." I slid down into the bed and prepared to fall asleep once again to the sound of Adam's voice on the other end of the line.

"Do tell, but I warn you, this sounds terrible already."

He didn't have to agree to be a comfort.

CHAPTER FIFTEEN
BAIT AND SWITCH

THE OPERATION COULDN'T GO into motion until Saturday because it required Val to be at work. Why else would I take Nina out without Val? Never mind that we'd been best friends since the dawn of time, Val would take offense if she wasn't included. Also, my conversation with Adam had taught me that Val wasn't a fan of the killer crush Gabe had developed on Nina.

"It was probably because she wanted to hook Gabe up with you," Adam had said, then his voice trailed off. "About that…"

"It's better this way," I answered a little too quickly.

Now, Nina and I were headed to The Calendar Club, the closest thing Birchwood had to a nightlife. Nina believed it was just going to be the two of us, going to see Nina's favorite local band, who was playing there all weekend. Gabe believed all four of us were meeting up to do the same.

Part one of the mission was accomplished. And all it had cost me was the requirement of wearing something other than a t-shirt and jeans.

Nina donned a white strappy sundress with a lilac print that came to her mid-thigh. On her feet, she wore matching white sandals. Though I didn't look quite as dressy, I definitely surprised her. I had picked out a dress in one of the local vintage shops. It was a charcoal A-Line dress that cut off just above the knee, paired with black booties and a matching wide-brimmed bowler hat. To top it off, I added a long silver necklace with a dragon pendant that dangled almost to my waist.

"Girl, you're wearing a dress," Nina said as we walked in the cooling evening, arm in arm. "I feel like I haven't seen your knees in ages."

"Shut up."

"What? They're admirable knees."

"So are yours," I said. "This might be one of the stranger complimentary tangents we've gone on."

She bumped my hip with hers. "Not as bad as the time we started comparing boobs."

"You're a boob," I teased.

"A smaller boob than you."

We erupted into embarrassingly childish giggling, and it felt good to giggle and be silly.

Once the laughter died down, I decided to make sure I didn't need to abort the plan before I pulled the pin out of the grenade.

"I wanted to ask you something," I said. "There is no right or wrong answer, but it's important. And whatever you tell me, I will take to heart."

Nina's brows furrowed. "O... kay. That doesn't sound scary at all."

"It's nothing bad. I just want to know if you have a thing for Gabe. Because we're not seeing each other."

Nina stopped in her tracks. "Where the hell did that come from?"

I tilted my head, put my hands on my hips, and gave her 'the look,' the one we'd been giving each other for years, which said 'you know I know you better than anyone, why would you even bother trying to sneak something by me?'

She met my gaze, her eyes hard, lips pressed together. Her hands moved to her hips. It lasted about five seconds before she threw her hands up in the air and let out an aggravated groan. "Fine, fine. Yeah, I like Gabe."

"Yeah, I know." I poked a finger into her shoulder. "And when were you going to tell me?"

"Oh, I don't know, when our collective universe stopped blowing up from one revelation or another?" Her shoulders slumped. "I didn't want to be another problem. And it didn't matter because I wasn't going to do anything about it. Not unless I was sure…"

"Yeah, I like him, but not like that. That seat is taken." It was out of my mouth before I'd even thought about it.

Nina made a face. "That sounded dirty."

"Slightly, yes."

"You talking about who I think you're talking about?"

"Of course. Murray."

Nina threw her head back and laughed. "I totally thought you were going to say Raphael."

"Ass."

"Whose?"

"Shut up!" I hid my face in my hands, and she wrapped an arm around me and pulled me to her.

"You wanted to ask me about Gabe, why?" She stretched out the last word, turning it into a song. God, it felt good to be having fun with her like we used to do.

"You want to date him?" We turned the corner, only a block away from the club.

"Yeah, sure, but he isn't asking."

"Yeah… I kinda…asked for him?" I cringed.

Nina shot me a look. "You're a jerk, but I already knew this, so stop cowering."

"What?"

"Gabe texted me and told me he was excited about coming to the club with us. Because *The Moonrakers* were playing tonight, and I'd told him how awesome they were." She growled playfully at me. "You should know by now that you can't hide things from me. Nina always knows."

"In this case, Nina always finds out, because Gabe is so crazy about you he can't keep his mouth shut." We slowed to a stop in front of The Calendar Club. "He came up with the idea to take you to see *The Moonrakers,* but wanted it to be a group thing because he's a chicken shit. We changed the plans on him."

"We, as in…"

"Me and Adam."

Nina groaned.

"What? We're helping our best friends find happiness. And at least with Gabe, I know your heart is safe. He's a good guy."

Nina slid me a look through the corner of her eye. "It will be strange, you actually liking a guy I'm dating."

We reached the front doors of the club, and I smiled. "I'm wearing a dress. It's a brave new world."

As the band tuned up their instruments, we headed past the bar toward the small round tables around the stage. We bumped through the people crowding in, and I tried to stand on my tiptoes to see over everyone's heads. Sometimes it sucked being so short.

Nina giggled. "Leave it to someone who can actually see over some of their heads."

I stuck my tongue out at her, because I was a mature future college student.

"I see Gabe!" Nina squealed, and my heart lifted, glad I could make this happen for her.

She grabbed my hand and weaved us through the crowd, accidentally making me hip-check and apologize to half the people I passed. She always seemed to forget I was wider than her.

When we made it to the table where Adam and Gabe sat, I breathed a sigh of relief.

"Hey!" She kissed Adam's cheek, then threw an arm over Gabe's shoulders. "This was such an amazing idea! Thanks for thinking of me."

Gabe scratched at the back of his neck. "Of course! I mean, it wasn't all my idea. I knew you liked this place and... I..."

Adam smirked at them.

I reached over the table and pinched Gabe's cheek. "Oh, don't be so modest." I took Adam's arm in mine. "That's our cue."

"Cue?" Gabe's mouth twisted into a confused frown, before immediately returning to its dopey grin.

"Yeah, man." Adam slipped an arm around my waist, and the movement sent a shiver through me. I hoped he hadn't noticed. "This was Brynn's brilliant idea. We're ducking out. Enjoy your date."

Gabe's eyes bulged. "What?"

Nina slid closer, resting her head on his shoulder. "Unless you're not interested?" She blinked up at him.

Gabe looked down at her, his mouth working for a moment before finally managing, "Um... interested." He did his best impression of a bobblehead.

Adam slugged him on the arm. "Smooth."

I planted a kiss on Nina's cheek, whispering in her ear, "Have fun." I began making my exit, waving back at them as I went. Weaving my way through the crowd, the feeling of a warm hand settling on the small of my back made me whirl around.

"Don't punch me!" Adam held up his hands defensively. "I was just guiding you through."

I laughed, holding up my clenched fingers to indicate how I'd nearly done it. "So close." I spun back toward the exit, my skirt flaring out around me as I strutted toward the door.

Adam laughed and rushed to catch up, his hand landing on the small of my back again. "I know you don't need me to guide you through the crowd," he teased, "but I'm doing it, anyway."

I shot him the finger, and as we left the club, we were both cracking up.

"You look nice," he said as our laughter died down. He studiously examined his black dress shoes.

He wasn't so bad himself, looking snazzy with his white short-sleeved button-down with a black bow tie and vest. He stuffed his hands into his jean pockets, shoulders up in a shrug as he rocked on his feet. With his hair slicked back, I missed his wild curls, but that wasn't enough to change the way my heart sped up just looking at him.

"So do you," I managed to squeeze out.

He cleared his throat. "Well, we're all dressed up with nowhere to go."

"We could go *some*where." I twisted back and forth like a shy little girl. *Ugh.* Why did he make me feel like I didn't know what to do with myself?

"Dinner?" he asked, perking up.

"They opened a new Mexican restaurant on Mountainview."

"Gabe told me I was taking my life in my hands if I tried Mexican food made in Birchwood." He impersonated Gabe's slightly deeper voice and the way he spat the name of our town like it was a curse. It was a surprisingly good impression.

"That's because Gabe is a city kid snob who thinks we can't have anything nice here." I winked. "What does he know?"

We headed over to the Mexican spot and ordered more food than we could or should eat, especially with the way my stomach backflipped and belly flopped. I hadn't expected him to order it to go, and when I asked, he just shrugged and told me we would sit outside to eat.

We got into his car and I held the takeout on my lap, the heat from the food seeping through the paper bag onto my thighs.

Adam guided the car along the twisting, narrow roads of the mountains as if he'd been driving this way his entire life. He controlled the car with a practiced ease, and I found myself torn between watching the beauty of the passing scenery and observing him to see what I could learn.

"Where are we going?" I asked to break the silence. I'd never been comfortable with silence from people I knew. People I didn't know, however, should always be silent.

"It's a surprise," Adam said, a smirk quivering on the edges of his lips.

"I don't like surprises."

"You'll like this one. It's right up your alley, trust me."

I did.

He maneuvered the car up a winding strip of road and slowed to a stop on a vacant expanse of land. We were on the crest of a hill, branches and pebbles cracking under the tires.

"We're here!" he announced with pride. He threw the door open, grabbed my water and his soda, and ducked out of the car.

I followed, takeout bag in hand. I stepped down onto a stretch of earth lined with cracks that sprouted weeds. Adam climbed onto the hood and sat atop it, his back to the windshield.

He waved me up. "Pass me the food and come up. I'll help you."

I did as he asked, but didn't need his assistance. I boosted myself up onto the car, then slid in a little closer, until Adam and I were shoulder to shoulder.

"Are you sure this is cool? Me sitting on your car?"

"Yeah, sure." His brows furrowed. "Are you sure this is okay? I didn't think to ask you how you felt about heights."

I shrugged, then glanced out ahead. The sky spread out before us, unmarred by a single cloud. Below, a series of jutting rocks acted like foot holds or a spiral staircase, leading a few hundred feet down to the swift-flowing river. A waterfall slid over the moss-covered stones. All around the ravine, the ground was shelved in green; trees, grass, and bushes coated every layer of exposed earth. Small copses of purple and pink flowers edged the river.

"When you see something you like," Adam said, his voice low, "your eyes widen and sparkle. Pure wonder. It's a good look on you."

I tore my attention away from the view and turned to him, my heart racing. He smiled crookedly, then jerked his chin out toward me. "Look that way."

An old lighthouse stood in the distance, a cylindrical guard dog against dangers that came with the darkness of night. It was weathered, the peeling paint clear, even from this distance. Some of its bricks looked a bit crumbly, but they felt less like a sign of weakness and more like scars won in a battle against the sea. The lighthouse remained strong despite its struggles.

"It's beautiful." The words came out breathy.

"I thought you'd agree." He took a sip of his fountain soda.

I settled in, opening the bag of food, and passed him his order. "So, how did you find this place?" I popped the cover off my nachos.

The smile melted off Adam's face. He took another sip.

I had asked the wrong question. I didn't know how I screwed up, but I had.

He fiddled with the wrapper of his enchilada before unrolling it on his lap. He fixed his eyes on his food. "That... is a question with a heavy answer. I don't mind answering it, but it might bum you out."

A lump formed in my throat, and though I was terrified to say what I wanted to, I managed. "Adam, you know you can tell me anything."

He glanced up for a moment before his eyes dipped back to the enchilada. "I just didn't want to ruin... yeah, okay." A quick nod. "When my mother died, I didn't take it well. I held on at first, but at some point during the funeral, something just... she was being lowered into the ground. And it became very real, all at once, that she wasn't there anymore, that she never would be again."

"Everybody loved her," I said when it seemed like he would not say anything further. "Every kid in Birchwood."

His head was still lowered, but his cheek lifted in the hint of a smile. "That night, I couldn't sleep. I climbed out of my window and I... I dunno... just left."

"Where were you going?" My voice sounded small, the very idea of him running away at night like that striking fear in my heart, twisting my stomach.

"Nowhere," he said. "No aim, no direction. For that one small moment, I didn't have a plan. I didn't stop running until I found this." He waved out one arm at the view before us. "It brought me peace. It was like my mother had led me here, had given me comfort when I needed it most, because how else could I walk in circles for hours and still know how to get home? And ever since then, I've been coming here when I can't sleep." He huffed a laugh and finally met my eyes. His were moist with the beginnings of tears, but his smile seemed to wipe them away. "I sound crazy. I found this place by magic." A shake of his head.

"I believe there's magic in the world," I said, thinking of Val. "I don't think we can ever plan for it."

"It's funny, because I've only ever not had a plan about three times in my life, and it always led me somewhere good."

"Yeah?"

"Dating Val—"

"You consider dating Val to be something that led you somewhere good?" I tried not to sound offended, but it was there. I grimaced.

"I had a great time with Val. I don't hate her. Things change. Feelings change. Val helped me find my way back into the world when I didn't want any part of it because I was still grieving. I needed to stop hiding. And if I hadn't, how would I have ever made my next not-plan?"

My lips twitched. "Not-plan?"

"Sitting here with you," he said casually. "You know, I've never brought anybody here before. I didn't actually plan to bring you. I just sort of... did."

I shifted, dread crawling through me. "Does it feel like an invasion?"

"No," Adam said. "I think you get it. I think you understood it was important before I even told you why."

I nodded, fighting down tears.

"Okay." He shook his head. "Let's bring ourselves out of that dark place I dove us into. Wanna hear something funny that literally just happened?"

"Like right now?" I teased. "Because literally doesn't mean what you think it means."

He nudged my shoulder and dove into his enchilada. "Well, yesterday, but whatever, professor. Yesterday I grabbed an old wiffle bat, and Gabe grabbed a broom handle, and we had a sword fight. We broke a lamp and my father contemplated killing me, but decided it was better if his son grew up to be a doctor so I could pay him back for the damages."

I grinned. "You guys are ridiculous."

"Oh, that's nothing," Adam said.

He launched into another of his exploits with Gabe, this one taking place in the city and involving a stupid moment where they rollerbladed holding onto the back of a bus. Spoiler: They fell and scraped the crap out of themselves.

We traded stories as we ate. Sometimes we would laugh, and sometimes we would speak softly to each other, hushed tones as we discussed our fears, our sadness, the people we didn't want to grow up to be. We spoke for hours until the fall of dusk shadowed his face.

I noticed it as he recounted a ridiculous story about his

mother and a bag of Oreos she tried to open. She pulled at the edges harder than necessary, and the bag tore in half, cookies flying all over the kitchen in a shower of crumbs worthy of a tub of cookies and cream ice cream.

"I saw an actual cookie rain, and my little kid self thought it was absolutely glorious."

I couldn't fight down a giggle. It wasn't the story. It was him. He shared the memory with bursting enthusiasm, his eyes dancing with contained laughter. I loved seeing that from him.

I loved him.

I had fallen in love with Adam Hernandez.

Hadn't I sworn it would never happen? It was like just by saying I would never love, I had drawn love to me. Or like Val fighting me about love had made me find it, but in exactly the last place she would have wanted.

Shit. Val.

"What?" Adam asked.

I snapped out of it, refocusing my attention on him, scrambling to figure out what I'd missed. "What what?"

His eyes narrowed, and his smile turned into a weird little half frown, like he still wanted to smile, but was waiting for the other shoe to drop. "Where did you go?"

"Nowhere," I said. "I'm right here. I just..." *Love you. And it's going to make everyone else I love hate me.* "... thank you. For taking me out. I kinda needed a pick-me-up."

"Cool." He slid down onto his back and motioned for me to do the same. He made an annoyed noise, whipped off his vest, balled it up, and placed it where my head would land. I took off my hat and laid down beside him.

We were shoulder to shoulder again, the warmth of his body so close. I thought I'd be nervous, but I wasn't. It was the most natural thing in the world.

"The stars are out," he said, pointing.

I took in at least two dozen twinkling lights in the sky, each their own suns, burning so far away that Adam and I, what we were doing here, felt inconsequential. And also so damn important.

"I didn't take you here because I thought you needed a pick me up," he confessed.

"No?" I turned to face him, and we were so close I could see flecks of green in his brown eyes. I'd never noticed them before. "Why then?"

"I just wanted to hang." He shrugged, slightly jostling me.

"Right. And Nina just stole Gabe away."

"I didn't want to hang with Gabe." A smile flickered along his lips, disappearing before it really got started. "You know, I never really noticed that lighthouse before coming up here. I've spent my entire life in Birchwood, and this lighthouse was here the whole time, I just never saw it, or I saw it and never paid attention to it." He sighed. "About a month ago, I heard there was a petition to renovate it over in Kramerville. The lighthouse doesn't need renovation. It's a perfectly functioning lighthouse, and it's beautiful as it is. But some townspeople said it didn't fit in with the rest of the 'mystique' of the town." He put up air quotes around the word 'mystique.' "I went to see it. I was curious if I would agree. I hadn't had an opinion on it before then. What do you think?"

I eyed the weathered white bricks of the house, took in its stature, its weight. It commanded attention, but radiated experience, like a well-worn shoe. "I think it's perfect the way it is. You?"

Adam smiled, his eyes brightening, and I swore my skin tingled where they settled on me. "I agree."

His fingers threaded with mine, and for a long time, we just watched the stars. I let my head fall to his shoulder, and I thought I heard him sigh.

Far too soon, my phone alarm went off. "Crap." I scrambled

up to a sitting position. "Unfortunately, we've got to start heading home before I turn into a pumpkin."

He picked up my hat and popped it on his head. "I'll show up in every house in Birchwood looking for the fair maiden who watched the stars in the sky with me. Only she will fit this hat."

I laughed. "*You* fit that hat. If that's your test, you'll find a lot of shes."

On the ride home, we talked about a lot of things——the senior trip on Monday, who worked the next shift at Scoopy Doo ——but we didn't talk about *it*. The big elephant in the room. What the hell was going on with us? Were we a thing? Weren't we? It certainly felt like we were, but neither of us was going to ask.

When we finally made it to my dad's, Adam leaned toward me, pressing a kiss to my cheek and lingering there for just a moment before pulling back and offering me a shy smile.

"Thank you for joining me today, Brynn."

I stole my hat back, tightening my grip on it so he couldn't see my hands shaking. "Thank you for trusting me with your place." I leaned forward and repeated his actions, stopping as I pulled away to give him time to meet my eyes. He did, and the look we shared was... something. Something tangible. Something I'd never even come close to sharing in my entire life.

I whispered goodnight to Adam, got out of the car, and didn't look back.

I wasn't sure I could keep my mouth shut if I did.

CHAPTER SIXTEEN
SPEAK NO EVIL

WHEN WE LEFT on our senior trip that morning, I hadn't expected to arrive at our destination to the tones of whining in my ear.

"Wake up, wake up, wake up!" Val punctuated each demand with a bruising kick to my calf, which finally roused me.

I jumped up in my seat. "What? WHAT? *WHAT?*" I punched Val hard in her shoulder. Not my most mature reaction, but nobody should be woken with kicks.

"Ow!" She shoved me just as I sat up, and I tumbled off the seat and into the middle of the aisle of the bus with a thump.

The fall knocked the wind out of me, and laughter erupted from the back of the bus. I rolled onto my knees, snatched Val by the front of her cotton candy-pink tank, and yanked her down to the floor with me.

"Ms. Stark, Ms. Kokinos, am I gonna have to separate you?" our chaperone, Coach Perl, yelled from the front.

Adam and Nina were assigned to one of the other two buses. When I realized I would be stuck with Val on a bus for three hours, I wanted to bolt and run all the way back home. I'd settled for taking a nap.

"Sorry, Coach," I said. "Val startled me when she woke me up."

Coach looked at me with a raised eyebrow, but when Val didn't argue, she nodded and turned back toward the driver.

Val rose and helped me to my feet. "Sorry. I got excited. We're almost there!"

"Oh!" I rubbed my eyes and stretched. "I didn't mean to sleep for the entire trip."

I had totally meant to sleep for the entire trip. Especially because the last few nights I'd been up texting or chatting with either Nina or Adam way too late. Nina was ecstatic, and also a bit alarmed, at how well she and Gabe clicked. Their first date had been astounding, and now they were inseparable.

Adam, on the other hand, confused me. He never discussed our evening together or gave me any further indication that we were more than friends. Perhaps somewhat touchy friends, but just friends. I didn't know what was happening, but having him as a friend was still a gain, so I happily accepted it, even if it would never be everything I wanted.

I could still pretend I had done nothing wrong, which was a happy side effect of a crappy ending.

"This... doesn't look like I imagined it." Val pressed her nose and hands to the bus window as we pulled up to our destination, The Rockin' Ranch. "It looks... dirty."

I rolled my eyes and looked past her. "It's a ranch. Were you expecting polished floors? We're not even inside yet!"

"I've seen nicer ones." Val shrugged.

"I'm shocked you even like stuff like this," I said.

"Seriously? I enjoy nature! I'm a goddess." She whispered that last bit. "My people invented nature." She flopped back into her seat, arms crossed over her chest. "Come to think of it, a ranch was kind of a dumb choice for our senior trip. We're not in touch with enough nature in a place named after trees?"

I shrugged.

"It's okay." She leaned forward and whispered in my ear. "I brought some goodies to keep everyone entertained."

My stomach dropped. "Goodies?"

"You'll see!" She clapped her hands together, once again filled with energy.

"I'm kinda scared to."

We slowed to a stop and Coach Perl shouted for us to grab our things and get off the bus in an orderly fashion. I snatched my messenger bag and slid out. Val grabbed a handful of the back of my t-shirt so she could stay close.

As we piled off the bus and waited for guidance, Coach Perl and Ms. Bratcher, one of the other chaperones, handed out maps. Unlike whatever Val had imagined, based on the map, the ranch was exactly what I expected. It was a large expanse of ground, with a lake in the center. Surrounded on its edges by quaint log cabins, there was a large open space for games and a trail that led off to a stable. Another trail led off into a wooded area.

I was finally getting excited about this trip.

"Hi everyone!" A short, older lady in a maroon t-shirt and beige shorts stood before the crowd of students forming between the parked busses. "My name is Desi Crawford, and I'm going to be your guide during your stay."

Someone tugged on my wrist, and I turned to find Nina beside me, Adam on her other side.

"Each of these cabins will house twelve of you. There is also a common area in each one if you want to hang out until lights out. We have some great activities planned for you over the next three days. We have hiking, horseback riding, paintball, time at the lake, a game room, sports, a rock-climbing wall, evening campfires, and food!" Ms. Crawford told us. "Each day, you'll have a schedule. So get settled in, and let's have a great time."

The parent chaperones divided us into groups of twelve and sent us to our assigned cabins to get settled. Nina, Val, and I stuck close together and were placed in the same cabin.

The cabins were rustic and surprisingly spacious. Our

common area was furnished with worn microfiber couches, enough love seats for ten people, and tables crafted from unfinished wood. The bunk beds in the two large sleeping spaces were crafted from the same wood, with three beds on each side.

Each bed had a cubby hole to store our things. I called the top bed on my side. Nina took the middle, and Val, who according to Nina was the sleeper most likely to roll off her bed in the middle of the night, got the bottom.

I climbed up to my bunk to unpack my stuff. As I emptied my tote, Nina and Val hissed and whispered at each other, too low for me to hear. Once I unpacked, I came down the ladder and settled on Nina's bed.

"What's going on?" I asked.

"Val is insane," Nina hissed.

"Nina, don't tell *her*," Val snapped.

"Val smuggled in three bottles of liquor from the liquor cabinet at home." Nina's eyes were bulging, her teeth gritted, and her hands clamped into fists.

"Nobody expects me to be a light packer." Val giggled. "Joke's on them. I packed a few light outfits, some vodka, and some tequila. We're gonna give these kids a *real* rite of passage."

"We're chaperoned," I said.

"Not after lights out. Do you see a room here for the chaperone?" Val asked.

"No, but they're going to come by," Nina argued.

"How many senior trips have you been on?" Val asked. "Just this one? That's what I thought. I've been going on senior trips like this in different towns for thirty years."

Nina coughed. "You *do* realize how disgusting that makes your relationship with Adam, right?"

"What relationship with Adam?" Val cut her eyes to me.

I rolled mine. "Whatever, the point is, that doesn't mean you'll be able to throw some kind of party tonight."

"I'm not going to throw it tonight," Val said. "I'm charming, not stupid. I need a day to see how things are run. Then we're going to have a wonderful time.".

"I could just tell Coach Perl what you have in your bag." I shrugged.

Now they were both looking at me. Nina broke the silence with another cough.

"You wouldn't," Val whispered.

I considered it. On the one hand, if either of my parents discovered I'd had a drink on this trip, they wouldn't be happy. On the other hand, she wasn't wrong about this being a rite of passage, and I wasn't some lame ass rule follower. Well, not most of the time. Who was I to impede on anybody else's good time?

Nina wheezed, capturing my attention. She made a face, then slapped a hand against her chest, as though that ever helped.

"You okay?" I took her hand as Val climbed up to her bunk.

"Where did you put your pump?" she asked.

"I got like this on the bus t—" Nina's response was cut off by a series of coughs, each more ragged than the one before.

"Arms up above your head." I grabbed both of her arms and pulled them up, then pushed down on her shoulders until she was sitting on Val's bed. "Val?"

Val's call of "can't find it!" was accompanied by an increase in rustling.

Nina brought her arms down, her face and eyes reddening as her cough persisted.

"Up, Nina."

She motioned from her shoulder to her hip.

"Brynn." Val handed a bottle of water to me, curls distorting my view of her face.

I grabbed the bottle and flipped it to Nina. "It's in her purse."

Val returned to her search with renewed vigor.

Nina sputtered and coughed around a few sips of water. Her eyes were watering.

"As much air as you can take, as many times as you can take it." I remembered the times in my life I had done this. After swim practice. When a particular scent we'd tested while perfume shopping was too strong. When she'd had a fight with Reeve. During a particularly bad bout with bronchitis. If she encountered too much bleach at Scoopy Doo. And sometimes, for no discernible reason at all.

Nina squeezed my hand, and I squeezed back.

"Got it!" Val yelled, tossing the pump at me and nearly braining me with it.

Nina took it from me with shaking fingers. She administered the medicine twice before her breathing settled. By the time she could talk again, Val had climbed down and curled up beside her, exchanging concerned glances with me.

"I think it's something they're growing over here," Nina said, her hands on her knees as she took greedy gulps of air. "Or it could be that the cabin's dusty. But I started feeling it before we even pulled up."

"Shit," I muttered. "Should we go home?"

"No!" Nina wheezed. "No, I'll be fine. I just need to keep my pump with me. I brought my nebulizer kit if I need a treatment."

"Nina," Val said, resting her head on Nina's shoulder. "I don't like this. We should call your parents."

Nina stood, straightened her canary yellow t-shirt and jean shorts, and tidied her ponytail. "I am going to enjoy my senior trip," she said, breathy but sounding mostly back to normal. "I'm not letting this get in the way. Now, come on. There is fun to be had."

Val pointed her round green eyes in my direction, her concern piercing. I shrugged. I could call Angie and Roman, but Nina would feel just as betrayed as Val would if I called them about her liquor bottles. For now, the best course of action was to shut up and enjoy myself.

THE MORNING CONSISTED of horseback riding, and the afternoon involved a lively game of paintball that left most of us battered and bruised. By the time it was *lights out*, we were all walking aimlessly around the cabin, ready for sleep.

Nina crashed early, which made me nervous, but I checked on her after an hour and she was sleeping soundly, her breathing deep and steady. Everyone else was asleep by eleven. Val paced the common area, waiting to see what the nighttime routine was so she could set her plan in motion.

My phone rested in my lap. Earlier, I was playing around on social media and posted a few pictures of our crazy day. As Val's feet plunked against the wooden floorboards, I wondered why I was still awake.

This was the time of day I normally talked to Adam. I was waiting for some kind of contact, signifying my current place in loserdom. I needed to give it up. I didn't know what was going on between Adam and me, but it wasn't an obligation. He would contact me if he wanted to.

Val dropped into the chair beside me, a bottle of liquor dangling from her fingertips.

"Val... what are you doing?"

Her glare could have chilled Frosty the Snowman. "I'm having a drink. Is that okay with you?" Her words came out slightly slurred.

I wanted to tell her no, it wasn't, but that wouldn't help. "Weren't you saving this for later? For whatever party you were going to try to pull off?"

"Oh, I will, I will." She flapped her hand at me. "We'll only be able to get away with it for a couple of hours, though. So I'm not looking to use all three bottles."

"That still doesn't explain why you're diving into the liquor today." She was about a third of the way through the bottle, and Roman and Angie never bought the cheap stuff.

"It's not the first time I've had a drink," she said. "As you girls so delicately pointed out earlier, I'm ancient."

"It wasn't meant as an insult."

"No? Nina said my relationship with Adam was disgusting." Her face screwed up tightly, and seeing the tears on her cheeks shocked me. "It may be odd, but there aren't exactly any other people around here who are a millennium old. And I look like a teenager. What was I supposed to do? Be alone forever?" Her eyes hardened, mood swinging faster than an amusement park ride. "I bet that's what you would have wanted."

"This isn't about whatever you think I want."

"Whatever I think?" She laughed. "You're going to tell me you don't want Adam?"

I opened my mouth to deny it, but I couldn't force the words out. I couldn't help how I felt, but I also couldn't lie to her face.

"You're lucky, you know that?" Val said. "In my prime, I would have destroyed you for this slight."

"So I've read," I said.

"Being banished amongst humans for so long has made me soft." She pouted.

"Val, I didn't do anything. I'm not gonna lie to you and tell you I don't have feelings for him. I do. I couldn't help it. But... I haven't... nothing has happened between us."

My phone buzzed in my pocket, and my gut twisted.

"How close have you come? Wait, don't answer that." Val's head tilted, her eyes narrowed, and I wanted to back up a step, but I stood my ground. "It's funny. I finally understand why my father banished me. He was teaching me a lesson. I had made a mistake, and I didn't understand the ugly, more dangerous side of love. Love, unrequited, is pain. You, Brynn, my dear, taught me all about that, didn't you?" Another odd head tilt. "I created love. And all love has ever created in return is madness and war." She clapped her hands. "No matter. Everything will change soon. Then you won't have to worry about the burden of your crush. You never wanted to fall in love, right? Well, once he stops avoiding me and lets me have a moment alone with him, I'm going to take him right off your hands."

"Off my..." My mind reeled.

The manic look in her eyes made my heart rate kick up. "What are you planning, Val?"

Val rose and took a step toward me, her voice low but cutting. "Was that insolence in your tone? Humanity certainly has changed, hasn't it? To speak to a goddess with superiority on your tongue would have earned you a death sentence in my prime."

I forced myself to meet her eyes, forced myself not to back down. "Times have changed."

"Yes, they have. They have changed so much that you believe you can tell me what to do about my Adam." She swayed a little, then righted herself, the snarl never leaving her lips. "You think because Adam is in love with you, you can tell me what to do?"

"What are you talking about?" I could barely force out the words.

"I can still feel love." She strutted around the room, speaking casually, as though she spoke of the weather, not her supernatural abilities. "The strong connections, especially, come through loud and clear. Like yours. And Adam's."

I tried to process what she was saying and what it could mean for Adam. "You're crazy. Adam and I are friends. That's it."

"You could be more than that," Val said. "Why do you think I've been so damn busy?"

Setting me up. Trying to make me look different. Act different. "You were trying to keep me away from Adam this entire time?"

"You were my friend, Brynn," she choked out. "I wanted you to be happy. Just with someone else, *anyone* else."

"I'm sorry, I never tried to—"

"It doesn't matter," she spat. "You didn't try to, and every single move I made to avoid it brought you closer. I was a fool. Fate can only be changed by one thing, and that is not the actions of a mortal. It is the will of a goddess."

"Val... what are you going to do?" The possibilities became clear, and they were horrifying.

"You know, it's funny," she continued like I hadn't spoken. "Getting Adam to love me always took a conscious effort. I wanted to do it fairly. For it to be real. I couldn't just charm him. I always had to *try*. I wield charm like a weapon. I could influence and cajole, but I could not make him love me. But then I realized, I have the tools right at my fingertips. I just wasn't using them correctly. I was trying too hard to be fair. But I can have what I want. And I will."

"You can't just make Adam fall back in love with you."

"Why not?" Val scowled at me. "Of course I can."

"Because it's...it's wrong," I scrambled to explain. "For, like, *so* many reasons. One being he decided he didn't want to be with you anymore, and also, you just don't do stuff like that. I can't believe I have to explain this to you!"

"No, *you* don't do stuff like that," she said. "You are a mortal, I am a goddess. Keep your icky morals out of my business."

"I'm going to let that go because you are drunk off your ass," I said. "But don't you dare——"

"I am not drunk!" Her voice squeaked like it always did when she was offended but knew she had no damn right to be. "You're just blurry. Now, begone peasant. I have work to do."

"Leave Adam alone, Val," I warned.

"Stop me."

And that was the crux of the problem, wasn't it? What was I going to do about it? She could have Adam in her thrall for the rest of his life, and there wasn't a damn thing I could do to stop her. That didn't mean I wouldn't try. It just meant I might risk my safety.

"I don't want to stop you," I said. "I want you to know better than to try. I want you to be human enough to realize this is wrong."

"You see, that's where *you're* wrong," she growled. "That's where you were always wrong, will always *be* wrong. Because I told you a long time ago that I was not cursed with mortality, and yet, you keep trying to see me that way."

"But... but..." I scrambled to find a convincing argument. "You love Nina. And Roman and Angie. You know they wouldn't be okay with this."

"I don't care what they think. I am going to choose the person I love and have the experience I've provided so many people, but never for myself. And nobody is going to stop me."

"I'm going to stop you." It didn't matter that I didn't know how. I'd find a way.

Her hands balled into fists. "Don't challenge me, Brynn."

"If you ever loved him, I wouldn't have to." I shook with fury, and all at once, I could picture it in my mind. Adam, a mindless zombie, trailing behind Aphrodite, heeding to her every whim. The image left me desolate and useless.

"For a moment, I forgot who I was. But I remember now." Her mouth twisted into a vicious, predatory smile. "You, in fact, aided my memory. For that, I am grateful, so I've allowed you to prattle on without warning. But, because I anticipate another outburst, I will inform you that your grace period has ended. If you attempt to engage in combat, you will be well met. Good night Brynn Stark." Her voice switched back to the bubbly excitement she normally radiated as Val. "Tomorrow night is gonna be awesome!"

She stalked off to bed without another word.

Tears pricked at my eyes as I watched her go. This was bad. Beyond bad- this was dreadful. And if I didn't find a way to do the impossible, I'd lose Adam forever. Hell, he'd lose himself.

I remembered the text I'd received earlier and tugged the phone from my jean pocket. It was Adam, because of course it was.

Trying to sleep in a room with five other guys? The days on this trip are fun, but the nights? They kind of suck.

He had no idea just how bad they were about to get.

CHAPTER SEVENTEEN

PARTY OR PERIL

THE FOLLOWING morning involved varied attempts to get Nina alone for more than a few minutes. I needed her help to figure out my next step. But every time I started to talk to her, Val showed up to shoot me a baleful glare to remind me of my "place."

Even if I was willing to risk Val harming me, I wasn't willing to endanger anyone else. Val knew the easiest way to get to me was through the others.

Our second day started with miniature golf, followed by two hours of unlimited play in the game room, climbing the rock wall, and a campfire under the stars. By the time we'd hit the campfire, Val was squirming, itching to get her party started. I wasn't certain she hadn't already started it. She offered to get something to drink for a few people—and playing waitress wasn't her thing.

The campfire was actually a series of campfires set in several firepits throughout the open areas between the cabins. Crowds of students surrounded each, eating, drinking, goofing off, and loudly gossiping. It was lovely, the fire licking at the night, the orange glow on all our faces, the excitement of this being one of the last nights we'd spend together as a cohesive group. After this, we may all be from Birchwood High, but we'd all be heading to a different college, moving in different directions, like the renegade flames that would sometimes spit free from the main fire.

I wish I could enjoy any of it.

"You want some soda, Brynn?" Val asked with a wink.

"Nah, I'm good," I said, stone-faced.

"I'll take one," Nina piped up from beside me.

Val disappeared into the crowd to retrieve her drink.

"You know she's spiking those," I whispered.

"Yeah, whatever." She cleared her throat, then coughed once, twice, three times. "You only live once, am I right?"

I glared at her, and she rolled her eyes.

"Fine, get one for me, too. I'll be right back."

I set out, looking for Adam in a sea of familiar faces. I waved and smiled at some or nodded, and deftly hid behind others to avoid Raphael, Tony, and Vinny. I finally spotted Adam sitting next to a few of the other well-known science geeks. I strolled up behind him, placing a hand on his shoulder. He spun on the bench to face me. "Hey Brynn!" he greeted me warmly. "How's it going? Having fun?"

"Do you have a minute to talk?"

"Sure." He stood. "You can even have more than a minute if you want."

"Great." I gave an abrupt nod and led him outside of the circle of campfires to the horseback riding trail, where I was sure nobody could hear us. I turned to face him.

"Brynn, are you okay?" he asked after one good look at my quivering lips and watery eyes. "What's going on?"

"Have you drunk anything Val's offered you today?" I asked.

"No. Why?" Adam's worry intensified, his lips tightening, his brows furrowing.

"Just don't, okay?"

"What, you think she's going to roofie me?" His jaw dropped as he watched me. "You do! You think she's gonna try to dose me?"

"I don't know." My thoughts raced. "Just...be careful around her."

"Brynn, I don't know what's going on, but you can't be serious." He shook his head. "Val can be a bit crazy, but I don't think she's capable of something that serious. Where did you get an idea like this?"

From Greek mythology. But it wasn't like I could say that. It wasn't like I could come clean with Adam to protect him. Not without making myself sound like a raving lunatic.

My knees were like rubber as I scrambled for a solution, and I paced in front of him, parsing out my options.

"It's that Val is..." I started, but I knew there was no way I could tell him. I was dealing with Adam here. He was too analytical to buy into the real story.

"What?" His eyes searched mine.

"She's... talking a lot of shit. So be careful when you're around her."

I turned and didn't look back. What I said would have to be enough for him to keep himself safe. I couldn't sustain this; there had to be a more permanent way to handle her, but I had no idea how.

I weaved my way back through the crowd, purposely losing Adam as I went. I didn't want him to ask any more questions because I had no answers. When I got back to our campfire, Nina was waiting for me, drink in hand, but she looked concerned.

"Where did you go?" She handed me my drink.

"I had to ask Adam something."

"Adam!" Val groaned, and I turned to watch her as she facepalmed. She hadn't been behind me a second ago. "That's who I forgot to bring a drink to!" She leaned over and kissed me on the cheek. "Thanks, Bree-baby!"

I bit back a growl and hoped Adam had listened to me.

Nina sighed. "I'm a loser, but I miss Gabe. Already."

I tried for a smile. "Ah, young love."

"Something like that." She shrugged. "He's great, but I'm also not enjoying watching Reeve flirt with... well, everybody."

I followed her gaze to where Reeve was whispering something in Sherri Tilden's ear. He smiled lasciviously at her, and I fought the urge to puke.

"Ugh," was the best I could come up with.

"The worst part is, I know. He was the worst, but I used to love him. What was I thinking? There is no *ugh* in the world big enough."

"You thought he was a decent guy. Now we know better."

"Yes, we do. And just in time for me to meet Gabe." She grinned.

"You know what Val told me last night?" I asked. "Fate is real, and nothing can change it except for the will of a goddess."

Nina frowned. "That sounds ominous."

"Only if you're me or Adam. If you're you? It's not so bad."

"What is she going to do?" Nina's concerned tone echoed my questions, my fears.

"I don't know." I shook my head to clear my mind. "Anyway, it's not important. You were right. You only live once. For now, let's party." I smiled and raised my cup.

Nina's eyes narrowed, but she bumped my cup with hers. "Let's party."

I DIDN'T LIKE ALCOHOL. Didn't like the taste. Didn't like the slightly swimmy feeling it created in my head. Didn't like the way it made me have to pee so urgently that I hadn't seen Adam enter the cabin. Now I didn't know where he or Val were.

Perhaps I didn't want to know.

What I *did* know was the alcohol was not helping my mood. I was pretty sure, after a couple of hours, I was no longer feeling the effects of that one drink. What I *was* feeling was morose.

I propped myself up against a wall in the corner of the room and sat on the bare floor. I didn't want to schmooze with anyone. I wasn't looking to have fun. I was just stuck with twenty-some-odd people in my cabin.

Nina lowered herself to the floor beside me. "What's going on?"

"Nothing."

"You're a liar now?"

"Shut up."

"Your face," she countered. "Why won't you talk to me?"

I sighed. "Val wants to force Adam to go back out with her."

Nina's eyes widened. "What? How?"

"Mind control? Charms? Magic? Who knows what the hell she does?" I snapped. "But whatever is going on, it's like the Val we've always known isn't in there. It's like she remembered she's Aphrodite."

"She's in there. She's just hurt and angry." Nina let her head drop back against the wall. "And unfortunately used to getting what she wants when it involves humans. Let me talk to her. Hopefully, I can get through. Any idea where she went?"

"I..." I was about to tell her I didn't know, and then I spotted them standing against the wall between the bedroom doorways.

Adam leaned slightly toward Val, who stared up at him adoringly. They were murmuring to each other and smiling, and she rose on her tiptoes, brushing her lips against his.

I should look away. I didn't want to witness this.

But my eyes remained fixed on the scene as Adam's eyes slid closed, his hand lowering to her waist. He pulled her closer. I remained riveted, even as I launched myself to my feet. I needed to get out of here. I needed to breathe.

Finally, I yanked my eyes away as I weaved through the

guests in the cabin, pushing and maneuvering until I'd reached the door.

A hand closed around my elbow. "Hey, Bree!" Raphael cheered, teetering on his feet, clearly drunk. He caught himself from falling, his eyes sliding to where I knew Val and Adam were kissing. He made a face and straightened his t-shirt. "Weren't we supposed to hang out? I feel like you're avoiding me."

"Maybe that's because I am?" I snapped. I was a fish flopping on the ground. Getting out of this cabin was my only way to water. "Would you stop following me around everywhere? You've moved up on my creepy scale. You're in the cushy spot between clowns and spiders."

He looked away. "Yeah, Val said you weren't as bitchy as I thought. Looks like you're both skanks." He glanced back at me, and his gaze was alight with mischief. "Hey, if you want to kill that reputation you've picked up, I can help. All you have to do is come upstairs with me and…"

I leaned in close to him and his voice trailed off.

"I need you to pay attention." I mustered my best attempt at a sensual voice, even while my heart felt bruised, and rage crashed against my temples, my view tinged crimson. "Are you listening?"

"I'm all ears, baby." He grinned, teeth like tiny pearls strung on a necklace.

"Excellent." Another centimeter closer, my eyes locked on his. "Eat shit and die."

I yanked my arm free and stormed through the door, slamming it behind me.

I plopped down onto the stairs leading up to the cabin and sent a wish out into the universe that Raphael wouldn't follow me. Perhaps I could punch him in the face if he did. By this point, he'd certainly earned it.

My eyes slid closed, but Adam kissing Val was all I saw, a

mocking vision of what I'd lost. What I'd foolishly believed I could have. But I could never have Adam. Love herself had chosen him, and even he didn't have a choice. As awful as that was, he'd loved her once. He had been happy. And I could never be sure how much of his behavior was her influence, and how much of it was him missing her.

Val was beautiful, and around most people, she was fun. She made Adam laugh all the time. He probably just realized what he'd lost, moving away from her and toward me.

I should be overjoyed for them. The feeling got stuck in my throat on the way to my heart. Tears sprang to my eyes. I sucked in a breath through my nose and held it before letting it stream back out between my lips in a screechy whistle.

A light flickered beside me, and I followed it to find a firefly hovering near my shoulder. "Stop glowing," I grumbled.

Something inside told me to go find Adam. I cursed myself for letting him become the first person I wanted to talk to when I cried. I still thought of Nina, of Dad, but I mostly wanted comfort from the boy who had hurt my heart to begin with, however inadvertently.

My chest was an excruciating void I ached to fill. Was this how Nina had felt when Reeve left? How Mom had felt when her marriage fell apart? Was Jesse the only way she'd managed to fill the emptiness?

I searched the night sky for an answer. If everything happened for a reason, had it all happened just so I could trip myself into this lesson? Because if it was, a virulent hate burned in my gut for whatever puppet master was trying to mold my life into a fable.

Val. I mean, who the hell else?

The door clicked open behind me. I wouldn't look. I didn't want to know.

"Hey. What's wrong?" Adam said.

"I'm fine." The hard edge in my tone was like a siren cutting through the silent night of his voice.

"You don't look fine."

"Then stop looking."

He knelt in front of me. "I know I screwed up."

I finally dragged my eyes up to meet his. He looked miserable, a desperation in his bright eyes I had never seen before.

"Please, Brynn. Talk to me."

"Why?" I asked. "It's not my business if you get back together with Val. It never has been." I tried to sound convincing, but the words caught in my throat, sounding choked and wrong.

He flinched, devastation written across his face, and even in my angry state, I knew this wasn't his fault.

"Look, I'm just angry. I want to be alone. You haven't done anything wrong. We're still friends."

"Yeah, no. As nice as it is that you won't hate me forever, that's not enough. We have too many things we're not saying. It might be easier that way, but it won't fix anything. We need to talk about this."

"Nah, I'm good."

"I don't know why I did it," he blurted, his hand landing on my upper arm like he was trying to hold me in place. "I...it was weird. We were talking. I was trying to patch things up with her. You know we're trying to stay friends. But I couldn't help but wonder about what you'd said earlier. So I went to find her, and we talked."

I had done this. It was like what Val had said about fate. By trying to interfere, I'd made it happen.

"She kissed me. And I kissed her back and I don't know why."

His brow was furrowed, his eyes red-rimmed and shining. It was all the confirmation I needed that this wasn't Adam still having feelings for Val, as much as the initial shock of seeing him kiss her had hurt. This was Val's ancient power exerting its will over him.

My hands curled into fists. Val didn't understand, but what she had done to Adam was an atrocious violation.

"But then I saw you," he added, "and it was like waking up. I realized what I was doing, and I stopped. I came out after you to try to explain."

"Adam, I have to tell you something." My voice came out breathy, and I shook out my hands to clear my nerves. "Val is actually——"

The door behind us clicked open, hitting the outer wall of the cabin with a bang. The light from inside silhouetted Nina's figure as she moved into the night, letting the door swing closed behind her. "There you are! I was worried."

"I thought you saw me run out here," I said.

"Not you," Nina said, sucking in a shallow breath. "Adam. I didn't see where he went when I went to flip out on Val."

"Why would you do that? We just broke up. It's not crazy that she kissed me..." He trailed off, and I wondered if maybe, somewhere deep down, he knew that wasn't true.

"But it is," Nina said, pulling in another shallow breath. "Adam, you don't understand." Another breath pulled in on a wheeze.

"Nina?" I asked.

"Do you have your pump?" Adam asked.

Nina nodded. "Inside." Her hand fluttered to her chest. "But we have to keep you away from Val."

Adam made a face. "You're crazy." He turned toward the door and tried to open it. It didn't budge. He tried again. Nothing.

"Adam?" I asked. Nina moved closer, leaning her shoulder against mine.

"What the hell?" Adam yanked on the doorknob with both

hands, bracing himself with one foot on the door frame. "It was just open!"

A raindrop fell squarely on my nose. I scrunched it, swiping at it with the back of my hand. "Maybe try knocking?"

He rolled his eyes but did what I said. As he knocked, more rain fell.

"Was it supposed to rain today?" I asked. Nina shrugged in response before launching into another stretch of coughing.

"I don't think so." Adam knocked again, then walked around the cabin, knocking at the windows, the sound barely audible over the music and chatter we could hear coming from inside.

The rain continued to come down, building like an orchestra bringing a piece to a crescendo, until sheets of water came down from the sky. Still, nobody answered the door.

"This is bullshit." He yanked out his phone, cupping a hand over it in a vain attempt to keep it safe from the deluge. The screen was already streaked with water. "No signal."

I hadn't taken mine outside with me.

Nina searched her pockets, then shook her head. "It's okay." Shallow breath. "Who else has asthma?"

"David Cohen." Adam bounced on the balls of his feet. "He's in my gym class. I think he's in cabin five."

A gust of wind almost swallowed his words. The chill it brought forced me to cram my hands in the pockets of my jeans.

"Val?" Nina rasped, rubbing her arms with her hands.

"Aphrodite doesn't control the weather. Zeus does." My stomach dropped as I uttered the words. Could Zeus be involved in this? I looked up to the slate gray sky and shivered.

"What the hell does that have to do with anything?" Adam asked.

The wind howled again, and the surrounding trees creaked and rocked.

"There's no time to explain. We have to get Nina a pump or a treatment!" I needed to yell to be heard over the sound of water cascading onto the earthen campground. "Which way is cabin five?"

He pushed his hand through his hair, water sluicing over his face, and tried to clean his glasses to no avail. "I need windshield wipers for these damn things." He jabbed a finger in my direction. "Further out that way."

I rushed in that direction.

"Wait," he called, and I stopped and looked back. The rain was so powerful I had to use my hand as a makeshift visor.

"It's too hard to see. We need to hold on to each other," he announced. On either side of me, Nina and Adam took my hands.

Cabin five was four cabins away, a seemingly endless distance, our clothes sticking to our skin, sucking sounds coming from our rain-filled shoes.

A crack split the night air. Leaves rustled. I jumped back, yanking Adam and Nina along with me. My feet slid in the mud, and the three of us fell hard into mud puddles that seeped through my shorts. A *whoosh* sang out, then an impossibly loud bang shook the ground beneath us. A tree had fallen directly between cabins eight and nine.

Right where we'd been standing moments before.

Adam erupted in a steady chorus of "shits." Nina's coughing and gasping intensified. My heart battered against my ribs, my breathing coming in rapid bursts.

"Is there another way?" I asked.

"To the cabin?" Adam shook his head.

"Where else would they have one?"

Adam's eyes lit up. "The main cabin. Registration." He scrambled to his feet and pulled me and Nina up after him. "It's just on the other side of the..."

We followed his gaze to the lake which was flooding, the water already lapping over the dock where the pedal boats were stationed.

Nina coughed long and hard, shuddering as she did. She leaned over, her hands on her thighs. Adam and I shared a concerned look over her head. We both knew we needed to get Nina to that main building. If there were medical supplies available, that's where they'd be.

"There has to be a better way," he said. "We could go around the other side. What are the chances there's a downed tree blocking that route, too?"

"Can't," Nina gasped. "Wasted time. Can't."

Adam looked to me, a question in his eyes.

Tears pricked at my eyes and my hands shook. "We took too long going this way. She doesn't have it in her to go back around. She doesn't think she can make it that far."

Adam's eyes widened. "But you think you can make it across the lake?"

Nina shrugged. Her entire body rose and fell with every breath, her lips taking on an odd color in the limited light.

"The lake it is." His eyes shone with fear. "At least the rain calmed down?"

Thank the gods for small miracles.

CHAPTER EIGHTTEEN

BREATHE AGAIN

THERE WAS no point trying to walk out onto the docks to get to the pedal boats. The water had risen over the wood planks, and the tarp-covered boats floated a few feet away, tethered to the docks by a rope. Adam walked into the water, ignoring my protests, and dragged one of the boats to where we stood on the lakeshore.

"Crap," Adam said. "I need something to cut the ties on the tarp."

The corners of Nina's mouth twitched, and she pulled a set of keys from her pocket. A bottle opener dangled from the keychain. Her hands shook, and the keys jangled. "Val's."

I nodded. "From the party."

Adam nodded back. "Nina, you step into this boat." He used the keys to cut through the ropes fastening the tarp. "I'll pedal for both of us."

Adam climbed in, and the boat bobbed in the water before it steadied out. I took Nina's hand as she stepped in. She stumbled, but Adam caught her and laid her against the seat. Her breathing was as choppy as the waters of the lake.

"What about me?" I asked, because this was dangerous, and Nina wasn't okay, and I didn't want to let either of them out of my sight.

"It will tip if anyone else gets in." He glanced around frantically. "Could you use that one?"

I followed his gaze to find a second pedal boat, as far off the other side of the dock as this one had been.

Adam took his glasses off and stuffed them in the breast pocket of his t-shirt.

"Yeah. I can do that," I said.

Adam placed the keyring in my hand and closed my fingers around it, gaze intense when it met mine. "I'll take care of her, I swear. You be careful."

With a nod, I rushed across the muddy ground, my sneakers squelching. Adam took off, pedaling as hard as he could, the boat rocking from the movement. The wind picked up as he moved, blowing the boat off course.

I thanked every god but Zeus and Aphrodite for the light coming from the main cabin, the only light available to guide our way. The camp staff must have had a backup generator.

A rumble rolled through the sky, and I picked up the pace, wading out into the water until it was up to my waist. I cut the bindings and tried to throw the tarp aside. It was heavier than I expected, and my feet slid out from under me. My ass brushed against the graveled bottom of the lake. Shoving the tarp aside, I struggled to my feet, pebbles scratching the backs of my legs. I stumbled forward to grasp the edges of the boat. Using my momentum, I launched myself over the edge and into the boat.

My knee struck the edge, and I hit the floor hard. The wind rushed out of me. Rainwater hit my face. I sputtered.

God, this is what Nina has felt like for minutes now. My heart clenched, and my nostrils burned from inhaling the lake water. I had been focusing on fixing the problem, but lying alone in the pedal boat's base, it all hit me at once. Nina could die.

I'd spent so many evenings with Angie and Roman in hospitals as Nina struggled, waiting for treatments to kick in. I'd held her hand at Scoopy Doo while waiting for an ambulance.

Later, I'd comforted her again as her parents fought with hospital staff in vain, fighting to get them to take direction from me, a minor, while they were stuck in traffic, trying to get to their little girl.

I wasn't with her now. Angie and Roman weren't there. I trusted Adam implicitly, but it wasn't enough. As much as Adam meant to me, Nina would always be my true soulmate, the one person who understood me more than anyone else ever would. It wasn't romantic love, but Nina trumped all that.

There will be boys, and they will come and go, but we are forever.

She had said that years ago. It was true. It always would be. I had trusted Adam with my greatest treasure. I hoped he understood what that meant.

I hoped I could get to her in time.

Untying the tether, I threw myself into the padded seat of the boat and pedaled as hard as I could. My wet sneaker slipped free from the pedal, the hard plastic swinging up and smacking me hard in the shin.

I'd never been good at riding a bike, either.

The rain grew heavier as I worked, and I had to squint through it to see Adam's boat. It floated in the middle of the lake, bobbing along with the force of his pedaling. Watching him, I found my rhythm.

The bright cut of lightning burned through the sky and the boom of thunder rolled through the surrounding air. My ears rang, purple and blue flashes overtaking my vision.

When it cleared, I looked for the other boat. The water near its last location sizzled and popped. Adam had only been there a moment before. On the boat, Adam's shoulders were hunched, body leaning forward, as he pedaled for his life. I pedaled like fire was at my heels. There might be, soon. I took hold of the steering mechanism.

I thought about action movies I'd seen, where heroes avoided gunfire. If Zeus was shooting lightning bolts at us from somewhere, we had to keep moving. If we stayed on a straight course, we'd be sitting ducks.

"Zig and zag, Adam!" I shouted. The wind picked up, swallowing my words, blowing my hair back and up from my face.

I prayed he thought of it on his own. There was nothing else I could do.

I pedaled faster, steering fifteen rotations to the right, fifteen straight, then fifteen to the left. Another lightning bolt hit just a couple of feet away. I shrieked, though I couldn't hear it over the echoing dullness in my ear from the thunder. My fearful twitch rocked the boat. I gripped the sides and planted my feet, stiffening. My eyes slammed shut, and I sucked in a breath in case the boat flipped over.

When a minute passed and the boat stabilized, I finally released my breath and returned to pedaling. I could barely make out Adam's boat as it touched land. I was only a few feet behind him and I pedaled faster as he disembarked in front of the main cabin.

By the time my boat made it near the dock, Adam had managed to help Nina out of theirs. I pulled myself onto the dock as Adam lifted Nina into his arms. Nina's skin, normally tawny brown, was ashen, her color drained as she continued battling for air.

I pushed myself to my feet, racing for the door so fast that I had to catch myself before I collided with the cabin's outside wall. I fumbled my way to the door, my fingers closing around the metal door handle. *Please open, please open, please open.*

The door swung open far too hard and crashed against the side of the cabin.

"We need a medic!" I screamed into the dimly lit front office, holding the door open for Adam and Nina.

By the time I entered the door behind them, two people had rushed out toward us, a woman coming from the back hallway and a man who was stationed at the front desk.

"She needs a nebulizer treatment!" I shouted.

"Follow me," the woman called in an authoritative voice. She rushed back down the hallway she'd come from and into a room. When the three of us caught up to her, she was already putting the medicine into the nebulizer, preparing it for Nina. "Lay her down on the table."

Adam did as he was told, and I took Nina's limp hand in mine. Her chest rose and fell rapidly, her stomach along with it, and it was only a moment before the woman who called us in handed a tube-like apparatus to Nina. The end facing her emitted a vapor of asthma medication, and Nina sucked it in.

It took five deep breaths of the vapor medication for her to stop the full body breathing she was doing. After what only amounted to five to ten minutes, but felt like hours, Nina's breathing steadied, and her skin regained color.

"I put two doses of albuterol in the nebulizer," the woman, Medic Garcia based on the name on her badge, told us as she busied herself with checking Nina's vitals. "Thankfully, we were notified of your asthma and prepared accordingly. You took your inhaler, and this still happened?"

"No," I said. "We walked out of our cabin for a minute, and the door got locked behind us. She hadn't taken her inhaler outside. And then the storm started. I knocked on the cabin's door, but nobody answered. It took us a while to get here."

Medic Garcia glanced at Adam, her eyebrow raised, before looking back to me. "That's your story?"

I nodded and hoped I looked as confident as I pretended to be. "That's my story."

"Because, you know, it could be possible that you guys snuck out for a party outside before the rain started, and that's how you ended up in this predicament. And if it was, and there were other people out there…"

"It was just us," Nina said with a gasp. "Just the three of us."

The medic nodded, then pushed a stool over to me. "She's

obviously got this bed. Now I need to figure out what the hell we're going to do with the two of you until the storm stops. You're not going back out in that." She moved out of the room, her combat boots clunking across the floor.

I lowered myself onto the stool, rolling it closer to the bed. "Hey." I brushed my fingers across the crown of Nina's head, smoothing out the soaking wet curls. "Better?"

Nina smiled, still breathing in the vapor, her eyelids flagging. "Better. Tired."

A warm weight landed on my shoulder. Adam's fingers gently squeezed. "She's shaking," he murmured.

"It's the medicine. It makes her jittery. And the work her body has done keeping her alive exhausts her."

I squeezed Nina's hand again, and she flashed me another fatigued smile. "Heroes, you two." Her body shook with laughter she fought to restrain for fear of making her breathing worse. "You did good."

I didn't bother arguing that Adam and I had done what anyone would do in the same circumstances. I'd had that argument with her before. Nina and I were more than friends-we were family.

We sat with her until Medic Garcia returned, carrying a stack of clothing and linens.

"Here's the deal," she announced with the same commanding tone she'd used earlier. "I've brought you two of our ranch uniforms. Go to the bathrooms to get changed so you're not in sopping wet clothes all night. Then go to the third room on your right. There are two cots in there for you. I'll help Nina change, stay with her, and monitor her vitals. Does that work for you kids?"

"Yes ma'am," Adam said.

She handed us each a uniform, a pillow, and a blanket. Then she grabbed a clipboard from a table covered in containers of first aid supplies and stacks of paperwork. "And your names are?"

"Brynn Stark and Adam Hernandez." I had a feeling that taking our names down wasn't the best sign.

"Noted," she said.

Adam and I said goodnight to Nina and went about following Medic Garcia's list of steps. The room she directed us to had two cots placed along opposite, empty walls. Adam strolled to the cot on the far end but turned to face me just before he reached it.

"I'm sorry. This whole night has been so damn strange. I mean, everything was weird since I got to your cabin, but the lightning bolts were the weirdest part. I mean, it was like they were out to get us. Like the damn weather was out to get us. Because lightning does not strike like that. It simply does not." He pushed his hands through his hair roughly. "And I sound crazy."

"No. You don't sound crazy." I leaned back against my cot. "It's that Val is Aphrodite."

Adam looked up, his mouth twisted into an unfamiliar expression. "Right, Val played Aphrodite in our presentation."

"No. Val *is* Aphrodite," I said. "And I know this sounds crazy, and there's no such thing, but hear me out. Val was determined to set me up, and we didn't know why, right?"

Adam nodded.

"It turned out it was because she can read people's emotional matches, and she found one she wasn't happy about. So she started moving us like chess pieces. She confessed her true identity to Nina and me." I shook my head. "I think the storm was caused by Zeus. Maybe he's pissed we left Val at the party, but—"

"—those lightning strikes were pretty targeted," Adam finished for me, the words dribbling freely as if they had escaped.

"And the tree," I said. "Right in our path."

"So what you're saying...is...Greek gods are real." His eyes were wide, unblinking.

"Yes."

For a moment, time moved like a thick viscous liquid, and Adam said nothing.

"Of all the world mythology, the Greek gods are real," Adam said, his voice even. "And Val is one of them. Wait, not only one of them, Val is *the* person, nope, sorry, goddess, that caused the Trojan War. We did a presentation on the Trojan War with Aphrodite herself."

I nodded, gazing pleadingly at him. I didn't know what I'd do if he didn't believe me.

"I broke Aphrodite's heart," Adam said, "and this was something you've casually known for a while now?"

"Well, I didn't know you were going to break her heart."

His lips pursed, his gaze hardening. He wrapped his hand around the crucifix dangling from his neck. Usually it rested under his shirt, like he forgot it was there. It had landed on top of the maroon uniform polo. "Dad's gonna be so disappointed."

"I'm not sure the existence of Aphrodite and Zeus disproves any other religious beliefs. I didn't ask Val when she sprung it on me."

"Yeah, I wouldn't imagine you would," Adam said. "Val is Aphrodite." He nodded slowly, then, "Val is Aphrodite?!"

"Yes. Valentina. So close to Valentine. She hid a clue in her own damn name."

His brow furrowed. "She told you this?"

"She showed me," I corrected. "She used her... abilities. She changed her appearance on a whim. Nina saw it too. I'm not crazy."

"I never said you were crazy." He released his crucifix. "What else can she do?" He winced and glanced behind him for the edge of the cot. He settled against it, his breaths coming out in puffs of air. The cot creaked beneath his weight, sliding backwards. He barely reacted.

"Are you okay?" I stepped toward him.

"Answer the question, Brynn." The words were sharp, a tone I wasn't used to him using with me.

I blinked back my shock. "Um... she can influence people..."

Adam paled even further.

I knew he wasn't upset because his worldview was knocked off course. It was because he thought Val had forced him to date her.

"Only for a short time," I added. "Not for months. You would have wondered why you were dating her. I think that's why Tony Lin changed his mind about me so fast."

Adam nodded for a long time, his eyes flitting around as he wiped his palms repeatedly on his jeans. "So, I wouldn't have dated her..."

"You would have known you didn't actually want to," I said. "But you did. You did want to, didn't you?" I took another step closer. I needed to hear the truth.

"Yes. Yes, I wanted to. At first." He met my eyes. "I care about her. Always will. But it wasn't what I thought it was. *She* wasn't who I thought she was. She was one person when we were getting to know each other. And then, when she was in her element, she... changed. She lived for attention, no matter who gave it to her. She flounced and flaunted. And I've always... well, I've never liked people like that."

Did he like the opposite? The question came to mind unbidden.

"But I still liked her. So I stayed. I tried to temper it."

"Why?" I hated myself for the edge that crept into my voice, getting sharper with every word. "I don't get it. I don't get it!"

Adam flinched. "What's there to get?"

"Why did you break up with Val?" I was sick of this, and angry, so damn angry, the heat of it licking its way along my face, lighting my cheeks with burning red. I was tired of the run-around. I was tired of Adam sending me mixed signals. I was tired of running from gods. I was tired of all of it. The burn spread, the tips of my ears so warm I could light a candle off them.

His eyebrows raised, and he turned his gaze on me, his cheeks flushed red. "She didn't tell you?"

"I know what you said and what she believes. I don't know which one is true. Did you lie to her?" It was an accusation, but hope sprouted deep within, tangling with vines of guilt.

Adam sighed. "You're angry at me?"

"Are you going to ask me questions without answering any of mine?" I wanted to stomp my feet, lose control like a child. He could be so frustrating sometimes.

He scrubbed his hands over his face before looking up at me through pained eyes. "You *are* angry."

"Also not an answer."

His head dropped back, his eyes searching the ceiling as though he'd find answers carved up there. "I broke up with her because I didn't like what she was doing to you." He released the information in a huff of air. "I didn't like that she was setting you up in these situations you didn't want to participate in, dressing you in clothes you didn't want to wear. She was being an enormous busybody and messing with your life like you were her puppet. The more I saw of what she put you through, the less I wanted her around. The less I liked her."

His answer nearly choked me, but I pushed forward, needing to see this through to the end, to understand what we were, what we weren't. "So, you told her the truth, but she saw what she wanted to see, and she was way off base."

He leaned forward, his head dropping into his hands, fingers spearing through his dark curls and tugging at the ends. He was silent for a long moment.

Would it really be that bad to bolt out into the storm? It couldn't be worse than staying in here.

"Not *way* off base."

My spark of hope reignited. "So, just a little off base?"

He pushed himself to his feet, the cot making an awful screeching noise that left me wincing. One step closer, and his eyes narrowed into that appraising look I always got from him. He watched me, and I wasn't sure what he saw, but he took a deep calming breath.

"Not off base. Not at all."

I swallowed hard. "Not off base?"

Another step closer. "No."

"So you..." I couldn't get the words out. I had demanded an answer, and now that I'd received one, I didn't know what to do with it. I was elated and overwhelmed, and suddenly very aware of my skin.

"Yes." Another step.

"And me?" My voice cracked. *Loser.*

"Is that what you want?" His voice was low, gravelly, and it moved through me, joining the blood rushing through my veins, pounding in my ears.

"You answered another question with a question."

"Does that bother you?" That delicious smirk of his overtook his face, and I half wanted to shake him for being so frustrating.

The other half... wanted things I'd never wanted before. Yearned for them.

I swallowed hard. "Why are you acting like this?"

"You just answered *my* question with a question." Another step.

"Yeah. What are you gonna do about it?" I raised my eyebrows.

He dove forward, taking my face in his hands, and held me there, his nose brushing mine, breath hot against my lips. "How 'bout this?"

"I'm game," I murmured breathlessly.

His lips brushed mine gently. Just once. A tiny tease of a

kiss. But it swelled my heart until it felt like my heart was all of me, easily bruised by the slightest wrong movement. My hands shook at my sides.

He moved forward again, this kiss firmer as his hands fell to my waist, gently tugging me closer. I slid my arms around his neck as I opened my mouth to him, my fingers tangling in the curls at the nape of his neck.

Wait. I couldn't just let this happen. I needed to understand what Adam wanted. I'd lost my anti-love battle the day he drove me to the airport. I'd known what was happening. I'd known, and I'd let Val do her work, hoping she could convince me to love somebody else, anybody but Adam.

Val had said love was worth any risk. And I believed that I loved Nina. In the end, I'd loved Nina enough that I couldn't risk loving Adam. Because then I would have hurt Val. And Val was Nina's family. So I ran away as hard and as fast as I could.

But I couldn't stop loving him, and I had to stop running.

I pulled back, the taste of his lips lingering on mine, as I pressed my forehead to his. Our breaths mingled in the air between us, and he wiggled his nose to move his glasses back into place. The motion was so cute, so incredibly *Adam* that I nearly kissed him again. I compromised, nipping at his nose instead.

He let out a warm chuckle. "I feel like I've wanted this forever."

Warmth spread through me, and for a moment it was difficult to speak. "And what is this? This thing between us?"

"Honestly?" he asked.

I raised my eyebrow. "Is there another way you're ever supposed to answer me?"

"Point taken." He took my hands in mine. "It feels kinda like magic. The kind I barely believed in before."

CHAPTER NINETEEN
FALLOUT

THE HEAT of the morning sun spread through the room, waking me. The storm must have moved on, which meant a return to reality, a chance to assess the fallout from the night before. I didn't want to do any of that, because as I lay on an old rickety cot that squeaked and screeched with my every movement, Adam was beside me.

He was beautiful when he slept, and I tried to memorize everything about him. The weight and heat of his arm curled around my waist. His hair, normally a curly but uniform mass, was now doing things an anime character could only dream of. He had unwisely fallen asleep with his glasses on (*I just want to look at you and actually see you, so I can convince myself you're really here*), and they were now pushed up and out from his face at a bizarre angle.

Adam had a somewhat large nose, but it fit his face. When he started to fall asleep, he'd woken himself with his own low snore. It made me want to pull him even closer. His lips were full, and his kisses were soft. But his morning breath was rancid enough to make me wince and observe him from a safer distance.

His clothes were rumpled. We'd lain down together on the cot with the blanket over us, but now it only covered our feet. Our legs were entangled, my head resting on his arm. I had never been this close to a human being that wasn't family for this long before.

I liked it, because this human being was Adam.

I cuddled a little closer, and he roused enough to pull me in, his arm tightening around my waist. It felt real and right, and I couldn't bring myself to regret any of it.

I may have screwed up with Val——with potentially dangerous consequences——but I knew I couldn't let go of Adam.

He stirred, eyes cracking open, and let out a pleased little hum. He caressed my cheek and pressed a chaste kiss to my lips. "Good morning, Brynn."

"Good morning." I smiled. "No regrets?" We'd only made out, but I needed to be sure he was truly in this.

"None. At. All." Another peck on the lips. "Don't ask stupid questions."

"You shouldn't be here." The strident voice of a ranch employee speaking from the other side of the closed door cut into our moment.

Adam and I exchanged curious glances.

"You should have waited until we declared travel safe ag—"

We scrambled upright. My feet caught in the sheet as I pushed myself out of the bed with my arms. I nearly flew sideways, but Adam caught me by both arms, his body thrown halfway across the cot.

"I know," another voice, thin and reedy, joined in. This one I recognized. Oh *god*, how I knew that voice. It was uncharacteristically bashful. "But I had to make sure my girl was safe. Stupid teenager, I know."

Adam was still pulling me onto the cot when the door opened.

"Brynn..." Raphael stood in the doorway, his eyes wide, mouth slightly open. He cleared his throat. "I've been searching for you. I wanted to make sure you were alright, because all anybody knew yesterday was that you three had gone out for air and then you never came back." He glanced from me and Adam sprawled across the cot to the other clearly unused cot in the room. "It's good to see you're safe." His words came out flat, empty.

I shrugged, not about to act guilty. I had done nothing wrong to Raphael, and maybe this would finally get my lack of interest in him through his thick skull.

"Didn't the guy at the front desk call to tell anyone where we were?" Adam asked.

"Gee, I thought you were out in that storm, dumbass," Raphael snapped. "It brought down a tree, and you think the phones are A-OK?"

Adam nodded, considering it. "Makes sense." He glanced at me. "Don't ever talk to me about important things before I've had my morning coffee."

I grinned. "Actually, that seems like it's *exactly* when I should talk to you about important stuff."

"I'm... gonna... go tell everyone you're all okay." Raphael bolted out of the doorway, pushing past the frowning ranch employee.

She made a face, something between pity and disapproval. "Sorry about that. I wouldn't have let him back here if I'd realized you were... otherwise engaged." She backed out the door, patting it. "I'm gonna leave this open from now on, understood?" She disappeared from our view.

I facepalmed. This looked *great*.

"Do you think he's jealous?" Adam asked, a smirk playing at the corner of his lips as he sat up, pulling me up with him.

"Doubtful," I said. "If anything, he's pissed because he didn't win the 'first to date Brynn Stark' prize he thought he was going to get for chasing me."

"And that has nothing to do with actually wanting to date you?" Adam asked, eyeing me warily.

I shrugged.

"I want to date you," he said, his wary look morphing into a frown. "You're aware, right?"

"I guess. Still haven't figured out why." The words were out of my mouth before I could stop them. "I shouldn't be surprised, really. Second place to my parent's arguments, second place to Nina once Val showed up, second place to Val with you…"

His frown became a glare. "You're second place to nobody, Brynn. Not to your parents, not to Nina, and definitely not to me."

Heat rose to my cheeks, and I ducked my head, stood up, and adjusted my clothes. "I don't know why I said that."

"I know why," Adam said, "but I think you're getting over it."

"What?" I asked.

"Whatever makes you hate yourself."

"Not you, too."

"Val wasn't wrong about that part." He rolled off the cot and straightened his clothes. "You hide. It's one thing to wear baggy clothes and all black. That's cool. It's another to walk with your eyes to the floor, or to feel like you don't have a permanent place in people's lives."

I swallowed hard. "It's not that I—" But it kind of was.

"Hey." He put a finger to my lips. "You don't have to explain to me. You don't have to change if you don't want to. I love who you are, and if I'm honest, I've crushed on you from way back. I've always known how amazing you are. But a little soul-searching might be in order."

I stared back at him, my thoughts snagging on one word. *Love.*

"Or…you know…not." He shrugged. "I'm not trying to dude-splain your life to you. I'm just trying to help."

"I love you, too." It was a whisper, almost a squeak. And it made him light up like the city skyline.

A loud rap on the door frame made us both jump and whirl in its direction. Coach Perl glared at us in all her scowling glory.

"Coach," Adam said, "it's *very* good to see you."

Coach Perl looked pointedly at the other, clearly untouched cot. "I'm sure it is... Anyway, I'm glad you're safe. Thank you both for getting Lopez to safety after her asthma attack."

"You're welcome, Coach." I smiled the biggest smile I'd ever managed to give an authority figure; it was pretty weak.

"Yes, that was great." She wrinkled her nose slightly. "How you were discovered in here, coupled with the fact that you were both at a party with liquor, is another thing entirely."

Adam winced. "We didn't drink."

I could have corrected him, but it didn't seem like a good time.

"That's beside the point, Hernandez." She leaned against the door, shrugging helplessly. "We called your parents the minute the phones came back online. There will be consequences for your involvement."

"Can we get bonus points for helping others?" I asked. "Like ten points for Gryffindor?"

"No."

Yeah, I didn't think so.

COACH PERL USHERED us out into the cafeteria on the other side of the cabin. There were other kids, all people who had taken part in the party the night before, most of whom I knew nothing about except for their names. They were clustered around the long tables, some standing, some sitting on the benches.

Adam and I chose the emptiest space on the far end of the

room. We climbed onto the benches and sat on top of the table. Nina joined us soon afterward and straddled the bench we were resting our feet on. She looked better than she had yesterday, although exhausted.

After a while, Val walked in. The smile she wore was tentative as she crossed the room to our table.

"Hey there, goddess," Adam practically snarled.

Val started, her eyes going wide. "Goddess? Well, that's a new and interesting little pet name you've cooked up." She giggled, but it was high-pitched and ugly.

"Right. We'll go with that." He crossed his arms over his chest. "How are you feeling this morning?"

Val pouted, choosing to sit as we did on the table facing us. "Hungover. And cranky."

"Poor baby," Adam said. "Nina almost died last night."

Val's head snapped up. "What do you mean?"

"It's self-explanatory," he said. "We all almost died last night, but Nina came the closest."

"Whoa. I wouldn't say I almost died." Nina held up a hand.

"No?" he asked. "Not from the asthma attack? Or the fallen tree? Or the trip across a lightning lit lake?"

Nina's mouth snapped shut.

"I'm still trying to figure out how you managed it all," he hissed. "You're the goddess of love, not the goddess of locked doors."

Val's gaze hardened, and she responded in the same harsh whisper. "I made the women of Lemnos emit a stench that frightened away their husbands and stoked the fires of anger that made them kill their men. I made Echo disappear, so that only the sound of her voice could be heard. And those are only the stories that made it in the mythology books. Still, you believe a locked door and bad cell reception are out of my purview? Foolish wretch."

"Heartless witch," Adam grumbled under his breath.

"Hey!" Val squeaked, losing her previous fire. "I heard that!"

Adam leaned forward, his gaze venomous. "You were supposed to. Doesn't it bother you that you nearly killed us?"

"Of course it does!"

I placed a restraining hand on Adam's shoulder, in case Adam had forgotten exactly who he was dealing with.

"Yes, Adam," Val said. "Heed your beloved's advice."

"Yes, Val," Adam mocked. "You're the wronged one here. You're the one who nearly died, right? No. You have a killer hangover and got to enjoy a fun party."

Val flinched and sucked in a shaky breath. Her eyes flitted around the room, finally landing on her white beaded sandals. Her voice dropped to a whisper. "I made a mess of things. I know that. I didn't create the storm. I asked Father to help me. I meant for him to take me home. I was just sad and I... didn't want to be here anymore."

"Take you home?" Nina asked. "You were just... gonna... leave?"

Adam's expression softened. "Why?"

"I hate it down here. Everything is so hard." Val kicked her foot out. "Not... I mean... I had two choices from the beginning. I could keep my distance, or I could blend in. And for so long, I took the first choice. I tried to be Aphrodite, living among the mortals. But over time, I started to care. You were silly children who didn't understand how the world worked, but despite that, you took risks, and you felt so much. I wanted to feel that. And I... I started to... but it wasn't enough."

I scooted closer to Val, resting a hand on hers where it gripped the edge of the table. "How wasn't it enough?"

"I love Angie and Roman, but Nina is their daughter. I love Nina, but you're her best friend, Brynn. And I love Adam, but... he doesn't love me, does he?" She shook her head, fat tears rolling over her cheeks. "The goddess of love, and I can't seem to grasp it, can't seem to capture it for my own. I can only see it in the air. Can only see the perfect matches I can't have. And remain second best."

An ache spread through my chest. Hadn't I said nearly the same thing to Adam? And Val, the one person in the world I assumed would never understand me, felt the same way. We just coped differently.

"Val," Adam said, "you have love. We all love you. Maybe not the way you want, but we do."

Val glanced up at him, her eyes glistening.

"Brynn Stark?" Principal Bowen's voice boomed across the cafeteria.

My head shot up. There, standing beside Mr. Bowen, looking frightened and frazzled, were Uncle Josh and my parents.

"SO, you're set up in the manager's office." Uncle Josh lifted a gold nameplate that named "Josie Farnsworth" as the manager. He flipped it over in his hands a few times before returning it to the desk. "What happens if the manager needs to... manage?"

"Joshua, this is no time for snark," Mom hissed at him, as though she could somehow go unheard by Mr. Bowen sitting two feet away.

"It's always time for snark," Josh and I said in unison. We exchanged a glance, and he smiled. It made the thumping of my pulse in my ears a little quieter.

Dad gave me a warning look from the other side of Josh, and a part of me had to laugh that they were so chickenshit about being around each other that they placed Josh between them. Hell, that was probably the only reason Josh was here—so Mom and Dad wouldn't have had to take the two-hour drive to the ranch without a buffer. It was like when I mediated their conversations. God forbid they sucked it up and dealt with each other.

Mr. Bowen's eyebrow inched up the dark skin of his bald head. "I suppose we should get to the matter at hand."

"Of course, sir," Dad said, using the contained, clipped tone he only ever used with business associates. "It appears you have quite a few students to get through today."

To get through made us sound like we were walking up to put our heads on a chopping block.

"Yes, unfortunately," Mr. Bowen intoned. "Brynn, could you please explain to your parents how you ended up here instead of your cabin during the storm?"

My hand twitched, almost forming into a fist, but I took a deep breath to calm myself. "There was a party in my cabin."

"Brynn," Dad groaned.

"And how long beforehand did you know there would be a party there?" Mr. Bowen asked.

"Around the time of the campfires," I lied. "Some of the drinks going around were spiked."

"Did you drink, Brynn?" Mom asked. I was getting tired of hearing my own name.

Josh opened his mouth to talk, but a vicious look from Dad caused it to shut with a clack.

"I had one drink," I said.

"You took a drink from a stranger." Mom sighed. "We taught you better than that."

"We did," Dad agreed. "Which is why it wasn't a stranger, right? Was it Val?"

Shit. "I'm not looking to point fingers."

"It was Val," Dad confirmed.

"Anyway, the party happened, and I didn't want to be there. I got upset at Val for... something... and I stormed out." I wiped my sweaty palms on my jeans. "I didn't expect them to, but Adam and Nina came out after me."

"Where were you going?" Mr. Bowen asked.

"To get some air. There were a lot of people in that little cabin, and I was upset, and…"

"Brynn likes to go for long walks when she's upset," Mom said tersely.

"Yes, I went for a long walk out the door and then plopped on the welcome mat, basically." I frowned at her. "Adam, Nina, and I talked, but Nina started having an asthma attack. It wasn't until we went to get her pump that we realized we were locked out of the cabin. And then the crazy rainstorm started. I don't know why no one heard us, but we knocked for a long time. Nina was still having her attack, so we cut our losses and found our way here. A fallen tree blocked one of the roads, so we took the boats across the lake."

"God, kid, you could have been killed," Josh said.

Dad slid his hand into mine.

"Yeah, but *Nina*," I said, by way of explanation. "She only came outside to help me. I had to make sure she was safe."

"And Adam helped you," Dad clarified.

"Yes."

"Speaking of Mr. Hernandez," Mr. Bowen said, "please complete your story, Ms. Stark."

My nose wrinkled in confusion. "Um, yeah, okay. We got here to the cabin, and they gave Nina a treatment. Then Adam and I went into the visitor room to sleep."

Mr. Bowen turned his attention to my parents. "At first we couldn't find any of the children and searched all the cabins. That was how we learned about the party." Mr. Bowen leaned forward slightly, his hands folded tightly on the desk. "When a student found Ms. Stark here, she was sharing one of the two cots in the visitor room with Mr. Hernandez."

Oh no. Oh my God.

Dad blinked. "Excuse me?"

I glared at Mr. Bowen. "Do you hate me? What have I ever done to you?"

He offered a kind smile in return. "Telling your parents isn't meant to be a punishment. It is our role as your guardians on this trip to be sure your parents are informed of anything they would want to know, anything that could potentially put you in danger."

"Sleeping is dangerous?" I spat.

"I'm assuming they were clothed. Correct?" Josh said, because thank Mt. Olympus for Josh.

"We were clothed," I said before anybody else decided to weigh in. "Can we continue this discussion anywhere but here?"

"Yes, please do." Mr. Bowen waved a dismissive hand. "I am aware there will probably be consequences handed down by each student's family. However, the school needs to hand out its own punishment for the party. Therefore, every senior that was in that cabin or not in their assigned cabin when we came looking for them this morning will not be attending prom."

"I understand." I hadn't planned to go, anyway. I had forgotten to buy a dress once Reeve broke up with Nina. Who knew if Val still intended to go, given her relationship status with Adam.

Mr. Bowen nodded. "Your parents have already packed up your room. You're free to go. Thank you all for coming on such short notice. If you could, please show the Lopez family back here."

"Thank you, Mr. Bowen," Dad said, standing and straightening his suit.

That's when I realized he was wearing a *suit*. We had interrupted him at work with this insanity.

"We're truly sorry for the inconvenience," Mom said, eyeing me as though I was the cause of said inconvenience.

Josh's hand landed on my shoulder, and I glanced at him, but his eyes were directed at Mom and Dad, a frown firmly in place.

"And Brynn," Mr. Bowen said. "Please exercise better judgment in the future. Soon you'll be on your own, making your own choices."

I nodded, but it felt wooden and wrong. I still couldn't understand what I'd done wrong, aside from not tattling on my friends. By most teenager's standards, I was still a goody-goody rule follower——even with the one alcoholic beverage and the smooches.

We headed out of the office and walked down the hall in silence until we reached the room where everyone else was gathered and waiting. It was only a matter of time before we found Angie and Roman, deep in an animated discussion with Val and Nina.

"Excuse me, Angie, Roman," Mom said as we approached. "I'm sorry to interrupt. Mr. Bowen is ready for you."

Angie's eyes slid to Nina and Val, then back to us. "Thank you. I'll call you when we get home, Chelsea."

"Thank you," Mom said, before turning and steering us all toward the exit.

I searched through the crowd of teenagers and their angry, disapproving parents until I found Adam. He sat on a bench, looking up at his father. William glared down at him, hands on his hips, expression darker than any I'd ever seen him wear. Adam motioned wildly with his hands, eyes wide with alarm. He was probably trying to explain how someone like him had somehow gotten sucked into this mess of a rebellion.

As Mom led me through the door, Adam caught my eye. Desperation and regret shone in his rich brown eyes as I was nudged out into the suffocating warmth of the summer air.

Mom wrapped her fingers around my wrist and all but dragged me to Dad's car, Dad and Josh following closely behind.

"Shotgun!" Josh raced to the passenger side of the car as Dad unlocked the doors.

"Really?" I shouted after him. "You suck so bad."

"Hey." He peeked over the car roof with a twinkle in his eye.

"It's your fault I rode out here by myself with them. Deal with the consequences."

"Yes," Mom deadpanned. "The consequences. Sitting next to me on the way home."

I shrugged, then slid into the back behind Josh.

We got settled in the back of the car, and Dad maneuvered the car onto the highway. For a while, I watched in silence, taking a second to calm the nerves that had been jumping since the night before when the door to the cabin wouldn't open. Even my brief respite with Adam had been interrupted by me waking several times to my panicked, racing heart.

"I have to ask," Mom said. "I know you don't want me to, but I have to."

"Nothing happened between…" I stopped myself. That was a lie I couldn't explain my way out of.

"Brynn?" Dad's eyebrows raised, his eyes searching as he glanced into the rearview mirror. The look was stern, but there was a softness to it, and I began to trust that I wouldn't be locked in for the rest of my life if I told him the truth. If he believed it.

"We made out," I blurted. "Just a little."

"So I guess Val figured out why she couldn't hook you up with anybody?" Dad asked.

I sighed. Because how could I really respond to a question like that?

Josh coughed a laugh, then straightened in his seat.

Mom glared at him before her eyes dropped on me like an anvil. "Just a little? On a cot?"

"There wasn't anywhere else comfortable to sit? And then we went to sleep. That's it."

Mom sunk back in her seat, her eyes searching the car interior as though it had somehow wronged her. "How many times have I talked to you about appearances?"

"I didn't sleep with him," I said. "I... slept with him. Um... next to... him."

"That doesn't matter!" Mom snapped.

"Really, I think it does," Dad said. "There's a big difference."

"And she's nearly an adult," Josh chimed in. "I'd be more concerned about whether she knew how to be safe about sex, not about whether or not she *had* sex."

"Stop talking," Mom said as if shooing away a pest. "You're not her parent."

"Josh raises a good point." Dad's eyes flicked to me in the rearview with all the superiority of an eye-to-eye Dad-Glare. "Were you safe about it?"

"I didn't have sex!" I screamed. I closed my eyes and took a deep breath. Then, softer, "But if I had, I would have been safe about it."

"I guess we should be thankful for that," Mom deadpanned. "Don't mind me. I'll just be over here having an existential crisis."

"Oh grow up, Chels," Josh grumbled. "Brynn is nearly eighteen. His normally jovial voice was edged with steel.

Mom practically growled at him before turning her attention back to me. "Isn't Adam Valentina's boyfriend? Can you explain that? And while you're at it, you can tell me where I went wrong as a mother."

"She doesn't have that much time, Chels," Josh muttered.

"They broke up," I said.

"Before or after last night?" Mom sat up a little straighter, dagger-eyes aimed my way. "I just want to see how much of a hypocrite I'm dealing with. Did you even wait until Adam and Val were over before swooping in?"

"Did Jesse?" The retort flew from my mouth before I could stop to think about the harm those words would cause Dad. I bit my tongue against anything worse, but Dad still cringed.

It was like the air was sucked from the car. We were puddles of still water, cordoned off from each other, untouched in our loneliness, in our inability to connect, to flow together.

But Josh... Josh was never still.

"You know," he said quietly. "And God help me, I never thought I'd say this. But Chelsea has a point."

"What?" Mom whipped her head in his direction.

"It's not exactly the same. There are enough similarities between what happened with them and what happened with you, Adam, and Val that it should make you think a bit. Like maybe you can see where they were coming from? Why this situation was so hard."

Dad muttered something from the driver's seat.

Josh chuckled. "It's true, whether you like the parallel or not."

I swallowed hard, trying to moisten a throat that was as dry as the humor in a Neil Gaiman novel. My stomach twisted, my heart constricting in my chest as I turned it over and observed the situation from all sides.

"I don't like that parallel because I don't like Jesse." I turned to Mom. "Because the big difference here isn't whether or not you and Dad separated. It wasn't the cheating. I should have been more important. You should have been thinking about how catching you like that would affect me." I sighed. "I was already frustrated with you anyway, which didn't help." I looked down at my lap, picking at a frayed thread on my shorts. "I like Adam for the same reason I get along so well with Josh and Dad. For the same reason I love Nina, and for the same reason I don't get along with Val. Because it's nice to not be judged for everything you do. And the day I walked in on you and Jesse, I learned you expect a level of 'decorum' from me that you don't even expect from yourself. And that's just not fair."

Mom sighed. "I screwed up. I've already said it to your father, but I'll say it again. Ian, I'm sorry. I shouldn't have let things get so out of hand. I should have talked to you both long before things got so far with Jesse."

Dad made a noise low in his throat. "The truth is, one of us should have cracked and gotten a divorce years ago instead of the bullheaded silent competition we engaged in." He glanced into the rearview, his eyes meeting mine. "I'm not mad about Jesse. I told you that. You shouldn't be either. And based on what your mom's told us, he isn't going anywhere. You're going to have to learn how to put this behind you and move forward with both of them."

Mom turned to me. "You never should have walked in on what you did. And you certainly never should have felt you had to be someone else to be loved. I know I can be a little quick to correct you—"

"She's like that with everyone," Josh supplied.

Mom made a face at him. "—but you are still my number one girl. No matter who you choose to be."

"You have a strange way of showing that," I said. "For instance, maybe don't look at me like it's a miracle if I dress up a little."

"But you are a miracle," she teased, nudging my side. "Even in all black and jeans."

I glared at her.

"Okay, okay, I get your point." She paused, drumming her fingers on the seat between us. "I didn't see it the way you did. I like when you dress up because it gives us something in common. And we used to have a lot of that, but you grew up and then... there was less." She offered me a sheepish smile. "From now on, I'll be more careful about celebrating the things we don't have in common, too."

The weight in my chest felt strange, as though Mom had lifted some of it.

I had been so ready to attack Mom because I didn't like how judgmental she could be, so ready to attack Val because I didn't like how similar they were, that I never stopped to look at them as people. Real people with real, breakable hearts.

I never imagined a simple apology and a promise to do better could do so much.

"We're not perfect," I said, a wry smile on my lips. "But we're all better than Jesse."

Mom shot me a warning glance.

"Alright, alright, I'll try to be nicer to him."

"He's a decent guy. I wanted you to like him. And he wanted you to like him because it's what I wanted," she said. "We talked after you moved in with your father. We'll try to be less... demanding." She brushed a hand through my hair, her fingers playing with the edges of my bangs.

"We all need to figure out how to get along," Dad said, "for your sake. Even if sometimes we want to bite each other's heads off."

"And we still will," Mom said. "We fought all the way over here. But we all decided you're more important than that. I want you to be able to come to us. Both of us."

"And to your cool Uncle Josh when they're too lame to understand," Josh teased.

Mom laughed. "Please try to avoid that."

"Please," Dad echoed.

"Yeah, fuck the both of you."

"Language," Mom said, but the word cracked in the middle like she realized it was a silly thing to say. "So... tell me about Adam..."

I had to take a moment to catch my breath. I needed this. I smiled. Then I told Mom all about Adam.

CHAPTER TWENTY

THE SENIOR EXPERIANCE

WE WERE ESSENTIALLY on house arrest until Wednesday. No hanging out, no cell phones, nothing. All communication took place through our parents. Dad had called William so he could let Adam know he couldn't call me until my phone privileges were returned on Thursday.

William had assured Dad that Adam and I were in the same boat. Mom had been in touch with Angie and Roman, and Nina was right there with us. Val's situation was understandably worse. As the ringleader of the party, she was grounded indefinitely, only allowed out for school and her shifts at Scoopy Doo.

I was worried, mostly because of Val. While I was still angry about her part in all of this, our talk with her while we waited for our parents had made me feel bad for her. She screwed up, yes, and she was a mess, but had she really meant to hurt anyone? Or was her view of the world just so skewed she hadn't realized what she was doing?

I also worried about Angie and Roman. If Val wanted to get out of being grounded, she would, whether or not Angie and Roman wanted her to.

By the time Thursday rolled around, I had caught up on the latest Leigh Bardugo duology and a solid Patrick Ness novel and reorganized my bookshelf. Again. I also spent loads of time watching grimy reality television with Josh that made me consider dragging him to a support group. If that was how he entertained himself, he had problems.

I was actively trying not to think about the prom, the last great senior activity before graduation, which would contain: people, which I hated; a cheesy Enchanted Forest theme, which I hated; dancing, which I hated; and a crucial part of "the senior experience," which I sort of wanted in spite of myself. It was tonight, and I was not allowed to go.

Either way, being angry at Val wouldn't bring back prom to me or the rest of the sad sacks who had been caught in our cabin. So, I dedicated myself to the task of picking out my next book. I had just settled on an author whose previous work I loved when a knock sounded on the front door.

When I'd last been downstairs, Josh had been hard at work, his laptop perched on the edge of his recliner, and Dad had been cooking dinner. With a groan, I rolled out of bed and onto my feet. "I got it!" I called, jogging down the stairs.

When I opened the door, my heart hiccupped. Adam leaned against the doorway, a tentative smile on his face. Behind him, Nina and Gabe carried stacks of boxes and garment bags.

"W-what are you doing here?"

Adam stuffed his hands into his jean pockets. "I had a feeling you'd be trying to pretend you weren't disappointed about missing prom." He cleared his throat. "So..I... uh... decided we should bring it here. To you." He motioned toward the collection of boxes the others carried. "Can we come in?"

I froze. And blinked. And didn't say a word.

"Yes, you may," Dad said. A glance over my shoulder revealed he was standing right behind me.

"Thank you, sir," Adam said, "but if you don't mind, I'd rather hear it from Brynn."

"Whoa, you finally got people to stop calling you Bree?" Uncle Josh yelled from the living room.

"You'll have to excuse my family." I spoke through a rictus of a smile. "They're nosy."

"They're just looking out for you." Adam rocked forward on his heels. "You deserve that."

"Smooth, bro," Gabe commented. "So, Brynn," he over pronounced, "what will it be?"

"Yeah," Nina said. "Gabe's arms are getting tired." She added a bag on top of the stack he already carried, the corners of her mouth twitching.

A smile cut its way across my face and I was helpless to stop it. I leaned back so I could see Uncle Josh on his recliner, feet up, laptop balanced precariously on the arm of the chair. "Yeah, Nina already asked me for permission to come over. And for the whole prom thing."

"Come in." I stepped aside, and they marched into the living room.

"Okay." Adam glanced around the house. "We have a lot to set up. Where's your room?"

"No. Nope," Dad said firmly, his head shaking. "No visits to Brynn's bedroom for you. You boys can go get changed in my room. Brynn…"

"I know, I know." I headed up the stairs, the others following me. "I don't know why you think you have to tell me this."

"Because you were found sleeping with him in a cabin?" Josh suggested.

"Super helpful," I said. "Thanks."

Adam's cheeks went scarlet and Josh shrugged, barely suppressing a grin. "I'm just sayin'."

I ignored him and turned to Dad. "We'll behave."

"Promise!" Nina chimed in before we disappeared into my room. "I picked out the perfect dress for you. You're gonna love it."

I practically growled. It was a very Val thing to say.

"Don't you dare look at me like that!" She leaned in, eyes narrowing. "Have I ever steered you wrong? Like, ever?"

No. She hadn't. But she didn't wait for an answer.

"I knew you were going to wait until the last minute. So, I talked to your mom. It took a little work, but by the end, I think she understood."

"Understood what?" I didn't know if I should be pissed or grateful. She'd gone to Mom behind my back and gotten me a prom dress? What if it didn't fit? What if I hated it? What horrible words of wisdom had Mom shared with Nina? We might be on better terms, but that didn't mean she understood anything about my style.

Nina bent to unzip the garment bag on the bed. "That you're you. And she needs to understand that. She agreed. And helped me buy you this."

She pulled the bag open to reveal an absolutely gorgeous— burgundy halter dress, trimmed with black satin and embroidered with spirals of black branches and thorns. Black ribbons criss-crossed up the midsection, and the skirt flared out. I ran my fingers over it in awe, inspecting it. The black satin was sleek, the ribbons soft like velvet, and a peek under the skirt revealed a few layers of black tulle.

"It's...wow," I admitted. I couldn't wait to put it on, a thought I'd never had before when looking at a dress.

"Well, don't just stand there," Nina said. "I've got wardrobe, hair, and makeup to do for both of us. Put it on."

For a moment, all I could do was stare, overwhelmed by how well she knew me. But she shot me a pointed look, and I could practically hear her thoughts. *Get to it, girl, I haven't got all day.*

As I changed into the dress, Nina dug into her own garment bag, producing a canary yellow organza dress with a sweetheart neckline and a skirt that ended around mid-thigh.

"So..." Nina said as she gathered her curls at the nape of her neck, turning away from me so I could zip her up. "... have you spoken with Adam about what happens after graduation?"

"No." I turned so she could tie my halter. "We haven't spoken about anything, really. Just... admitted we liked each other. Kissed a bit. There was some mention of dating... and... well... the L-word was exchanged..."

"You told him you loved him?" She squeaked.

"He said it first, or something like it anyway," I said. "How do you think I should wear my hair?" I faced the mirror and wrinkled my nose.

"Or something like it?" Nina held her curls up, peering into the mirror, considering.

"He loves me the way I am," I said, and I had to struggle not to hide the goofy grin or the blush that caused. "And then I just... said it. The words."

"You're super casual about this," Nina said.

"Trust me." I smiled. "I'm really not. We do have to talk about it, and we would have, if we hadn't been caught."

"Good." She combed her fingers through my hair. "I'm happy for you."

"And I'm happy for you and Gabe. Now, about my hair, spiky or brushed down?" I reached forward and plucked a fallen eyelash from her cheek.

"Spiky would be striking with that dress. I brought gel." She motioned to what looked like a suitcase filled with hair and makeup items.

I picked up a tube of clear mascara and rolled it between my fingers. "I have my own gel, you know."

"I know." Her smile slipped, the look in her eyes darkening slightly. "Sorry, just excited." She shook her head hard and began unpacking various supplies. "Gabe is taking Adam to New York City with him in a few weeks. He talked to my dad and told him they would help view the apartments Dad has lined up for us."

"Wow, really?" It was a sweet gesture, but it triggered a sick feeling in my chest.

"Gabe says he and Adam intend on spending a lot of time there." She poked me in the arm, her lips crushing together, suppressing a smile.

The sick feeling bubbled over, exiting my mouth as, "How's Val?"

Nina shrugged. "Heartbroken. Pissed off at herself. Not really talking to me. Not really talking much at all." Another shrug, this one more defeated. "She isn't mad at me, but she isn't opening up." She looked up, sparkling green eyes meeting mine. "If we move out to New York City, me and you, Gabe and Adam... what happens to her? Do we just leave her here?"

"Doesn't seem right, does it?" I asked.

"It doesn't."

We looked away from each other. I straightened one of the ribbons on my dress. She adjusted her dress strap. Both of us frowning, worrying.

"We'll figure it out," I said.

"We always do." She glanced around the room and took a deep breath. "We have all summer for that. For now, let's get dolled up. It's a special occasion." Her smile grew deep enough to highlight the dimple in her cheek.

"Just this once," I teased.

"WOW!" Dad said when we reached the base of the stairs. "You girls look beautiful."

Josh gaped. "They look like grown-ups. I don't like this."

Dad side-eyed him. "Weren't you the one who recently reminded me and Chelsea that Brynn is nearly an adult?"

Josh's gape morphed into a pout. "That was different." He folded his arms over his chest.

"Let me get a picture of you two." Dad snatched his phone from the couch and motioned for us to pose. "I'll get one with your dates when they come back in."

I looped an arm around Nina's waist and grinned. Dad snapped a series of pictures before the screen door to the backyard rattled, and Gabe and Adam's good-natured ribbing floated to the front of the house.

"Stop!" Dad yelled to them. "Stop right there. I want video of this." I couldn't see the guys from where I stood, but whatever they did made Dad roll his eyes. "Not of *you*. Of you when you see *them*." Dad motioned us forward, Nina first, then me.

The boys... well, they didn't say anything. They were both decked out in rented tuxes and slick, gelled hair. They would have looked dignified, except they kept elbowing each other. I looked to Nina for an answer.

"I think they're wondering if this is real life. They don't believe what they're seeing." Her eyes twinkled with amusement.

Of course Nina was amused. She was used to attention like this. I, on the other hand, was heating up.

"Pictures," Dad prompted again. "Pictures or Chelsea and Angie will kill me."

Nina complied first, walking to the guys and shoving Adam aside so she could stand next to Gabe. Adam took the hint and scooted around them, making his way to me.

As Dad played photographer, Adam took my hand in his and brought it to his lips.

"You look beautiful," he whispered, "and like yourself." He flashed me a smile.

"Nina and my mother picked it out for me. A little more hard rock and a little less ballerina, don't you think?" I winked, and he laughed, that coarse bark of a laugh that made something in my chest twist. I didn't think I'd ever get bored with hearing it.

"You two now." Dad placed a hand on my shoulder and ushered me into place by the back door.

Adam slid a shy glance my way before looping his arm around me, his hand settling at my waist and pulling me against his side. He smiled for the camera, all teeth. I couldn't help but smile just as widely in return.

———

I GLANCED to where Adam sat on the worn wooden picnic bench beside the patio table in my father's small backyard. I'd settled down beside him as soon as we'd come outside, and Adam had spent the last five minutes awkwardly taking in the scenery.

While we had been upstairs getting dolled up, Adam and Gabe had been stringing fairy lights between trees and along the patio, placing a tablecloth over the picnic table and tinsel along the patio railing. A bowl of punch rested on the table. Dad immediately tested it for alcohol, something he never would have done before the ranch fiasco.

Once Dad and Uncle Josh decided things were on the level, they headed back inside. Gabe started grilling some burgers, and Nina rigged her phone up to Josh's Bluetooth speakers. The night was warm, but not stifling, a delicate breeze in the air. It was still light out, but it was growing darker, and I breathed in, capturing this moment in my mind as a reminder of the awesome nature of friendship.

"So, how much are you going to eat this time?" Gabe asked.

"Enough to give myself a little bloat baby." Nina ran her hand over her stomach and preened.

Gabe let out a low chuckle. "You're nuts." He put some corn cobs on the grill. "Have you ever tried ketchup on corn?"

Nina cringed. "That's disgusting. You're lucky you're cute."

Circles of red dotted Gabe's cheeks. "I'm cute?"

"Also a little lame." She pinched his side.

He jumped, then straightened his tie and flexed his fingers. I could practically feel the electricity of his nerves.

I shook my head, as much out of fondness as out of disgust, and pointed at the lovebirds. "They're gross."

"I've been told we're not any better." Adam wiped his hands on his pant leg. He rose and turned, one hand extended toward me. "Dance with me?"

I slid my hand into his and allowed him to lead me into the center of the backyard, our dance floor. We both tried to put our hands on each other's shoulders, then snatched them back.

"Okay, let's try that again," he said with a laugh.

I reached for his waist just as he reached for mine.

Adam took my hands in his. "If I lead, will you follow?" He maneuvered my arms around his neck, then glided his hands back down to my elbows. His touch was feather light, and I shivered at the contact.

"Only if you follow when it's my turn to lead." I stepped closer as his hands came to rest at my waist.

"Anywhere." His voice was a hoarse whisper, his breath warm against my face as he led us in a movement that was barely a dance. I leaned into him and he swayed us to the rhythm.

My heart fluttered as I stared into his eyes, at the intent I saw there. I was swept away by his enduring kindness, the endearing nature of his awkwardness. He leaned forward slowly, his eyelids sliding closed as his lips brushed mine, soft, testing.

The sudden flash of lightning and rumble of thunder came in such quick succession that I knew how close the bolt had struck the ground, even without the heat licking at my ankles, as the grass beside me erupted into flames.

Adam hauled me backwards almost before our lips separated. Nina was shrieking, but the sound of it had a padded, clouded quality around it, like I was hearing it through layers of gauze. I pushed my hands against my ears like I could rub the haze away.

Nina dumped the entire punch bowl on the fire to put it out.

"Well..." Gabe remarked blankly as he maneuvered closer to us. "That should confirm the lack of alcohol content to your father."

We froze for only a moment, eyes ticking between us to make sure we all saw what we thought we saw.

A burst of rain poured from the sky like a waterfall. A mere moment passed, and we were soaked from head to toe. My dress clung to my torso, the skirt weighed down by the water. The almost chlorinated smell of ozone built around us and my muscles tensed. Something bad was about to happen, just like it had at the ranch.

A sharp flash of light rent the air, not entirely unlike the lightning bolts we'd previously encountered, but more like a solid spotlight descending from the sky. I threw myself into Adam, pushing us both out of the way.

It struck the ground, fissures and tremors scattering from the crater it formed in my backyard. The force of the crash was like a hand, tossing Adam and me aside carelessly. We landed in a heap, elbows and knees knocking together. Mud seeped into the back of my dress, and I swore.

We scrambled to our feet. I needed to see what happened. I needed to be ready to run.

"Brynn!" Dad dashed out onto the porch, immediately followed by Uncle Josh. Both stopped abruptly, jaws dropping as they took in the disaster.

A crater had formed in the middle of the yard. A man draped in white robes knelt in the middle of the hole. White curls fell to his shoulders as he leveled his gaze on our small group. Thick white whiskers covered his chin. He rose to his full height, towering over us, his barrel-like chest exposed where his robes were loosened. Flowy white material surrounded his legs, and he remained untouched by the rain.

"Brynn Stark." The man's voice was thunder rolling along the ground. "Adam Hernandez. I have arrived to deliver judgment upon you."

"That doesn't sound good," Adam whispered, his tan skin going pallid.

"You'll do no such thing," Dad said, his words shooting spikes of panic through my veins.

"Dad, no."

"She is my daughter. If you have something to say to her, you can say it to me instead."

I swore loudly.

"Ian Stark," the man boomed, "I have no qualms with you. My issue is only with the two before me."

I wanted to cower. I wanted to be afraid. But I was also truly sick of this shit. I stepped forward, pushing Adam behind me.

"You're looking for me? You've got me. How can I help you, Mister..."

"King of Olympians!" His shout rattled my brain in my skull. "Father of the gods. I am Zeus, and you will show your god respect!"

Dad and Josh stepped forward until they stood on each side of us. It was a sweet gesture, but I couldn't stand behind them. I had gotten myself into this mess, and I would either get myself out, or...

Or...

"I'm sorry, sir," I said. "But you are not my god. You're my friend's father. And let's face it——if you were an infallible god, you would have hit us with a lightning bolt without even coming down for a visit. Are you having trouble with your aim? Because you could have hit us many times by now."

"Brynn..." Adam took a step closer, but I planted my hand against his chest, facing Zeus head on.

He narrowed his already squinty eyes at me. They were a startling shade of green. "Ms. Stark. Would you like for me to try my aim at this closer range? I'm sure you will find it has vastly improved."

"Leave her alone," Dad snarled.

I spoke over him. "A blind man with vertigo could hit me at this range." I ignored the way my heart shifted in my chest, as though it was pounding out of place. "But never mind that. Why are you here? What could you possibly hope to accomplish?"

"I think I can answer this for you, Father." A comparatively smaller, more elegant being slunk out from behind him, her body sinuous, her face gentle and open.

"Great. Brynn, what the fuck am I seeing?" Josh asked.

Dad's eyes snapped to me.

"Val," I whispered hoarsely. "Valentina Kokinos. Aphrodite."

Val's arrival made the whole thing seem more real, and suddenly I wasn't the hero of a novel, stepping out in front of my loved ones and defending them in front of some pretender to a throne I wasn't even sure existed. I had seen Val's power. I had been subjected to her whims.

Zeus may not be able to aim his lightning bolts, but Val could still worm her way under our skin, and that made her more frightening.

"He is here because I called him," she said. "I asked him for help in a weak moment. And he is obliging. Which is funny. Not funny 'ha-ha,' but funny 'how dare you come when I call after banishing me for millennia' These are my friends. You will not be hurling more lightning bolts at them any time soon."

Pride and a kind of helpless gratefulness swelled in my chest. She may look like Aphrodite now, but the girl standing before us was 100% our Val. And I had never been so happy to see her.

Zeus turned to face his daughter in one sweeping movement, slow enough to leave me trembling in anticipation of his next move. His shoulders drooped, his face screwing up in consternation. "I don't understand. You called me just days ago. You asked me to heal you, for your heart was broken. It took me some time to regain the strength required to come here, to get close enough to harm them with my lightning. Non-believers and imperfect aim won't save them now. I am here *for you*. And you *shun* me?"

The wind and rain tapered down. It seemed Zeus couldn't maintain his confusion and theatrics at the same time.

"I'm not shunning you," Val said, her voice thick with emotion. "Don't you see, Father? I have made a spectacular mess, yet again. I have learned nothing from my time here, have learned nothing from my banishment. All I ever do is damage the humans in my charge. Forget my earlier words, for they were born of selfishness and anger. Instead, I ask that you hear my plea——take me back home. If you do, I will no longer attempt to bend the will and whims of humanity. I will answer solely to you."

"And then what?" Nina piped up from her corner of the yard, her hand clutching the arm of Gabe's suit jacket. "Will love even exist if you leave?" Her eyes glistened with tears, and my heart clenched. This was her sister, talking about leaving forever, and for all our differences, the idea of Val leaving and never speaking to us again left me with a sense of dread.

"Oh Nina, my dear sister." Val shook her head. "I have long since lost control over my creation. Love remains untouched with or without me."

"What did you do?" Adam asked, his voice cracking halfway through the statement. As he spoke, Zeus's glow dulled. "What made him send you here in the first place?"

The Val before us shifted into the Val we'd all grown to love. "I caused the Trojan War by mucking in the affairs of humanity, by trying to force love to fit what I wanted for it. Does that sound familiar, my love?"

Adam swallowed hard. "It does."

"I have spent so long here in continued foolishness," Val said. "I have made the same mistakes over and over again, only leading to heartbreak. I hurt the only true friends I ever had in the pursuit of selfishness. Brynn and Adam may not have been innocent, but..."

"This was the very reason I sent Hephaestus down to assist you," Zeus interrupted her. "However, he took too long to announce himself and was sidetracked from his mission."

"His... mission?" Val asked. "I never once saw Hephaestus. I would have recognized his ugly mug anywhere."

"I sent him in the perfect disguise, as a boy who moved away at the end of last summer. A stranger disguised as one of their own."

Nina and Adam exchanged a glance, Nina's face screwing up in disgust, Adam's head bobbing in a nod. "Raphael," they groaned in unison.

"It wasn't really him?" I asked. "No wonder he got so weird."

"I *knew* I hated that guy!" Val shrieked.

Thoughts swirled in my head and I struggled to tack them in place. The studying we had done for that stupid presentation. Everything we had learned about Aphrodite. Everything I now understood about Val. The stupidity surrounding Raphael. It all added up to one thing. Clarity.

"But he wasn't here for Val," Adam said. "He was here for Brynn."

"He was attempting to make Aphrodite jealous," Zeus said, then reluctantly added, "at first."

"Hephy did that for me?" Another shriek, her hands coming up to cup her face. I could practically see the cartoon hearts in her eyes. "That's so sweet. Sure, he's hung up on Brynn, but that's my fault. I cast a net for susceptible minds. Apparently, it works differently for fellow gods." A wicked gleam filled her eyes. "So, he's in love with Brynn now. I can fix tha—"

"Aphrodite has learned her lesson!" I shouted over her. "Wherever you gods have holed up, you should take her home. She misses you. And she doesn't enjoy being here."

"This from the very girl she believes she has wronged?" Zeus intoned. "How interesting."

"She has wronged me," I agreed. "And I've wronged her. But people fuck up sometimes." I winced. I hoped Zeus didn't mind a swear here or there. "That's what it means to be human. And if you were trying to teach her more about the humans she's manipulated, you've done that. I think she understands us now better than she ever has.

"Adam and I made a mess of things," I continued, turning to Val. "We hurt you, but we never wanted to."

"I should have stepped back when I saw what was happening between you." Val's gaze dropped to her elegantly sandaled feet.

My heart twisted at the sorrow so evident in her low, careful voice. I stepped closer, sliding my hand into hers. "Maybe. But we all messed up. In the end, the most important thing is what you learned. What we all did. That mortals screw things up, and that when you try to twist things in your favor, you may be causing happiness for yourself, but you're invariably hurting others. Just like what went down with us. Or what happened between my parents. Or what happened between Nina and Reeve. Love is powerful, but it can also hurt."

"Even when it's magic," Adam said, stepping in from behind me. "It's always a risk. You made it that way for a reason. Glorious and terrifying. And that was the miracle you granted us. But I think you now understand the power you wield."

Val tore her eyes away from the ground she'd been focusing on and met his eyes. "Yeah?"

"We all believe in you." Nina stepped up, dragging a completely confused Gabe beside her. "And because of that school assignment, we all know what you're capable of, and who you are now. You're a pain in the ass, but you've grown."

"By, like... a lot," I chimed in.

Val glanced between us and Zeus. "I want to go home, Father. I want to do better."

Zeus laughed, and I jumped at the grand bellowing sound. "There truly isn't much for us to do anymore. Your... friend... had it right." He nodded toward me. "In this world that doesn't believe, our powers are not what they were, and our Pantheon... well, it is far more... human than it once was."

Val's eyes went round, tears brimming along the edges.

"All the better for you to find your place again." Zeus smiled, draping a large, muscular arm over her shoulder and giving her a squeeze. "I will come for you soon. Let your caretakers know your true family has found you. For now, enjoy those you have chosen as your companions."

With another raucous boom and a flash, Zeus disappeared.

Val longingly watched him go before turning back to the rest of us.

"Um... property damage," Uncle Josh called, motioning at the crater like a mad man. "An actual act of a god. Just my luck."

Dad was pale to the point of translucence, his head shaking back and forth. "What?" he finally uttered.

"We've got a lot to explain," I said. "Sorry about your back-yard, Uncle Josh."

"Yeah, I'm also gonna need an explanation." Gabe shot a pointed stare at Adam, who simply shrugged.

"So, what now?" Val asked. The look in her eyes was distant, her gaze frosted over, and she inched closer to us, grasping my hand on one side and Nina's on the other.

Adam leaned toward the three of us. "I'll handle the explanations. Give you ladies some privacy." He motioned to Gabe. "You, come with me." As he entered the house behind Dad and Josh, I heard him say, "Brynn and Nina will join us soon, I swear. They just need a minute to make the Greek god on our doorstep feel better first."

Meanwhile, I struggled for an answer for Val. What was it like to want something so badly for so long, and suddenly, surprisingly, get it? Actually, I knew that feeling——my parents' divorce had that same bittersweet vibe.

"What now? I think... well, I think you think it over for a while," Nina said.

"And for now? Until you do?" I said. "I think...you dance."

"Dance! Dance! Dance!" Nina chanted, reaching behind her to turn the stereo back on. I had no idea how it had turned off to begin with.

When the music started once again, I grabbed Val by the hand and gave her a good spin.

CHAPTER TWENTY ONE

LOVE HEALS

AN INCESSANT BEEPING broke through my perfectly enjoyable dream. I smacked at my bedside table——once, twice, three times——before I finally found the source of the noise. I switched the alarm off and sat up in bed.

Rubbing the sleep from my eyes, I smiled despite myself. The dream was boring and wonderful and perfect.

I shot Adam a text.

Dreamed about you.

It didn't take him even a second to reply.

Was it a sexy dream?

The dream was about me and Adam... discussing books.

You wish.

That was better than letting him in on the inner workings of my subconscious.

He was just teasing. It wasn't like we didn't do anything sexy, but I was taking my time getting there, and Adam respected that and didn't push for more. I didn't want to run headfirst into anything. We had time. As far as I was concerned, we had all the time in the world. Neither of us intended on going anywhere.

"Brynn?" Dad called. "You coming down for breakfast?"

I stretched and let out a roar of a yawn. "Be right down!"

Eating breakfast now. See you at the thing.

I threw off the covers and rolled out of bed. My phone buzzed before I made it halfway down the stairs.

I'll be the one in the cap and gown!

He was such a dork.

"Good morning, honey. What are you grinning about?" Dad stood in the middle of the kitchen, a plate of eggs and sausage in hand.

"Adam being cute." I flopped into the chair beside Uncle Josh.

"Barf." Uncle Josh groaned. "Are you guys gonna be like this forever?"

I barely looked up at him as I made grabby hands at Dad so he would pass me my plate.

"It's going to be at least this bad until I move to the city with him. Then you won't have any clue how bad it is."

Josh choked on his eggs a little.

"Dammit, Brynn." He kicked Josh's chair leg. "And that's for getting me caught in your cross-fire."

I laughed despite myself. "Oh Dad, you know I'm just playing."

He narrowed his eyes at me. "Eventually you won't be."

"You see, this is why I'm going to miss you when you go to college. Not only do you give as good as you get, but you trip yourself into trouble whenever you do and it's endlessly entertaining. It's been nice having someone around who can appreciate my humor. Besides, it's been almost like I got a chance to be a parent. Experience done. Bucket list entry, checked. I can get back to being a bachelor again." He winked.

"Hey, you never know. Maybe Val will show up and find you a surprise significant other, too." I grinned at him. I was going to miss him too.

I was just teasing, though. Josh seemed perfectly happy to be single. And if that was how he wanted to live, he had every right to continue that way. As long as he was happy.

The same was true for my actual parents. Dad seemed happier now than he had with Mom. And Mom's quirks, which had frustrated Dad to no end, seemed perfectly reasonable to Jesse.

It turned out, after a couple of dinners and a long discussion about what he'd done to piss me off, Jesse wasn't so bad. I still wasn't happy about how they'd gone about starting their relationship, and he was not my new daddy, because nobody ever would be, but he was all right. And he made Mom happy, which mattered a lot.

Love did suck while you searched for the right fit, but when you found it, love could actually be wonderful.

"Dad, you should start dating again," I announced.

He didn't look away from what he was working on by the stove. "When the person is right. You know, I did meet this woman at work."

"Really? You didn't mention anybody." Josh pouted.

"Sure. Her name is Athena, she looks great in body armor..."

"Shut up, Dad."

He laughed heartily, not speaking again until he'd lost some steam. "So what's the plan for today?" He ambled over from the kitchen to our small dining nook and slid a plate of food and a cup of coffee my way before returning for his own.

"Breakfast." I motioned at my plate. "Thank you, by the way."

Dad nodded, a smile playing at the corners of his lips, and he settled at the table.

"Then we get dressed. We have to be at the school by 9:30. The ceremony starts at ten." I took a break to shovel eggs into my mouth.

"You'll have to sit between me and Chelsea during the graduation." Dad waved a forkful of eggs at Josh. "And Jesse is coming."

Josh's eyes widened in terror. "I'm still having nightmares

about that drive to and from the ranch." A shiver. "And after that is dinner with the Lopezes, right?"

"Speaking of Nina's parents, has Val made her decision yet?" Dad asked.

"She hasn't told us, but..." *Oh look! Eggs!* The eggs on my plate were very interesting. Enthralling, even.

"But you think you already know."

"I do." I sighed. "Because if she was staying, she would have said something."

"And are you okay?" Dad leaned forward, catching my averted gaze.

"Well, if she leaves, she'll be with her real father again."

"She never should have left him in the first place," Josh muttered.

"Yeah, but she set some important things in motion," Dad said. "Will you miss her?"

"Yes and no," I said. "She was my friend. Sort of. Even if she wasn't great at it." That didn't feel like enough. "I didn't really know her. She spent a school year here, and she was a goddess in disguise the entire time, so..." I shrugged.

"Yes." Dad nodded sagely. "But you loved who you believed she was. And she changed your entire worldview. It's very complicated and..."

"Or," Josh cut him off, "she was half-a-bitch, half-a-friend, so it's very complicated."

"Must you?" Dad asked.

I smiled at Josh, and he grinned. "Yeah, kid. That's what I thought."

But if I was right, and Val was leaving... I was going to miss her, as crazy as she was. We went to school together, we worked together, and somewhere deep inside we loved each other. It would be hard to see her go.

THE GRADUATION CEREMONY was beautiful in its own, Birchwood Grove-ish kind of way. Small, but folksy and heartfelt, our farewell to the high school was pitched in exactly the same tone one would pitch a farewell to the town. After all, a large portion of the high school senior population of Birchwood left when they went off to college, even if they eventually returned.

We all gathered for dinner at The Pine Steakhouse, the only place in town I'd never been to. Paid for by Angie and Roman, they had requested the presence of my family and Adam's at the event.

Mom loved the opportunity to schmooze with the upper crust from the rich side of town.

"This place makes me uncomfortable," Jesse admitted, glancing around at the polished wood floors, the dark wooden bar, the modern art on the walls, the immaculately set tables, and the almost sofa-like seating.

We couldn't all be my mother.

"Amen," Josh muttered.

"For Nina and Val," I said by way of explanation.

Josh and Jesse both nodded and grunted, then glanced away from each other, as though disturbed they were getting along. It *was* disturbing, but I wasn't going to point that out. Josh and Dad stood on one side of me, and Mom and Jesse were on the other, all waiting eagerly to be seated.

It didn't take long for us to get through the line and find our way to the large table in the back where Gabe, Adam, and Adam's father, William, waited with Angie, Roman, Val, and Nina. A chorus of greetings filled the air when we spotted each other, and we traded hugs and cheek kisses, happy as always to see each other.

It was enjoyable, having this large family, a patchwork quilt sewn together by Nina, Adam, and me. It was good to have them all together for our last high school milestone.

Even Jesse. Maybe. A little.

We filled in our spaces at the table and got to the business of ordering our meals. The parents had allowed the graduates to choose the appetizer and gave me the honors of ordering it. We chose a charcuterie board.

"Sure," the waiter said. "We have a wide variety of fresh meats and cheeses for the board. They will be served with grapes, apricot jam, honey, and flatbread. You can choose your meats and cheeses from here." He pointed out the correct spot on the menu.

"Um…" I hated ordering. "For meats, we want prosciutto, salami, and ham. For cheeses, we want sharp cheddar, feta, and Camembert."

"It's Cam-em-bear, darling," Mom admonished, correcting my pronunciation. Because no matter how far we'd progressed recently, she was still Mom.

A blush roared to my cheeks. I had to stop myself from hiding my face behind my hands. Silly me for not realizing the 't' was silent.

Across the table, Adam shrugged. "That just means she's only ever read it in a book, and she's never had to say it out loud before. Nothing wrong with learning from a book."

A warm feeling spread through my chest. When it reached my face, it manifested as a goofy smile. Adam always knew the right thing to say.

After ordering the rest of dinner and a debate between the adults about whether it was acceptable to allow us a little champagne, our food arrived with a bottle. Angie herself took the time to fill every glass.

"Everybody," Angie said, flashing a dazzling smile I recognized as a cover-smile, one she only used during particularly sad moments. Like when she found out she couldn't have another child just before our spring concert in fifth grade. My heart lurched.

"Our darling Valentina has an announcement to make."

All attention turned to Val where she stood beside Roman at the head of the table. Her eyes darted between us, and she quietly cleared her throat. "Sorry to interrupt your conversations, everyone. I wanted to tell you all that I will be leaving Birchwood Grove at the end of the summer and going to live in Greece, my parents' homeland."

My stomach took a dip. Around the back of my father's chair, Nina clasped my hand in hers.

Mom's hand fluttered to her heart. "But... your family is here. Your life—"

"I won't disappear," Val said. "I'll remain in touch with everyone."

"Where will you stay?" William asked, glancing at Adam for his reaction.

"With my father," she said. "You see, I moved to the US with my mother when I was very young. Only a few short years later, my mother passed away. She hadn't left behind any information about my father, and though he looked, he lost me in the system. But now he's found me, and since I'll be turning eighteen in July, my father no longer needs to appeal to the US courts to have me sent back to him. I have long known who he was but had no way of finding him. So, I will get to know the parts of my birth family I never had the chance to know. It's all very exciting." Her eyes sparkled, the dimple in her cheek flickering.

"I know Val hasn't told anybody about this," I said, looking to Angie and Roman, "but she's been struggling with this decision since the senior trip. It's part of what happened there. I'm glad she picked the choice that makes her happy."

Val smiled, toothy and brilliant.

"I hope you meant what you said about coming to visit," Nina said, her voice taking that stern edge that made me want to duck and hide from her reprimand. "And I'm not just talking about Mom and Dad. I want you to visit our apartment in the city."

"We can show you around," Adam said. He offered Val a shy smile, and Val returned it fondly. "Even though you've been there before."

"It will be way better with you guys as my tour guides." For a moment, her expression slackened, eyes rounding with sadness, but she shook it off, blonde curls bouncing along her shoulders like a cascading river. "Anyway, that's my big news. Let's eat."

It was a perfectly timed announcement, finished just as the waiters arrived with our food.

Primly, she lifted her fork, gazing over her grilled salmon. "And Brynn?"

I glanced at her, ignoring the wonderful scent wafting off the juicy-looking steak before me. "Yeah?"

"Thank you for helping me find my way. As twisted as the road there became." She giggled, leaning in to whisper, "I'm glad I did my job in the end, as fate would have it."

"I really believed I'd never find someone to love."

"Well-" she sipped at her champagne- "never say never. Someone's bound to take it as a challenge."

"SO THAT'S THAT, HUH?" Nina said later that night, strolling into her basement hangout room with popcorn and a bag of plain potato chips. The parents were upstairs having a drink or two while we partook in our weekly movie night.

"That's it." Val had a bowl of spinach and artichoke dip in one hand, a bowl of sour cream and onion in the other. "I'm going to Mt. Olympus."

She and Nina settled the food on the table.

"Does anybody ever think to climb it?" I asked from the

couch. "I mean, does anybody ever find any of you guys up there?"

"If they did, they wouldn't remember it," Val answered.

"Now, you see, I find that to be playing a little dirty." Adam pulled himself to his feet after inserting a DVD into the player below the television. "If humans are able to find the gods, why can't they be rewarded for it?"

"Rewarded?" I tossed a popcorn kernel into Val's bouncing curls. "Is that what you call this?"

Val ruffled my hair, and I swatted her hands away. She turned to Adam instead. "You were always too pure for this world, Adam Hernandez." She made a face. "I don't know how I didn't see you were better off with Brynn."

He stuck his tongue out at her.

"I'll allow you to retain the memory." Val waved her hand dismissively.

"How benevolent of you." Nina winked.

"I picked *Can't Hardly Wait*." Adam shrugged. "Dad says it was my mother's favorite movie, back when they were teens. It's about a post-graduation party."

"You see, I like that," Gabe said. "It's gotta become like a generational thing."

"Yes!" Val punched the air. "To making new traditions and saying to hell with the old!"

"I like that." Nina tossed a bag of chocolates at Val, and she caught it just before it hit her in the stomach.

"So, the gods, huh?" I asked. "That's one helluva extended family you're going to live with."

Adam grinned. "Just when you think your family is full of drama…"

I pressed a finger to my lips. "Sssshhhh, they can hear you." I bumped him with my shoulder, and he wrapped an arm around me.

"Which ones? The family upstairs? Or Val's folks?" He laughed.

"Potentially both," Nina said, curling up across Gabe's lap and resting her head on my lap and her feet on Val's.

"This shouldn't be comfortable," I said.

Nina just inclined her head slightly in my direction and winked.

Adam hit play, but the chatting didn't stop. It slowed down, but we quipped, and quibbled, and shifted positions, and before long, we were on the floor, laid out on our bellies, leaning on each other to help get the right angle to see the TV without craning our necks.

While the others seemed to really be watching the movie, I thought about where I'd be in a few weeks, a few months, a few years, because graduations made you sentimental, whether or not you wanted to be.

And then I thought of my mom and dad, happy apart. Of Josh, happy on his own. Of Angie and Roman, Nina and Gabe, happy to be together. Of Val, happy to be returning to her family. Of Adam, happy——for reasons I grew more and more capable of understanding——with me. And of all of us, happy just to be in each other's lives.

And I realized love didn't suck at all. Actually, it was pretty damn awesome.

Not that I would ever admit it to anyone outside of this house.

ACKNOWLEDGMENTS

Some people have a writing tribe. I have a writing city. I have been so very blessed to have grown that city over the time I've been working on this novel, from the time it was but a spark in my eye, to when it became a true novel, and I have so many to thank. I tend to be rather verbose and effusive, but that's because so many people in my life rock. If you're reading this, get yourself friends like these. If yours wouldn't do these things for you, dump 'em.

First and foremost, thank you to the amazing Sword & Silk Books crew. The founders, Laynie Bynum and MaryBeth Dalto-McCarthy. I knew MaryBeth before S&S was a thing, and she'd always been gracious with her guidance and her friendship. It wasn't surprising to learn Laynie was quite the same. I am forever lucky you took a chance on me and chose Brynn to be your first strong heroine. I know good things are in store for this group. Thank you to Jennia Herold D'Lima, my editor at S&S--your witty commentary wasn't nearly as essential as your ability to pick out exactly what I was trying to say when I struggled to say it, but both were valued highly. I'm overjoyed to have sat you in the front seat of Brynn's roller coaster of emotions.

Thank you to Lucy Rhodes for producing such a gorgeous cover and graphics. We work well together, and I thank you for reading my mind. Thank you also to Kristin Jacques, Nicole Bezanson, and J.M. Jinks and to my fellow authors at S&S Haleigh Wenger and Alys Murray (check out their books, ya'll!). I am so lucky to have such a hands-on, supportive team at my side for this one.

To the super supportive Twitter Writing Community at large, and, more importantly the Writer in Motion chat for containing a constant source of advice and warmth and a place to vent my frustrations when this business gets me down. I'm lucky to have a group of writers like you, championing my victories.

To the Sisterhood of the Traveling Pantsers, Maria Tureaud, Jeni Chappelle, Megan Manzano, R. Miotto, Ari Augustine. There are some people who change the entire course of your experience and put you on a new path. They teach you about yourself, they teach you about your industry, they mourn your losses and celebrate your wins. I've been very lucky to have you be my safety net. Thank you for everything you do. Specifically to Maria, Jeni, and Megan--you each read this story in various stages of its infancy, and you've all contributed to improving upon it in your own ways. Maria, you single-handedly rewrote my synopsis on the desk of the hotel room, the day after we first met in person. I credit that with helping open doors for me. Even funnier was Megan randomly contributing in her some-what hung-over state and then returning to sleep. We don't get to see each other in person often, but any time with you guys is cherished beyond words.

To the staff and community of WriteHive and the students at my writing classes there. You are, always, an inspiration.

To the Minners and Manzano families at large. The tremendous support you give to me and my guys is so appreciated and so very necessary. Thank you for being there for us.

How to say this without it sounding weird or offensive? To

my parents, Doris and John Minners, who taught me so much about love and loss, divorce, and that being an adult didn't always mean being right. I've lived and loved and flourished and fallen with you both, and I'm glad for the lessons each of you have taught me.

For my father specifically, I think I got my gift with words from you, and that is the greatest gift you've ever given me. Thank you.

For my mother specifically, thanks for your constant support and belief in me. You were my first fan and you continue your zealous support for me. Your faith in me is why I have the courage to try anything. Thank you.

To my blood brother and sister (Jon and Melissa) and the sisters I've gained through them (Kristy and Dorothy) for being my forever partners-in-crime, never hesitating to share your best and worst with me. Melissa, Jon, I never would have survived my teen years without your wisdom and constant willingness to step between me and whatever raging bull or self-created problem I got myself into. You guys are the best. And Jon, thank you for getting me my first job, at Carvel.

To the Carvel team, who worked with me in my teen years, especially Jon, Vinny, Mike, and Brian, who were usually stuck with me and my terrible shake skills. Craig's first day was based on my entire time there with you guys, but you all eased the pain. Here's to the time SOMEONE (truly not me) threw a broom through the ceiling and somehow hid it for years, and the time I accidentally stabbed a box cutter into my hand and one of you gave me a scoop of ice cream so I didn't pass out. Stories like those will make it into a book one day. It's only a matter of time. Joe--the old store owner, if by some crazy chance you're reading this...I'm sorry. HA HA HA.

To all my various wonderful kiddos, Millie and Wynnie M., Moira and Wynnie F., Genaro, Kaitlyn and Chloe, Wilkins, Eduardo, and the fabulous Ms. Angelica. You guys have made sure I remember what it's like to be young--an important thing, when you're an old writing books for teenagers. ;)

To friends who are family, Denise, Jose, Marissa, Fruhmann, Julian, Jennine, Anthony, Heather, Liz, Christian, J'vania, Christopher and Victor. Thank you for being a cherished and necessary part of our inner circle, and our lives. You guys are the glue that holds us together, and our trio is blessed to have you in our world. We appreciate and love you guys more than you know.

To Ismael, the man who taught me that falling in love could truly be a happily ever after. I was probably more of a Val when I met you, with my declaration that we were forever. I was probably terrifying, but thankfully, I was also correct. Twenty-four years later, and I'm really glad I didn't scare you away. Thank you for always seeing through my weirdness, and embracing my drive. The years of being each other's right hands have been an absolute pleasure. There's nobody I'd rather regularly embarrass myself around.

To Logan, the little man who has taught me more in my life than anybody else could ever teach me. Thank you for shouting to everyone that will listen that your mom is a writer and always listening to me rambling about my various ideas. The older you get, the more you become a partner in my writing career--reading my stories, sharing your ideas, and brainstorming ideas with me. When I had you, I knew we were creating another family member--I had no idea I was creating a new teammate. Love you, little dude.

To all the boys I've hated before, you know who you are. You and all of the others who dated my friends along the way inspired the various terrible boys Brynn has the displeasure of knowing. Enjoy your moment of immortality.

To Soul Sisters in general--this book is about love, but not just romantic love. Even more than that, this book is about the bond between friends, more particularly, the bond between girls. So, here's to my soul sisters.

To Allegra, it's so hard to believe that we met through Ismael, with how close we've become. I never would have imagined that a shared love for Farscape and Buffy would blossom into a friendship I can't live without. In our twelve year friendship, we've been lucky to experience college courses, girl's nights, drama, several jobs, new careers, weddings, pandemics and, best of all, motherhood. I'm so glad you called Logan a bowling pin in his sonogram picture. Apparently, it was the perfect foundation for a lifelong friendship. I love you!

To Megan, thank you for always being there to listen to book industry rage, family rage, geek rage and every other kind of rage in between. Oh, and the happy things too. I don't know how we turned out to be variations on the same person (you, the more bitter, anti-social version, me the stranger, more gregarious one), particularly because we share no blood relation, but there's nobody I'd rather be the same person as than you. I am more proud of your accomplishments in this business, and in life, than you will ever know. Thanks for giving me my very first (and only!) kid sister, and for inspiring Brynn. I enjoyed living in a brainspace so close to yours. I love you!

To Joy, you are the Nina to my Brynn. We have spoken before about your belief that you can have several soulmates, and if that's true, there's no question that you are one of mine. I didn't know you all my life, the way Brynn knew Nina, but I've never had anyone in my life who I instantly understood and who instantly understood me, the way we have. I always know that even when I'm making no sense, I make sense to you. We've always said we'd be old ladies living next door to each other, sitting on our porches in rocking chairs and reveling in sharing the same space. I know we'll make it there. Thank you for being the only person who understands me when I speak with my mouth full. I will always know what you mean when you ask me to get you "the thing on the thing." Our language is the best language. I love you!

And finally, to any of you who have read this story and loved it, and anyone else who has supported me through the years that I missed, every ounce of support is appreciated and cherished. I only hope I give you as much enjoyment when you read my work. Here's to many more shared times together.

ABOUT THE AUTHOR

Justine Manzano is an author of YA Urban Fantasy novels
including The Order of the Key and Never Say Never.
A freelance editor, she lives in Bronx, NY with her husband,
son, and a cacophony of cats. She can usually be found at her
website, www.justinemanzano.com, and she's on all the usual
social media haunts. If you've looked in all these places and
can't find her, she's probably off reading fanfiction.
She'll be back soon.

facebook.com/justinemanzanoauthor
twitter.com/justine_manzano
instagram.com/justine_manzano
goodreads.com/justine_manzano
pinterest.com/justinehmanzano

ALSO BY JUSTINE MANZANO

Order of the Key

Jacklyn Madison never expected to be attacked by a beast on an evening snack run. Turns out, her parents were once members of the Order of the Key, gifted humans that protect humanity from creatures spilling through inter-dimensional rifts. Unable to control her newfound abilities, Jacklyn and her family rejoin the Order. After an attack on their headquarters leaves Jacklyn questioning their leadership the boy who led her initial rescue reveals a darker secret. The Order's leader may be corrupt. Drawn into the search for proof, Jacklyn must use her guts and magical brawn to protect her family, her friends, and herself from the monsters spilling from rifts, and those hiding within the order.

A SPECIAL THANK YOU TO OUR KICKSTARTER BACKERS FROM SWORD AND SILK BOOKS

Patrick Lofgren, Meghan Sommers, Rebecca Fischer, Bridh Blanchard, William Spreadbury, Wm Chamberlainq, Marisa Greenfield, Anne-Sophie Sicotte, Jenn Thresher, Casey, Kris McCormick, Adam Bertocci, Susan Hamm, Jamie Provencher, Paula Rosenburg, Morgan Rider, Elizabeth Sargent, Greg Jayson, Melody Hall, Jamie Kramer, Ara James, Sarah Lampkin, Karen Gemin, Stuart Chaplin, Amanda Le, Rae Alley, Arec Rain, Megan Van Dyke, Kathleen MacKinnon, Paul Senatillaka, Christine Kayser, Jennifer Cremes, Bonnie Lechner, Amber Hodges, Kathrine Pocock, Mary Anne Hinkle, Jess Scott, Ella Burt, Sarah Ziemer, Stacy Psaros, Mel Young, Claire Jenkins.